IT'... ... IX W... ... ...APOCALYPSE DESTROYED THE WORLD AS WE KNOW IT. ONLY POCKETS OF HUMANITY REMAIN.

SAVAGE STREET GANGS RULE THE DAY WHILE FEAR AND SUPERSTITION RULE THE NIGHT.

WHEN ANGELS FLY AWAY WITH A HELPLESS GIRL, HER SEVENTEEN-YEAR-OLD SISTER PENRYN WILL DO ANYTHING TO GET HER BACK.

INCLUDING MAKING A DEAL WITH THE ENEMY.

About the Author

Susan Ee has eaten mezze in the old city of Jerusalem, surfed the warm waters of Costa Rica, and played her short film at a major festival. She has a life-long love of science fiction, fantasy and horror, especially if there's a touch of romance. She used to be a lawyer but loves being a writer because it allows her souped-up imagination to bust out and go feral.

Angelfall (Penryn & the End of Days, Book One) is her debut novel. Book Two in the series will be available in autumn 2013.

Visit Susan's website at www.susanee.com, find her on Facebook and on Twitter @Susan_Ee.

ANGELFALL

SUSAN EE

HODDER &
STOUGHTON

Originally published in the United States by Amazon
Publishing, 2012. This edition made possible under a license
arrangement originating with Amazon Publishing.

First published in Great Britain in 2013 by Hodder & Stoughton
An Hachette UK company

A CIP catalogue record for this title is available from the British Library

ISBN 978 1 444 77851 9

Typeset by Hewer Text UK Ltd, Edinburgh

Hodder & Stoughton Ltd
338 Euston Road
London NW1 3BH

www.hodder.co.uk

ANGELFALL

1

Ironically, since the attacks, the sunsets have been glorious. Outside our condo window, the sky flames like a bruised mango in vivid orange, red, and purple. The clouds ignite with sunset colors, and I'm almost scared those of us caught below will catch on fire too.

With the dying warmth on my face, I try not to think about anything other than keeping my hands from trembling as I methodically zip up my backpack.

I pull on my favorite boots. They used to be my favorites because I once got a compliment from Misty Johnson about the look of the leather strips laddering down the sides. She is – was – a cheerleader and known for her fashionable taste, so I figured these boots were my token fashion statement even though they're made by a hiking boot company for serious wear. Now they're my favorites because the strips make for a perfect knife holder.

I also slip sharpened steak knives into Paige's wheelchair pocket. I hesitate before putting one into Mom's shopping cart in the living room, but I do it anyway. I slip it in between a stack of Bibles and a pile of empty soda bottles. I shift some clothes over it when she's not looking, hoping she'll never have to know it's there.

Before it gets fully dark, I roll Paige down the common hall to the stairs. She can roll on her own, thanks to her preference for a conventional chair over the electric kind. But I can tell she feels more secure when I push her. The elevator is useless now, of course, unless you're willing to risk getting stuck when the electricity goes out.

I help Paige out of the chair and carry her on my back while our mother rolls the chair down three flights of stairs. I don't like the bony feel of my sister. She's too light now, even for a seven-year-old, and it scares me more than everything else combined.

Once we reach the lobby, I put Paige back into her chair. I sweep a strand of dark hair behind her ear. With her high cheekbones and midnight eyes, we could almost be twins. Her face is more pixie-like than mine, but give her another ten years and she'd look just like me. No one would ever get us mixed up, though, even if we were both seventeen, any more than people would mix up soft and hard, warm and cold. Even now, frightened as she is, the corners of her mouth are tipped up in a ghost of a smile, more concerned for me than herself. I give her one back, trying to radiate confidence.

I run back upstairs to help Mom bring her cart down. We struggle with the ungainly thing, making all kinds of clanking noises as we wobble down the stairs. This is the first time I'm glad no one's left in the building to hear it. The cart is crammed full of empty bottles, Paige's baby blankets, stacks of magazines and Bibles, every shirt Dad left in the closet when he moved out, and of course, cartons of her precious rotten eggs. She's also stuffed every pocket of her sweater and jacket with the eggs.

I consider abandoning the cart, but the fight I'd have with my mother would take much longer and be much louder than helping her. I just hope Paige will be all right for the length of time it takes to bring it down. I could kick myself for not bringing down the cart first so Paige could be in the relatively safer spot upstairs, rather than waiting for us in the lobby.

By the time we reach the front door of the building, I'm already sweating and my nerves are frayed.

'Remember,' I say. 'No matter what happens, just keep running down El Camino until you reach Page Mill. Then head for the hills. If we get separated, we'll meet at the top of the hills, okay?'

If we get separated there's not much hope of us ever meeting anywhere, but I need to keep up the pretense of hope because that may be all we have.

I put my ear to the front door of our condo building. I hear nothing. No wind, no birds, no cars, no voices. I pull back the heavy door just a crack and peek out.

The streets are deserted except for empty cars parked in every lane. The dying light washes the concrete and steel with graying echoes of color.

The day belongs to the refugees and raid gangs. But at night, they all clear out, leaving the streets deserted by dusk. There's a strong fear of the supernatural now. Both mortal predators and prey seem to agree on listening to their primal fears and hiding until dawn. Even the worst of the new street gangs leave the night to whatever creatures may roam the darkness in this new world.

At least, they have so far. At some point, the most desperate will start to take advantage of the cover of night despite the risks. I'm hoping we'll be the first so that we'll be the only ones out there, if for no other reason than that I won't have to drag Paige away from helping someone in trouble.

Mom grips my arm as she stares out into the night. Her eyes are intense with fear. She's cried so much this past year since Dad left that her eyes are now permanently swollen. She has a special terror of the night, but there's nothing I can do about that. I start to tell her it'll be all right, but the lie dries up in my mouth. It's pointless to reassure her.

I take a deep breath, and yank open the door.

2

I instantly feel exposed. My muscles tighten as if expecting to get shot at any moment.

I grab Paige's chair and wheel her out of the building. I scan the sky, then all around us like a good little rabbit running from predators.

The shadows are quickly darkening over the abandoned buildings, cars, and dying shrubbery that hasn't been watered in six weeks. Some tag artist has spray-painted an angry angel with enormous wings and a sword on the condo wall across the street. The giant crack that splits the wall zigzags through the angel's face, making it look demented. Below it, a wannabe poet has scrawled the words, *Who will guard against the guardians?*

I cringe at the clattering noise my mother's cart makes as she shoves it over the doorway and onto the sidewalk. We crunch over broken glass, which convinces me even more that we've stayed hidden in our condo for longer than we should have. The first floor windows have been broken.

And someone has nailed a feather on the door.

I don't believe for a second that it's a real angel feather, although that's clearly what's being implied. None of the new gangs are that strong or wealthy. Not yet, anyway.

The feather has been dipped in red paint that drips down the wood. At least, I hope it's paint. I've seen this gang symbol on supermarkets and drug stores in the last few weeks, warning off scavengers. It won't be long before the gang members come to claim whatever's left on the higher floors. Too bad for them we won't be there. For now, they're still busy claiming territory before the competing gangs get to it first.

We sprint to the nearest car, ducking for cover.

I don't need to check behind me to make sure Mom is following because the rattling of the cart wheels tells me she's moving. I take a quick glance up, then in either direction. There's no motion in the shadows.

Hope flickers through me for the first time since I made our plan. Maybe tonight will be one of those nights where nothing happens on the streets. No gangs, no chewed-up animal remains to be found in the morning, no screams to echo through the night.

My confidence builds as we hop from one car to another, moving faster than I'd expected.

We turn onto El Camino Real, a main artery of Silicon Valley. It means 'The Royal Path,' according to my Spanish teacher. The name fits, considering that our local royalty – the founders and early employees of the most cutting-edge tech companies in the world – probably got stuck on this road like everyone else.

The intersections are gridlocked with abandoned cars. I'd never seen a gridlock in the valley before six weeks ago. The drivers here were always as polite as can be. But the thing that really convinces me that the apocalypse is here is the crunching of smartphones under my feet. Nothing short of the end of the world would get our eco-conscious techies to toss their latest gadgets onto the street. It's practically sacrilegious, even if the gadgets are just deadweight now.

I had considered staying on the smaller streets but the gangs are more likely to be hiding where they are less exposed. Even though it's night, if we tempt them on their own street they might be willing to risk exposing themselves for a cartful of loot. At that distance, it's unlikely they'll be able to see that it's only empty bottles and rags.

I'm about to pop up behind an SUV to scope out our next hop when Paige leans through the gaping car door and reaches for something on the seat.

It's an energy bar. Unopened.

It is nestled among a scattering of papers as if they'd all fallen out of a bag. The smart thing to do would be for us to grab it and run, then eat it in a safe place. But I've learned in the past few weeks that your stomach can pretty easily override your brain.

Paige rips open the package and snaps the bar into thirds. Her face is radiant as she passes the pieces around. Her hand trembles with hunger and excitement. But despite that, she gives us oversized pieces and only keeps the smallest for herself.

I break mine in half and give half of my share to Paige. Mom does the same. Paige looks crestfallen that we're rejecting her gifts. I put my finger to my lips and give her a stern look. She reluctantly takes the offered food.

Paige has been a vegetarian since she was three years old when we visited the petting zoo. Although she was practically a baby, she still made the connection between the turkey that made her laugh and the sandwiches she ate. We called her our own little Dalai Lama until a couple of weeks ago when I started insisting she eat whatever I manage to scrounge off the street. An energy bar is the best we can do for her these days.

All our faces relax in relief as we bite into the crispy bar. Sugar and chocolate! Calories and vitamins.

One of the pieces of paper flutters down from the passenger seat. I catch a glimpse of the caption.

Rejoice! The Lord is Coming! Join New Dawn and Be the First to Go to Paradise.

It's one of the fliers from the apocalypse cults that sprang up like pimples on greased skin after the attacks. It has blurry photos of the fiery destruction of Jerusalem, Mecca, and the Vatican. It has a hurried, homemade look to it, like someone took still shots from the news videos and printed them on a cheap color printer.

We gobble up our meal, but I'm too nervous to enjoy the sweet flavor. We are almost at Page Mill Road, which would take us up to the hills through a relatively unpopulated area. I figure once we near the hills, our chances of survival will dramatically increase. It's full night now, the deserted cars lit eerily by the half moon.

There's something about the silence that puts my nerves on edge. It seems there should be some noise – maybe the skittering of a rat or birds or crickets or something. Even the wind seems afraid to move.

My mother's cart sounds especially loud in this silence. I wish I had time to argue with her. A sense of urgency builds in me as if responding to the buildup before lightning. We just need to make it to Page Mill.

I push faster, zigzagging from car to car. Behind me, Mom's breathing gets heavier and more labored. Paige is so silent, I half suspect she's holding her breath.

Something white floats gently down and lands on Paige. She picks it up and turns to show me. All the blood drains from her face and her eyes are enormous.

It's a fluffy piece of down. A snowy feather. The kind that might work its way out of a goose down comforter, only a little larger.

The blood drains out of my face too.

What are the chances?

They mostly target the major cities. Silicon Valley is just a plain strip of low-storied offices and suburbs between San Francisco and San Jose. San Francisco's already been hit, so if they were going to attack anything in this area, it'd be San Jose, not the valley. It's just some bird flying by, that's all. That's all.

But I'm already panting with panic.

I force myself to look up. All I see is endless dark sky.

But then, I do see something. Another, larger feather floats down lazily toward my head.

Sweat prickles my brow. I break out into an all-out sprint.

Mom's cart rattles crazily behind me as she desperately follows. She doesn't need explanations or encouragement to run. I'm scared one of us will fall, or Paige's chair will tip, but I can't stop. We have to find a place to hide. Now, now, now.

The hybrid car I was aiming for suddenly crumples under the weight of something crashing down on it. The thunder of the crash almost makes me jump out of my boots. Luckily, it covers Mom's scream.

I catch a flash of tawny limbs and snowy wings.

An angel.

I have to blink to make sure it's real.

I've never seen an angel before, not live anyway. Of course, we've all seen the looping footage of golden-winged Gabriel, Messenger of God, being gunned down from the pile of rubble that was Jerusalem. Or the footage of angels plucking a military helicopter out of the sky and tossing it into the Beijing crowd, blade-first. Or that shaky video of people running from a blazing Paris with the sky filled with smoke and angelic wings.

But watching TV, you could always tell yourself it wasn't real, even if it was on every news program for days.

There's no denying that this is the real deal, though. Men with wings. Angels of the Apocalypse. Supernatural beings who've pulverized the modern world and killed millions, maybe even billions, of people.

And here's one of the horrors, right in front of me.

3

I almost tip Paige in my rush to spin around and change direction. We skid to a halt behind a parked moving truck. I peek out from behind it, unable to stop watching.

Five more angels swoop down on the one with the snowy wings. Judging by their aggressive stances, it's a fight of five against one. It's too dark to see any details on the landing angels but one of them stands out. He's a giant, towering over the rest. There's something about the shape of his wings that strikes me as different. Their wings fold too fast when they land for me to take a good look and I'm left wondering if there actually was anything different about that one.

We hunker down and my muscles freeze, refusing to move from the relative safety behind the truck's tire. So far, they don't seem to notice us.

A light suddenly flickers and turns on above the crushed hybrid. The electricity has come back on and this street lamp is one of the few that hasn't yet been broken. The lone pool of light looks over-bright and eerie, highlighting contrasts more than illuminating. A few empty windows light up along the street as well, giving enough light to show me the angels a little better.

They have different colored wings. The one who smashed into the car has snowy white wings. The giant has wings the color of night. The others are blue, green, burnt orange, and tiger-striped.

They're all shirtless, their muscled forms flexing with every movement. Like their wings, their skin tones vary. The snowy-winged angel that crushed the car has light caramel skin. The night-winged one has skin as pale as an egg. The rest range from gold to dark brown. These angels look like the type to be heavily scarred by battle wounds, but instead they have the kind of perfectly unmarred skin prom queens around the country would kill their prom kings for.

The snowy angel rolls painfully off the crushed car. Despite his injuries, he lands in a half crouch, ready for an attack. His athletic grace reminds me of a puma I once saw on TV.

I can tell he's a formidable opponent by the way the others warily approach him even though he is injured and far outnumbered. Although the others are muscular, they look brutish and clumsy compared to him. He has the body of an Olympic swimmer, taut and muscled. He looks ready to fight them barehanded even though almost all his enemies are armed with swords.

His sword lies a few feet from the car, where it landed during his fall. Like the other angel swords, it is short with two feet of throat-slitting, double-edged blade.

He sees it and shifts to lunge for it. But Burnt Angel kicks the sword. It spins lazily across the asphalt away from its owner, but the distance it moves is surprisingly short. It must be as heavy as lead. It is still far enough away, though, to ensure that Snowy Wings doesn't have a prayer of reaching it.

I settle in to watch the angel execution. There's no question of the outcome. Still, Snow puts up a good fight. He kicks the tiger-striped one and manages to hold his own against two others. But he is no match for all five of them together.

When four of them finally manage to pin him down on the ground, practically sitting on him, Night Giant walks up to him. He stalks like the Angel of Death, which I suppose he could be. I get the distinct impression that this is the culmination of several battles between them. I sense history between them in the way they look at each other, in the way Night yanks at Snow's wing, spreading it out. He nods at Stripes, who lifts his sword above Snow.

I want to close my eyes against the final blow but I can't. My eyes stay glued open.

'You should have accepted our invitation when you had the chance,' says Night, straining against the wing to hold it away from Snow's body. 'Although even I wouldn't have predicted this kind of end for you.'

He nods again to Stripes. The blade whips down and slices off the wing.

Snow shrieks his fury. The street fills with echoes of his rage and agony.

Blood sprays everywhere, showering the others. They struggle to hold him down as the blood makes him slick. Snow twists and kicks two of the bullies with lightning speed. They end up rolling on the asphalt, curling around their stomachs. For a moment, as the remaining two angels fight to keep him down, I think he'll manage to bust loose.

But Night stomps his boot on Snow's back, right on the raw wound.

Snow hisses in a breath filled with pain but does not scream. The others take the opportunity to slink back into position, holding him down.

Night drops the severed wing. It lands with the thud of a dead animal on the asphalt.

Snow's expression is furious. He still has fight in him, but it's draining fast along with his blood. Blood soaks his skin, mats his hair.

Night grabs the remaining wing and yanks it open.

'If it was up to me, I'd let you go,' says Night. There's enough admiration in his voice to make me suspect he might mean it. 'But we all have our orders.' Despite the admiration, he doesn't show any regret.

Stripes's blade, poised on Snow's wing joint, catches the moon's reflection.

I cringe, expecting another bloody blow. Behind me, the tiniest sympathetic sound escapes Paige.

Burnt suddenly tilts his head from behind Night. He looks right at us.

I freeze, still crouched behind the moving truck. My heart skips a beat, then races triple time.

Burnt gets up and walks away from the carnage.

Straight toward us.

4

My brain clamps shut in fear. The only thing I can think to do is to distract the angel while my mother pushes Paige to safety.

'Run!'

My mother's face freezes wide-eyed in horror. In her panic, she turns and runs off without Paige. She must have assumed I'd push the wheelchair. Paige looks at me with terrified eyes dominating her pixie face.

She swivels her chair and rolls as fast as she can after Mom. My sister can roll her own chair, but not nearly as fast as someone can push her.

None of us will make it out alive without a distraction. With no time to consider the pros and cons, I make a split-second decision.

I sprint out into the open straight toward Burnt.

I dimly register an outraged roar filled with agony somewhere in the background. The second wing is being cut. It's probably already too late. But I'm at the place where Snow's sword lies, and there's not enough time for me to come up with a new plan.

I scoop the sword almost from under Burnt's feet. I grab it

with both hands, expecting it to be very heavy. It lifts in my hands, as light as air. I throw it toward Snow.

'Hey!' I scream at the top of my lungs.

Burnt ducks, looking as surprised as I feel at the sight of the sword flying overhead. It's a desperate and poorly thought-out move on my part, especially since the angel is probably bleeding to death right now. But the sword flies much truer than I expect and lands hilt-first right in Snow's outstretched hand, almost as if it was guided there.

Without a pause, the wingless angel swings his sword at Night. Despite his overwhelming injuries, he is fast and furious. I can understand why the others had to dramatically outnumber him before cornering him.

The blade slices through Night's stomach. His blood gushes out and mixes with the crimson pool already on the road. Stripes leaps to his boss and grabs him before he falls.

Snow, stumbling to regain his balance without his wings, bleeds rivers down his back. He manages to swing his sword again, laying open Stripes's leg as he runs off with Night in his arms. But that doesn't stop them.

The two others who'd backed off as soon as things got ugly rush to grab Night and Stripes. They pump their powerful wings while running with the injured, leaving a trail of blood dripping to the ground as they take off into the night.

My distraction is a shocking success. Hope surges in me that maybe my family has found a new hiding place by now.

Then the world explodes in pain as Burnt backhands me. I fly backward and slam onto the asphalt. My lungs contract so hard I can't even begin to think about taking a breath. All I can do is curl into a ball, trying to get a sip of air back into my body.

Burnt turns to Snow, who can no longer be called snowy. He hesitates with all his muscles tense, as though considering his odds of winning against the injured angel. Snow, wingless and drenched in blood, sways on his feet, barely able to stand. But his sword is steady and pointed at Burnt. Snow's eyes burn with fury and determination, which is probably all that's holding him up.

The bloodied angel must have one hell of a reputation because despite his condition, the perfectly healthy and beefy Burnt slams his sword back into his sheath. He gives me a disgusted glare and takes off. He runs down the street, his wings taking him airborne after half a dozen steps.

The second his enemy turns his back on him, the injured angel collapses to his knees between his severed wings. He looks like he's bleeding out pretty fast and I'm pretty sure he'll be roadkill in a few minutes.

I finally manage to suck in a decent breath. It burns as it goes into my lungs, but my muscles unclench as they get oxygen again. I revel in relief. I unwind my body and turn to look down the street.

What I see sends a jolt through me.

Paige is laboriously wheeling herself down the street. Above her, Burnt stops his ascent, circles like a vulture, and begins to swoop down toward her.

I'm up and running like a bullet.

My lungs scream for air but I ignore them.

Burnt looks at me with a smug expression. His wings blow my hair back as I sprint.

So close, so close. Just a little faster. My fault. I pissed him off enough to hurt Paige out of sheer spite. My guilt makes me all the more frantic to save her.

Burnt yells, 'Run, monkey! Run!'

Hands reach down and snatch Paige.

'No!' I scream as I reach out to her.

She's lifted into the air, screaming my name. 'Penryn!'

I catch the hem of her pants, my hand gripping the cotton with the yellow starburst sewn onto it by Mom for protection against evil.

Just for a moment, I let myself believe I can pull her back. For a moment, the tightness in my chest begins to relax with anticipated relief.

The fabric slips out of my hand.

'No!' I jump for her feet. My fingertips brush her shoes. 'Bring her back! You don't want her! She's just a little girl!' My voice breaks at the end.

In no time, the angel is too high to even hear me. I yell at him anyway, chasing them down the street even after Paige's screams fade into the distance. My heart practically stops at the thought of him dropping her from that height.

Time stretches as I stand panting on the street, watching the speck in the sky shrink to nothing.

5

Long after Paige disappears into the clouds, I turn around, looking for my mother. It's not that I don't care about her. It's just that our relationship is more complicated than the usual daughter–mother relationship. The rosy love I'm supposed to feel for her is slashed with black and splattered with various shades of gray.

There is no sign of her. Her cart lies on its side with its junk contents strewn beside the truck we were hiding behind. I hesitate before yelling out.

'Mom?' Anyone or anything that might have been attracted by noise would already be here, watching in the shadows.

'Mom!'

Nothing stirs in the deserted street. If the silent watchers behind the dark windows lining the street saw where she went, nobody is volunteering to tell me. I try to remember if I had maybe seen another angel grab her, but all I can see is Paige's dead legs as she is lifted from the chair. Anything could have happened around me at that time, and I would have been oblivious to it.

In a civilized world where there are laws, banks, and supermarkets, being a paranoid schizophrenic is a major problem. But in a world where the banks and supermarkets are used by gangs as local torture stations, being a little para- noid is actually an advantage. The schizophrenic part, though, is still a problem. Not being able to tell reality from fantasy is less than ideal.

Still, there is a good chance that Mom made herself scarce before things got too ugly. She is probably hiding somewhere, most likely tracking my movements until she feels safe enough to come out.

I survey the scene again. I see only buildings with dark windows and dead cars. If I hadn't spent weeks secretly peer- ing out of one of those dark windows, I might believe I was the last human on the planet. But I know that out there, behind the concrete and steel, there are at least a few pairs of eyes whose owners are considering whether it is worth the risk of running out into the street to scavenge the angel's wings along with any other part of him they can cut off.

According to Justin, who was our neighbor until a week ago, word on the street is that somebody has put a bounty on angel parts. A whole economy is being created around tear- ing angels to pieces. The wings fetch the highest price, but hands, feet, scalp, and other, more sensitive parts, can also fetch a nice sum if only you can prove they're from an angel.

A low groan interrupts my thoughts. My muscles tense instantly, ready for another fight. Are the gangs coming?

Another low moan. The sound is coming not from the buildings, but directly in front of me. The only thing in front of me is the bleeding angel lying on his face.

Could he still be alive?

All the stories I've heard say that if you cut off an angel's wings, he would die. But maybe that is true in the way that if you cut off a person's arm, he would die. Left unchecked, he would simply bleed to death.

There can't be that many chances to get yourself a piece of angel. The street might be flooded with scavengers any minute. The smart thing to do would be to get out while I still can.

But if he's alive, maybe he knows where they took Paige. I trot over, my heart beating furiously with hope.

Blood streams down his back and pools on the asphalt. I flip him over unceremoniously, not even thinking twice about touching him. Even in my frantic state, I notice his ethereal beauty, the smooth rise of his chest. I imagine his face would be classically angelic if not for the bruises and welts.

I shake him. He lies unresponsive, like the Greek god statue he resembles.

I slap him hard. His eyes flutter, and for a moment, they register me. I fight the panicked urge to run.

'Where are they going?'

He moans, his eyelids dropping down. I slap him again, as hard as I can.

'Tell me where they're going. Where are they taking her?'

A part of me hates the new Penryn I've become. Hates the girl who slaps a dying being. But I shove that part deep into a dark corner where it can nag me some other time when Paige is out of danger.

He groans again, and I know he won't be able to tell me anything if I don't stop his bleeding and take him to a place where the gangs aren't likely to swoop down and chop him into little trophies. He is shivering, probably going into deep shock. I flip him over onto his face, this time noticing how light he is.

I run over to my mother's upended cart. I dig through the pile looking for rags to wrap him with. A first aid kit is hidden at the bottom of the cart. I hesitate only a second before grabbing it. I hate to waste precious first aid supplies on an angel who will die anyway, but he looks so human without his wings that I allow myself to use a few sterile bandages as a layer on his cut.

His back is covered with so much blood and dirt that I can't actually see how bad the wounds are. I decide it doesn't matter, so long as I can keep him alive long enough to tell me where they took Paige. I wrap strips of rags around his torso as tightly as I can, trying to put as much pressure on the wounds as possible. I don't know if you can kill a person by making the bindings too tight, but I do know that bleeding to death is faster than death by almost any other way.

I can feel the pressure of unseen eyes on my back as I work. The gangs would assume that I'm cutting out trophies. They're probably assessing whether the other angels are likely to come back and whether they have time to run out to wrestle the pieces out of my hands. I have to bundle him up and get him out of here before they grow too bold. In my haste, I knot him up like a rag doll.

I run over and grab Paige's wheelchair. He is surprisingly light for his size, and it's far less of a struggle than I'd anticipated to get him into the chair. I suppose it makes sense when you think about it. It's easier to fly when you weigh fifty pounds rather than five hundred. Knowing he is stronger and lighter than humans doesn't make me feel any warmer toward him.

I make a show of lifting him and putting him into the chair, grunting and staggering as though he's terribly heavy. I want the watchers to think the angel is as heavy as he looks, because maybe then they'll conclude that I'm stronger and tougher than I look in my underfed five foot two frame.

Is that the beginning of an amused grin forming on the angel's face?

Whatever it is, it turns into a grimace of pain as I dump him into the chair. He is too big to fit comfortably, but it'll do.

I quickly grab the silken wings to wrap them in a moth-eaten blanket from my mother's cart. The snowy feathers are wondrously soft, especially compared to the coarse blanket. Even in this panicked moment, I'm tempted to stroke the smooth down. If I pluck the feathers and use them as currency one at a time, a single wing could probably house and feed all three of us for a year. That is, assuming I can get all three of us back together again.

I quickly wrap both wings, not fretting too much about whether the feathers are being broken. I consider leaving one of the wings here on the street to distract the gangs and encourage them to fight amongst each other instead of chasing me. But I need the wings too much if I am to entice the angel into giving me information. I grab the sword, which is amazingly as light as the feathers, and stick it unceremoniously in the seat pocket of the wheelchair.

I take off at a dead run down the street, pushing him as fast as I can into the night.

6

The angel is dying.

Lying on the sofa with bandages enveloping his torso, he looks exactly like a human. Beads of sweat cluster around his brows. He is fever-warm to the touch, as though his body is working overtime.

We're in an office building, one of countless structures housing tech startups in Silicon Valley. The one I picked is in a business park full of identical blocks. My hope is that if someone decides to raid an office building today, he'll pick one of the others that look just like this one.

To encourage others to pick another building, mine has a dead body in the foyer. He was there when we got here, cold but not yet rotting. At the time, the building still smelled of paper and toner, wood and polish, with only a hint of dead guy. My first instinct was to move on to another place. In fact, I was on my way out when it occurred to me that leaving would be almost everyone's instinct.

The front doors are glass and you can see the corpse from the outside. Two steps inside the glass doors, the dead man lies faceup with his legs akimbo and his mouth gaping. So I picked this building as home sweet home for a while. It's been cold enough in here to keep him from smelling too badly, although I expect we'll have to move soon.

The angel is on the leather couch in what must have been some CEO's corner office. The walls are decorated with framed black-and-white photos of Yosemite, while the desk and shelves sport photos of a woman and two toddlers in matching outfits.

I picked a single-story building, something low-key and not fancy. It's a plain building with a company sign that says Zygotronics. The chairs and couches in the lobby are over-sized and playful, favoring fuzzy purples and overly bright yellows. There's a seven-foot blow-up dinosaur by the cubicles. Very retro Silicon Valley. I think I might have enjoyed working in a place like this if I could have graduated from school.

There's a small kitchen. I just about broke down in tears when I saw the pantry stacked full of snacks and water bottles. Energy bars, nuts, fun-sized chocolates, and even a case of instant noodles, the kind that come in their own cups. Why hadn't I thought to look in offices before? Probably because I'd never worked in one.

I ignore the refrigerator, knowing there's nothing in there worth eating. We still have electricity but it's unreliable and often goes off for days at a time. There must still be frozen meals in the freezer because the smell is not unlike my mother's rotten eggs. The office building even has its own shower, probably for those overweight executives trying to lose weight at lunchtime. Whatever the reason, it came in handy for rinsing off the blood.

All the comforts of home without, of course, my family, who would make it home.

With all the responsibilities and pressures, hardly a day has gone by when I haven't thought I'd be happier without my family. But it turns out that's not true. Maybe it would be if I wasn't so worried about them. I can't help but think how happy Paige and my mother would have been if we'd found this place together. We could have parked here for a week and pretended that everything was all right.

I feel adrift and clanless, lost and insignificant. I begin to understand what drives the new orphans to join the street gangs.

We have been here two days. Two days in which the angel has neither died nor recovered. He just lies there, sweating. I'm pretty sure he's dying. If he wasn't, he would have awakened by now, wouldn't he?

I find a first aid kit under the sink, but the Band-Aids and most of the other supplies are really meant for nothing worse than paper cuts. I rummage through the first aid box, reading the labels on the little packages. There is a bottle of aspirin. Doesn't aspirin reduce fevers as well as get rid of a headache? I read the label, and it confirms my suspicions.

I have no idea if aspirin will work on an angel, or if his fever has anything to do with his wounds. For all I know, this could be his regular temperature. Just because he looks human doesn't mean he is.

I walk back to the corner office with aspirin and a glass of water. The angel lies on his stomach on the black couch. I tried to put a blanket over him that first night, but he just kept kicking it off. So he just has his pants, boots, and bandages wrapped around him. I thought about taking off his pants and boots when I sprayed the blood off him in the shower, but decided that I wasn't here to make him comfortable.

His black hair is plastered to his forehead. I try to get him to swallow some pills and drink some water but I can't wake him enough to do anything. He just lies there like a burning piece of rock, totally unresponsive.

'If you don't drink this water, I'm just going to leave you here to die alone.'

His bandaged back moves up and down serenely, just as it's been doing for the last two days.

In the meantime, I've been out four times looking for Mom. But I haven't gone far, always afraid the angel would wake while I was gone and I would miss my chance to find Paige before he died on me. Crazy women can sometimes fend for themselves on the streets, while wheelchair-bound little girls never can. So each time, I rushed back from my search for Mom, relieved and frustrated to find the angel still unconscious.

For two days, I've been mostly sitting around eating instant noodles while my sister . . .

I can't bear to think about what's happening to her, if for no other reason than my sheer lack of imagination as to what angels would want with a human child. It couldn't be enslavement. She can't walk. I shut down those thoughts. I will not think about what may be happening or what may already have happened. I just need to focus on finding her.

The anger and frustration swamp me. All I want to do is throw a tantrum like a two-year-old. I'm overwhelmed by a strong urge to hurl my glass of water at the wall, tear down the bookshelves and scream my head off. The temptation is so strong my hand starts to tremble, and the water in the glass shakes, threatening to spill.

Instead of hurling the glass against the wall, I throw the water on the angel. I want to smash the glass after it, but I hold back.

'Wake up, damn you. Wake up! What are they doing to my sister? What do they want with her? Where the hell is she?' I scream at the top of my lungs, knowing I could be bringing on street gangs and not caring.

I kick the couch for good measure.

To my utter amazement, his eyes open blearily. They're deep blue and glaring at me. 'Can you keep it down? I'm trying to sleep.' His voice is raw and full of pain, but somehow, he still manages to inject a certain level of condescension.

I drop down on my knees to look directly into his face. 'Where did the other angels go? Where did they take my sister?'

He deliberately closes his eyes.

I slap his back with everything I've got, right where the bandages are bloodied.

His eyes fly open, his teeth gritting. He hisses through his teeth but he doesn't cry out in pain. Wow, does he look pissed off. I resist the urge to take a step back.

'You don't scare me,' I say in my coldest voice, trying to tamp down the fear. 'You're too weak to even stand, you're practically bled out, and without me, you'd already be dead. Tell me where they took her.'

'She's dead,' he says with absolute finality. Then he closes his eyes as though going back to sleep.

I could swear my heart stops beating for a minute. My fingers feel like they're freezing. Then my breath comes back to me in a painful heave.

'You're lying. You're lying.'

He doesn't respond. I grab the old blanket that I left on the desk.

'Look at me!' I unroll the blanket onto the floor. The torn wings come tumbling out of it. Rolled up, they compressed to a tiny fraction of their wingspan. The feathers almost seem to have disappeared. As they tumble out of the blanket, the wings partially open, and the fine down lifts as if stretching after a long nap.

I imagine that the horror in his eyes would be exactly like that of a human's if he saw his own amputated legs rolling out of that moth-eaten blanket. I know I'm being unforgivably cruel, but I don't have the luxury of being nice, not if I ever want to see Paige alive again.

'Recognize these?' I hardly recognize my own voice. It's cold and hard. The voice of a mercenary. The voice of a torturer.

The wings have lost their sheen. There is still a hint of golden highlights in the snowy feathers, but some of the feathers are broken and sticking out at odd angles. Also, blood is splattered and congealed all over the wings, making the feathers clump and shrivel.

'If you help me find my sister, you can have these back. I saved them for you.'

'Thanks,' he croaks, surveying the wings. 'They'll look great on my wall.' Bitterness tinges his voice, but something else is also there. A tiny bit of hope, maybe.

'Before you and your buddies destroyed our world, there used to be doctors who could attach a finger or a hand back onto you if it happened to be cut off.' I don't mention anything about refrigeration or the usual need to reattach a body part within hours of being severed. He'll probably die anyway and none of this will matter.

The tense muscle in his jaw still stands out on his cold face, but his eyes warm just a fraction, as if he can't help but think of the possibilities.

'I didn't cut these off you,' I say. 'But I can help you get them back. If you'll help me find my sister.'

As an answer, he closes his eyes and appears to fall asleep.

He breathes deeply and heavily, just like a person in deep sleep. But he doesn't heal like a person. When I dragged him in here, his face was black, blue, and swelling. Now, after almost two full days of sleeping, his face is back to normal. The dent from his broken ribs has disappeared. The bruises around his cheeks and eyes are gone, and the numerous cuts and marks on his hands, shoulders, and chest are completely healed.

The only things that haven't healed are the wounds where his wings used to be. I can't tell if they're better through the bandages, but since they're still bleeding, they're probably not much better than they were two days ago.

I pause, thinking through my options. If I can't bribe him, I'll have to torture it out of him. I'm determined to do what it takes to keep my family alive, but I don't know if I can go that far.

But he doesn't have to know that.

Now that he's awake, I had better make sure I can keep him under control. I head out to see if I can find something to hold him.

7

When I walk out of the corner office, I find that the dead man in the foyer has been messed with. He seems to have lost all dignity since the last time I saw him.

Someone has arranged for one hand to be propped on his hip while the other hand reaches up to his hair. His long, shaggy hair has been spiked as though electrocuted, and his mouth is smeared drunkenly with lipstick. His eyes are wide open with black felt lines radiating like sun rays from his sockets. In the middle of his chest, a kitchen knife that wasn't there an hour ago sticks out like a flagpole. Someone stabbed a dead body for reasons only the insane can fathom.

My mother has found me.

My mother's condition is not as consistent as some might think. The intensity of her insanity waxes and wanes with no predictable schedule or trigger. Of course, it doesn't help that she's off her meds. When it's good, people might not guess there's anything wrong with her. Those are the days when the guilt of my anger and frustration toward her eats away at me. When it's bad, I might walk out of my room to find a dead-man-turned-toy on the floor.

To be fair, she has never played with corpses before, at least, not that I've seen. Before the world fell apart, she'd always been on the edge and often several steps beyond it. But my dad's desertion, then later the attacks, intensified everything. Whatever rational part that had been holding her back from diving into the darkness simply dissolved.

I think about burying the body, but a cold part of my mind tells me that this is still the best deterrent I could have. Any sane person who looks through the glass doors would run far, far away. We now play a permanent game of I-am-crazier-and-scarier-than-you. And in that game, my mother is our secret weapon.

I walk cautiously toward the bathrooms where the shower is running. Mom hums a haunting melody, one that I think she made up. She used to sing it to us when she was in her half-lucid state. A wordless tune that is both sad and nostalgic. It may have had words to it at one point because every time I hear it, it evokes a sunset over the ocean, an ancient castle, and a beautiful princess who throws herself off the castle walls into the pounding surf below.

I stand outside the bathroom door, listening to her. I associate this song with her coming back from a particularly crazy phase. Usually, she hummed it to us as she patched up whatever bruises or slashes she had caused.

She was always gentle and genuinely sorry during these times. I think it might have been an apology of a sort. Never enough, obviously, but it may have been her way of reaching back to the light, of letting us know that she was surfacing out of the darkness and into the gray zone.

She hummed it incessantly after Paige's 'accident.' We

never did find out exactly what happened. Only Mom and Paige were in the house at the time, and only they will ever know the real story. My mother cried for months after, blaming herself. I blamed her too. How could I not?

'Mom?' I call out through the closed bathroom door.

'Penryn!' she calls out over the shower splashes.

'Are you okay?'

'Yes. Are you? Have you seen Paige? I can't find her anywhere.'

'We'll find her, okay? How did you find me?'

'Oh, I just did.' My mother doesn't usually lie, but she does have a habit of being vaguely evasive.

'How did you find me, Mom?'

The shower runs freely for a while before she answers. 'A demon told me.' Her voice is full of reluctance, full of shame. The world being what it is these days, I might even consider believing her, except that no one but her sees or hears her personal demons.

'That was nice of him,' I say. The demons usually took the blame for the crazy, bad things my mother did. They rarely got credit for anything good.

'I had to promise I'd do something for him.' An honest answer. And a warning.

My mother is stronger than she looks, and when given the upper hand of surprise, she can do serious harm. She's been contemplating defense all her life – how to sneak up on an attacker, how to hide from The Thing That Watches, how to banish the monster back to Hell before it steals the souls of her children.

I consider the possibilities as I lean against the bathroom door. Whatever it is she's promised her demon is guaranteed to be unpleasant. And quite possibly painful. The only question is who the pain will be inflicted upon.

'I'm just going to collect some stuff and hole up in the corner office,' I say. 'I might be in there a day or two, but don't worry, okay?'

'Okay.'

'I don't want you coming into the office. But don't leave the building, okay? There's water and food in the kitchen.' I think about telling her to be careful, but of course, that's ridiculous. For decades, she has been careful about people and monsters trying to kill her. Since the attacks, she's finally found them.

'Penryn?'

'Yeah?'

'Make sure you wear the stars.' She's referring to the yellow asterisks she's sewn on our clothes. How I can *not* wear them is beyond me. They're on everything we own.

'Okay, Mom.'

Despite her star comment, she sounds lucid. Maybe that's not the healthiest thing after desecrating a corpse.

I'm not as helpless as the average teen.

When Paige was two years old, my father and I came home to find her broken and crippled. My mother stood over her in deep shock. We never did find out exactly what happened or how long she stood frozen over Paige. My mother cried and pulled almost all her hair out without saying a word for weeks.

When she finally came out of it, the first thing she said was that I needed to take self-defense lessons. She wanted me to learn to fight. She simply took me to a martial arts studio and prepaid in cash for five years' worth of training.

She talked with the sensei and found out that there were different kinds of martial arts – tae kwon do for fighting when you have a little distance, jujitsu for up close and personal, and escrima for knife fighting. She drove all over town signing me up for all of them and then some. Shooting lessons, archery lessons, survivalist workshops, Sikh camps, women's self-defense, anything she could think of, everything she could find.

When my father found out about it a few days later, she had already spent thousands of dollars we didn't have. My dad, already gray with worry about hospital bills for poor Paige, lost all color in his face when he learned what she had done.

After that rush of manic activity, she seemed to forget about ever having signed me up. The only time she asked me about it was a couple of years later when I found her collection of newspaper articles. I'd seen her cut them out now and then but never wondered what they were. She saved them in an old-fashioned photo album, a pink one that said Baby's First Album. One day, it was out on the table, open and inviting me to glance at it.

The bold title of the article carefully pasted on the open page read, 'Killer Mom Says the Devil Made Me Do It.'

I flipped to the next page. 'Mother Throws Toddlers into Bay and Watches Them Drown.'

Then the next. 'Child Skeletons Found in Woman's Yard.'

In one of the news stories, a six-year-old kid was found two feet from the front door. His mother had stabbed him over a dozen times before she went upstairs to do the same to his little sister.

The story quoted a relative who said that the mother had tried desperately to drop off the kids at her sister's place only a few hours before the massacre, but the sister had to go to work and couldn't take the kids. The relative said it was as though the mother was afraid of what might happen, as if she felt the darkness coming. He described how after the mother snapped out of it and realized what she had done, she nearly tore herself to pieces with her horror and anguish.

All I could think about was what it must have been like for that kid who tried so hard to make it out of the house to get help.

I don't know how long my mother stood there watching me looking through the articles before asking, 'Are you still taking your self-defense classes?'

I nodded.

She didn't say anything. She just walked past with wooden boards and books stacked in her arms.

I found them later on the lid of the toilet seat. For two weeks, she insisted we keep them there to keep the demons from coming up through the pipes. Easier to sleep, she said, when the devil wasn't whispering to her all night.

I never missed a single training session.

8

In the office kitchen, I collect instant noodles, energy bars, duct tape, and half the candy bars. I put the bag into the corner office. The noise doesn't bother the angel, who seems to be enjoying the sleep of the dead again.

I go back to the kitchen just as the sound of the shower stops. I run several bottles of water to the office as fast as I can. Despite being relieved that she has found me, I don't want to see my mom. It's good enough that she's safe and in the building. I need to focus on finding Paige. I can't do that very well if I'm constantly worried about what my mother is up to.

Trying not to look at the corpse in the foyer, I remind myself that Mom can take care of herself. I slip into the corner office, close the door, and bolt it with the door lock. Whoever had this office must have enjoyed his privacy. It works for me.

I felt safe from the angel when he was unconscious, but now that he's awake, him being wounded and weak is not enough to guarantee my safety. I don't actually know how strong angels are. Like everyone else, I know close to nothing about them.

I duct tape his wrists and ankles together behind his back so that he's hog-tied in the most uncomfortable-looking position. It's the best I can do. I consider using twine to rein-force the duct tape, but the tape is strong and I figure if he can get past that, the twine isn't really going to add much to it. I'm pretty sure he barely has enough energy to lift his head, but you never know. In my nervousness, I use almost the entire roll of tape.

It's not until I'm done and looking at him that I notice that he is looking back at me. All that hog-tying must have woken him up. His eyes are so blue they're almost black. I take a step back and swallow the absurd guilt that surfaces. I feel like I've been caught doing something I shouldn't be doing. But there's no question the angels are our enemies. No question that they're my enemies, so long as they have Paige.

He looks at me with accusation in his eyes. I swallow an apology because I don't owe him one. While he watches, I unfurl one of his wings. I pick up scissors from the desk drawer and bring them close to the feathers.

'Where did they take my sister?'

The briefest emotion flickers in his eyes, gone so fast that I can't identify it. 'How the hell should I know?'

'Because you're one of the stinking bastards.'

'Ooh. You cut me to the bone with that one.' He sounds bored, and I'm almost embarrassed by my lack of a stronger insult. 'Didn't you notice I wasn't exactly chummy with the other fellas?'

'They're not "fellas." They're not anywhere near human. They're nothing but leaking sacks of mutated maggots, just like you.' Looks-wise, he and the other angels I'd seen were closer to living Adonises, complete with godlike faces and presences. But inside, they were maggots for sure.

'Leaking sacks of mutated maggots?' He raises his perfectly arched eyebrow as though I've just failed my verbal insult exam.

In response, I cut through several feathers of his wing with a cruel snap of my scissors. Snowy down floats gently onto my boots. Instead of satisfaction, I feel a wave of uneasiness at the expression on his face. His fierce glare reminds me that he had been outnumbered five to one by his enemies, and he had nearly won. Even hog-tied and wingless, he sure could give an intimidating look.

'Try doing that again and I'll snap you in half before you know it.'

'Big words from a guy who's trussed up like a turkey. What are you going to do, wobble over here like an upside-down turtle to snap me in half?'

'The logistics of breaking you are easy. The only question is when.'

'Right. If you could do it, you would have done it already.'

'Maybe you entertain me,' he says with supreme confidence, as if he's in control of the situation. 'Like a monkey with an attitude and a pair of scissors.' He relaxes and rests his chin on the couch.

A flush of anger heats my cheeks. 'You think this is a game? You think you wouldn't be dead already if it wasn't for my sister?' I practically yell this last part. I viciously chop through more of the feathers. The once exquisite perfection of the wing is now tattered and jagged at the edges.

His head pops back up from the couch, the tendons on his neck straining so hard that I wonder just how weak he really is. The muscles in his arms flex, and I start worrying about the strength of the bindings around his limbs.

'Penryn?' My mother's voice floats through the door. 'Are you all right?'

I look to make sure the door is locked.

When I look back at the couch, the angel is gone, with only shreds of duct tape where he should be.

I feel a breath on my neck as the scissors are snatched out of my hand.

'I'm fine, Mom,' I say with a surprising degree of calm. Having her nearby will only endanger her. Telling her to run will probably make her freak in panic. The only sure thing is that her response will be unpredictable.

A well-muscled arm slides around my throat from behind and begins to squeeze.

Grabbing his arm around my neck, I tuck my chin down hard, trying to transfer the pressure of his arm onto my chin rather than my throat. I have about twenty seconds to get out of this before either my brain shuts off or my windpipe collapses.

I crouch as low as I can. Then I spring backward, slamming us both into the wall. The impact is harder than if he'd weighed as much as a normal man.

I hear an 'Oof' and the clattering of photo frames, and I know those gashes on his back must be screaming from the sharp frame edges.

'What's that noise?' my mother demands.

The arm squeezes viciously around my throat, and I decide the term 'angel of mercy' is an oxymoron. Not wasting my energy on fighting the choke, I gather myself for another slam into the wall. The least I can do is cause a lot of pain while he takes me out.

This time, his groan is sharper. I would get a lot of satisfaction out of that, except that my head is feeling light and spotty.

One more slam and dark spots bloom all over my vision.

Just as I realize my vision is going out, he loosens his grip. I fall to my knees, gasping for air through my raw throat. My head feels too heavy on my neck, and it's all I can do to not fall flat on the floor.

'Penryn Young, you open this door right now!' The doorknob jiggles. My mother must have been calling out all this time, but it hadn't really registered.

The angel groans like he's in real pain. He crawls past me and I see why. His back bleeds through the bandages in spots that look like puncture wounds. I glance behind me at the wall. Two oversized nails that used to hold up the framed Yosemite poster stick out from the wall, their heads dripping with blood.

The angel is not the only one in bad shape. I can't seem to take a breath without doubling over in a coughing fit.

'Penryn? Are you okay?' My mom sounds worried. What she imagines is happening in here, I can't begin to guess.

'Yeah,' I croak. 'It's okay.'

The angel crawls onto the couch and lies on his stomach with another groan. I flash him an evil grin.

'You,' he says with a dirty look, 'don't deserve salvation.'

'As if you could give it to me,' I croak. 'Why would I want to go to Heaven anyway when it's crammed full of murderers and kidnappers like you and your buddies?'

'Who says I belong in Heaven?' It's true that the nasty snarl he's giving me belongs more to a hellion than to a heavenly being. He mars the fiendish image with a wince of pain.

'Penryn? Who are you talking to?' My mother sounds almost frantic now.

'Just my own personal demon, Mom. Don't worry. He's just a little weakling.'

Weak or not, we both know he could have killed me if that's what he wanted. I won't give him the satisfaction of knowing I was scared, though.

'Oh.' She sounds calm suddenly, as if that explained everything. 'Okay. Don't underestimate them. And don't make them promises you can't keep.' I can tell by her fading voice as she says this that she's reassured and walking away.

The baffled look the angel shoots at the door makes me chuckle. He glances my way, giving me a you're-weirder-than-your-mom look.

'Here.' I toss him a roll of bandages from my stash. 'You probably want to put pressure on that.'

He catches it neatly even as he closes his eyes. 'How am I supposed to reach my back?'

'Not my problem.'

He relaxes his hand with a sigh, and the bandage rolls onto the floor, leaving a ribbon on the carpet.

'You're not sleeping again, are you?'

His only response is a muffled, 'Mmm,' as his breathing turns heavy and regular like a man in deep sleep.

Damn.

I stand there, watching him. This is obviously some kind of healing sleep by the look of his previously repaired injuries. If he wasn't so gravely injured and exhausted, there's no doubt he would have kicked my ass to kingdom come and back, even if he chose not to kill me. But it still irks me that he sees me as such a small threat as to actually fall asleep in my presence.

Duct tape was a bad idea that only made sense when I thought he was weak as wet paper. Now that I know better, what are my options?

I dig around the office kitchen drawers and supply room and come up with nothing. It's not until I go through someone's gym bag under a desk that I find an old-fashioned bike lock, the kind with heavy chains wrapped in plastic, with a key in the lock. There's something to be said for an old-school chaining.

There's nothing in the office to chain him to, so I use a metal cart sitting next to the copier. I sweep the stacks of paper off it and roll it into the corner office. My mother is nowhere to be seen, and I can only assume she is giving me the professional courtesy of letting me deal with my 'personal demon' in private.

I roll the cart next to the sleeping man – angel, I mean angel. Careful not to wake him, I loop the chain tightly around each of his wrists, then wrap it several times around one of the metal legs of the cart so that it takes up all the slack. Then I snap the lock shut with a satisfying click.

The chain can slide up and down the cart leg but can't escape it. This is an even better idea than I first realized because I can now move him around without him being able to run off. Wherever he's going, the cart will go with him.

I roll up his wings in the blanket and stow them away in one of the large metal filing cabinets beside the kitchen. I almost feel like a grave robber as I pull the files out of the drawer and stack them on top of the cabinet. I run my fingers along the stack. Each of these files used to mean something. A home, a patent, a business. Someone's dream left to collect dust in an abandoned office.

As an afterthought, I drop the key to the chain lock in the drawer where I stored the angel sword on the first night.

I trot back through the lobby and slip into the corner office. The angel is still asleep or comatose, I'm not sure which. I lock the door and curl up on the executive chair.

His beautiful face blurs as my eyelids get heavier. I haven't slept in two days, afraid to miss the one chance I might have if the angel woke, only to die on me. Asleep, he looks like a bleeding Prince Charming chained in the dungeon. When I was little, I always thought I'd be Cinderella, but I guess this makes me the wicked witch.

But then again, Cinderella didn't live in a post-apocalyptic world invaded by avenging angels.

*   *   *

I know something is wrong before I wake. In the twilight between waking and sleeping, I hear glass breaking. I'm wired and alert before the sound fades.

A hand clamps onto my mouth.

The angel shushes me with a whisper lighter than air. The first thing I see in the dim moonlight is the metal cart. He must have jumped off the couch and rolled it over here in the split second it took for the glass to break.

It dawns on me that if, for the moment, the angel and I are on the same side, then someone else is a threat to us both.

9

Below the door, light plays back and forth in the semidarkness.

The fluorescent lights were on when I fell asleep but now it's dark with only the moonlight streaming in through the windows. The light moving in the crack beneath the door looks like a flashlight jerking back and forth. Either an intruder came in with flashlights, or my mother turned one on when the lights went off. A sure sign of habitation.

It's not that she's unaware of the risks. She's far from stupid. It's just that her brand of paranoia makes her fear supernatural predators more than natural ones. So sometimes, lighting the dark to ward off evil is more important to her than avoiding detection by mere mortals. Lucky me.

Even chained and pulling a metal cart, the angel moves like a cat to the door.

Dark stains seep through his white bandages like Rorschach patterns on his back. He may be strong enough to break a roll of duct tape, but he is still wounded and bleeding. Just how strong is he? Strong enough to fight off half a dozen street thugs desperate enough to roam at night?

I suddenly wish I hadn't chained him. It's a good bet that whoever the intruder is, he's not alone, not at night.

'Hell-ooo,' a man's voice calls out playfully through the dark. 'Anybody home?'

The lobby is carpeted, and I can't tell how many of them there are until things start to crash from different directions. It sounds like there are at least three of them.

Where's Mom? Did she have time to run and hide?

I gauge the window. It won't be easy to break, but if the gang members could do it, I should be able to. It is certainly large enough for me to hop through. Thank whatever goodness is left in the world that we're on the ground floor.

I push at the glass, testing the sturdiness of it. It would take time to break this. Plus, the noise would echo throughout the building as I bang repeatedly on the window.

Outside, the gang calls to each other. They hoot and holler, smash and crash. They're performing for us, making sure we're good and scared by the time they find us. By the sound of things, there are at least six of them now.

I glance again at the angel. He's listening, probably figuring out his odds. Being wounded and chained to a metal cart, his chance of outrunning a street gang is about zero.

On the other hand, if the gang is drawn by the noise of the window breaking, they would be fully occupied as soon as they saw the angel. The angel is like the proverbial gold mine and they the lucky miners. Mom and I could get away during the chaos. But then what? The angel can't tell me where to find Paige if he's dead.

Maybe the gang will just break a few things, raid the food in the kitchen, and leave.

A woman's scream pierces the night.

My mother.

Men's voices shout and tease. They sound entertained, the way a pack of dogs might sound if they'd cornered a cat.

I grab a chair and smash it against the window. It makes a huge bang and flexes, but doesn't break. I want to make as much of a distraction as I can, hoping the noise will make them forget about my mother. I bang it again. And again. Frantically trying to break the window.

She screams again. Shouts come my way.

The angel grabs his cart and hurls it at the window. Glass explodes in every direction. I cringe but a distant part of my mind is aware that the angel has shifted, using his body to block the shards from hitting me.

Something thumps hard against the locked door of our office. The door rattles but the locks hold.

I grab the cart and pull it up to the windowsill, trying to help the angel get out.

The door crashes open, bouncing off the wall with broken hinges.

The angel spares me a quick, hard glance and says, 'Run.'

I vault out the window.

I land running. I dash around the building, looking for the back entrance or a broken window to jump through. My mind is crowded with what might be happening to my mother, to the angel, to Paige. I have an almost irresistible urge to hide under a bush and curl up in a ball. To shut off my eyes, ears, and brain, and just lie there until nothing exists anymore.

I shove the horrible, screaming images in my head into the dark, silent place in my mind that is getting deeper and more crowded each day. One day soon, the things I stuff in there will burst out and infect the rest of me. Maybe that will be the day the daughter becomes like the mother. Until then, I am still in control.

I don't have to go far to find a broken window. Considering how many times I banged at my window and still failed to break it, I hate to think about how amped up the guy who broke this one must be. That doesn't make me feel any better about sneaking back into the building.

I run from office to office, cubicle to cubicle, whisper-shouting for my mother.

I find a man lying in the hallway leading to the kitchen. His chest is bare, his shirt torn away. Six butter knives stick out of his flesh in a circular pattern. Someone has drawn a powder-pink lipstick pentagram with the knives at the end of the points. Blood bubbles up from each of the knives. The man is all eyes and shock as he stares at the ruin of his chest as though unable to believe it has anything to do with him.

My mother is safe.

Seeing what she did to this man, I can't help but wonder if that's a good thing. She has purposely missed his heart, and he will slowly bleed to death.

If we had been back in the old world, in the World Before, I would have called an ambulance despite the fact that he had attacked my mom. The doctors would have fixed him up, and he would have had all the time he needed to recover in jail. But unfortunately for all of us, this is the World After.

I step around him and leave him to his slow death.

Out of the corner of my eye, I catch a glimpse of a woman-shaped shadow slipping out through a side door. She stops before the door closes and looks back at me. My mother frantically waves her hand at me to come with her. I should join her. I take two steps in her direction, but I can't ignore the grunting and crashing of the colossal fight at the far end of the building.

The angel is surrounded by a gang of scruffy but deadly looking men.

There must be at least ten of them. Three are strewn about at odd angles beyond the circle of the fight, unconscious or dead. Two more are taking a beating from the angel as he swings the cart like a giant mace. But even from here, even in the thin moonlight streaming in through the glass doors, I can see the crimson stains seeping through his bandages. That cart must weigh a hundred pounds. He is visibly exhausted and the others are moving in for the kill.

I've sparred with multiple opponents in the dojo, and last summer, I was one of the assistant instructors of an advanced self-defense course entitled 'Multiple Assailants.' Still, I've never fought more than three at a time. And none of my opponents have ever wanted to actually kill me. I'm not stupid enough to think that I can take on seven desperate guys with the help of a crippled angel. My heart tries to gallop out of my chest just thinking about it.

My mother waves at me again, beckoning me toward freedom.

Something smashes on the far side of the lobby and a grunt of pain follows it. With every hit to the angel, I feel Paige slipping away from me.

I wave my mother away, mouthing the word *go*.

She beckons me once more, more frantic this time.

I shake my head and wave her away.

She slips into the darkness and disappears behind the closing door.

I bolt over to the filing cabinet beside the kitchen. I quickly think through the pros and cons of using the angel sword and decide against it. I might slice up one person with it, but without training, I'm sure it would be taken away from me in no time.

So instead, I grab the wings and the key to the angel's chain. I stuff the key in my jeans pocket and quickly unwrap the wings. My only hope is that the gang's fear and desire for self-preservation will be on my side. Before my brain can kick in and tell me what a harebrained, dangerous idea this is, I rush over to the dim hallway where the moonlight is bright enough to silhouette me, but not bright enough to show much detail.

The gang has the angel cornered.

He's putting up a good fight, but they've realized that he's injured – not to mention chained to an awkward, heavy cart – and won't give up now that they smell blood.

I cross my arms behind me and hold the wings behind my back. They wobble, out of balance. It's like holding up a flagpole with my arms contorted. I wait until I can hold them steady, then step forward.

Desperately hoping that the wings look right in the shadows, I kick over a side table with a surprisingly intact vase on it. The unexpected crash gets their attention.

For a second, everyone is silent as they look on my dark silhouette. I hope to all that's holy and unholy that I look like an Angel of Death. If it was well lit, they would see a skinny teenage girl trying to hold oversized wings behind her back. But it's dark, and they are hopefully seeing the one thing that makes their blood run cold.

'What have we here?' I ask in what I hope is a tone of deadly amusement. 'Michael, Gabriel, come see this,' I call out behind me as though there are more of us. Michael and Gabriel are the only two angel names I can think of. 'The monkeys seem to think they can attack one of our own now.'

The men freeze. Everyone stares at me.

In that moment, while I hold my breath, possibilities roll around the room like a roulette wheel.

Then, a really bad thing happens.

My right wing wobbles, then slips down a notch or two. In my rush to right it, I wiggle to get a better grip, but that just brings more attention to it as the wing waves up and down.

In the long second before everyone absorbs what just happened, I see the angel rolling his eyes heavenward, like a teenager in the presence of overwhelming lameness. Some people just have no sense of gratitude.

The angel is the first one to break the silence. He heaves his cart up and swings it at the three guys in front of him, crashing through them like a bowling ball.

Three of the others come for me.

I drop my wings and scuttle to their left. The trick with fighting multiple assailants is to avoid fighting them all at the same time. Unlike in the movies, attackers don't wait in line to kick your ass; they want to pounce all at once like a pack of wolves.

I dance in a semicircle around them until the guy closest to me is in the way of the other two. It only takes a second for them to run around their buddy, but that's enough time for me to snap a solid kick to his groin. He doubles over, and though I'm dying to accept the invitation to knee him in the face, his buddies take precedence.

I dance around to the other side of the doubled-over guy, making the others fall back into a line to get around him. I sweep the injured guy's feet, and he comes crashing down on wifebeater number two. The remaining guy pounces on me and we roll on the ground in a grapple for the top position.

I end up on the bottom. He outweighs me by a hundred pounds, but this is a position I've practiced fighting from over and over.

Men tend to fight differently with a woman than they do with men. The overwhelming majority of fights between men and women start with the man attacking from behind, and almost instantly end on the ground with the woman on the bottom. So a good female fighter needs to know how to fight on her back.

As we struggle, I wriggle my leg out from under him for leverage. Brace. Then tip him over to one side with a twist of my hip.

He flips onto his back. Before he can get his bearings again, I slam my heel down on his groin.

I'm up in a flash and kicking his head before he recovers. I kick him so hard his head whiplashes back and forth.

'Nice.' The angel stands watching in the moonlight behind his bloody cart.

Around him are the moaning bodies of our intruders. Some of the bodies are so still I can't tell if they're alive. He nods appreciatively as though he sees something he likes. I let myself have an internal tongue-lashing when I realize I'm pleased by his approval.

A guy staggers up and runs for the door. He holds his head as though afraid it will fall off. As if that was their cue, three more get up and stumble out the door without looking back. The rest lie panting on the ground.

I hear a weak laugh and realize it's the angel.

'You looked ridiculous with those wings,' he says. His lip is bleeding and so is a cut above his eye. But he looks relaxed as his smile lights up his face.

I dig out the bike lock key from my pocket with trembling hands and toss it to him. He catches it even though he's still chained.

'Let's get out of here,' I say. It sounds less shaky than I feel. The post-fight adrenaline has me literally trembling. The angel unlocks himself, stretches, and cracks his wrists. Then he rips a denim jacket off one of the groaning guys on the floor and tosses it to me. I gratefully put it on even though it's about ten sizes too big.

He goes back into the corner office while I quickly roll his wings in the blanket. I run to the filing cabinet to grab the sword, then meet him in the lobby as he comes back out with my pack. I strap the blanket onto the pack, trying not to cinch it too hard under his gaze, then load up. I wish I had a pack for him but he wouldn't be able to carry it on his wounded back anyway.

When he sees the sword, his face breaks into a glorious smile as if it's a long-lost friend rather than a pretty piece of metal. His look of sheer joy stops my breath for a moment. It's a look I thought I'd never see again on anyone's face. I feel lighter just being close to it.

'You had my sword the whole time?'

'It's my sword now.' My voice comes out harsher than the situation calls for. His happiness is so human that I forgot for an instant what he really is. I dig my nails into my palm to remind myself never to let my thoughts slip again.

'Your sword? You wish,' he says. What I wish is that he would stop sounding so damned human. 'Do you have any idea how loyal she's been to me over the years?'

'She? You're not one of those people who name their cars and coffee mugs, are you? It's an inanimate object. Get over it.'

He reaches for the sword. I step back, not wanting to hand it over.

'What are you going to do, fight me for her?' he asks. He sounds like he's close to laughing.

'What are you going to do with it?'

He sighs, seeming tired. 'Use it as a crutch, what do you think?'

There is a moment when a decision hangs in the air. The truth is that he doesn't need the sword to beat me now that he's free and on his feet. He could just take it, and we both know it.

'I saved your life,' I say.

He arches an eyebrow. 'Questionable.'

'Twice.'

He finally drops the hand that had been reaching for the sword. 'You're not going to give me back my sword, are you?'

I grab Paige's wheelchair, stick the sword in the seatback pocket. So long as he's too tired to argue, I'm better off maintaining control. Either he really is exhausted, or he's decided to just let me carry it for him like a knight's little squire. By the way he glances at the sword with a half grin, I'm guessing it's the latter reason.

I wheel Paige's chair around and roll out.

'I don't think I'll be needing that chair anymore,' says the angel. He sounds exhausted, and I'm willing to bet he wouldn't say no if I offered to push him in the chair.

'It's not for you. It's for my sister.'

He is silent as we walk into the night, and I know he thinks Paige will never see the wheelchair.

He can go to Hell.

10

Silicon Valley is about half an hour by car from the forest in the hills. It's also about forty-five minutes away from San Francisco if you're driving on the freeway. I figure the roads will be clogged with deserted cars and desperate people. So we head for the hills where there are fewer people and more places to hide.

Until a few weeks ago, rich people lived along the lower hills, either in three-bedroom ranch houses that cost a couple million dollars, or in fairytale mansions that cost ten million dollars. We stay away from those, my logic being that they probably attract the wrong kind of visitors. Instead, we pick out a little guesthouse behind one of the estates. A not-too-fancy kind of guesthouse that won't attract any attention.

The angel just follows me without comment, and that works fine for me. He hasn't said much since we left the office building. It's been a long night, and he can barely stand by the time we reach the cottage. We make it to the house just before a storm hits.

It's strange. In some ways, he's shockingly strong. He's been beaten, mutilated, and bleeding for days, yet he can still fight off several men at a time. He never seems to get cold despite being shirtless and jacketless. But the walking seems hard on him.

When we finally sit in the cabin as the rain starts, he eases off his boots. His feet are blistered and raw. They're pink and vulnerable as though they haven't been used much. Maybe they haven't. If I had wings, I'd probably spend most of my time flying too.

I dig through my pack and find the small first aid kit. In it, there are some blister packs. They're like adhesive bandages but bigger and tougher. I hand the packages to the angel. He opens one up and stares at it like he's never seen one before.

He first looks at the skin-colored side, which is a shade too light for him, then at the padded side, then back at the skin-colored side again. He puts it up to his eye like a pirate's eye patch and makes a grimace.

My lips crack into a quarter smile even though it's hard for me to believe I can still smile. I grab it out of his hand. 'Here, I'll show you how to use it. Let me see your foot.'

'That's a pretty intimate demand in the angel world. It usually takes dinner, some wine, and sparkling conversation for me to give up my feet.'

That calls for a witty comeback.

'Whatever,' I say.

Okay, so I won't be getting the Witty Woman of the Year Award. 'Do you want me to show you how to use this or not?' I sound surly. It's the best I can do right now.

He sticks out his feet. Angry red spots scream for attention on his heels and big toes. One foot has a burst blister on the heel.

I look at my meager supply of blister packs. I'll have to use them all on his feet and hope that my own will hold out. The small voice pipes up again as I gently place the adhesive around his burst blister: *He won't be with you for more than a couple of days. Why waste precious supplies on him?*

He pulls a glass splinter out of his shoulder. He's been doing that the whole time we've been walking, but he keeps finding more. If he hadn't stepped in front of me when he broke through the window, I'd be peppered with glass shards too. I'm almost sure he didn't protect me on purpose, but I can't help but be grateful that he did.

I carefully soak up pus and blood with a sterile pad, even though I know that if he is going to get an infection, it would come from the deep wounds on his back, not from a few blisters on his feet. The thought of his lost wings makes my hands gentler than they would be otherwise.

'What's your name?' I ask.

I don't need to know. In fact, I don't *want* to know. Giving him a name makes it sound like we're somehow on the same side, which we can never be. It's like acknowledging that we could become friends. But that's not possible. It's pointless to make friends with your executioner.

'Raffe.'

I only asked him his name to distract him from thinking about having to use his feet instead of his wings. But now that I know his name, it feels right. 'Rah-fie,' I repeat slowly. 'I like the sound of that.'

His eyes soften as though he smiles even though his

expression doesn't change from his stony look. For some reason, it makes my face heat up.

I clear my throat to break the tension. 'Raffe sounds like Raw Feet. Coincidence?' That gets a smile out of him. When he smiles, he really does look like someone you'd want to get to know. Some otherworldly handsome guy a girl could dream about.

Only he's not a guy. And he's too otherworldly. Not to mention that this girl is beyond dreaming about anything other than food, shelter, and the safety of her family.

I rub my finger firmly around the adhesive to make sure it won't fall off. He inhales sharply and I can't tell if it's from pain or pleasure. I'm careful to keep my eyes down on my task.

'So, aren't you going to ask me my name?' I could kick myself. That sounds just like me flirting. But I'm not, of course. I couldn't be. At least I'd managed to keep the tone from being giggly.

'I already know your name.' Then he mimics my mother's voice perfectly. 'Penryn Young, you open this door right now!'

'That's pretty good. You sound just like her.'

'You must have heard the old adage that there's power in knowing someone's true name.'

'Is it true?'

'It can be. Especially between species.'

'Then why did you just tell me yours?'

He leans back and gives me a bad boy, devil-may-care shrug.

'So what do they call you if they don't know your name?'

There's a brief pause before he answers. 'The Wrath of God.'

I take my hand off his foot in a slow controlled motion to keep it from shaking. I realize then that if someone could see us, it might look like I am paying him homage. He sits in a chair while I kneel at his feet with my eyes downcast. I quickly stand up so that I am looking down at him. I take a deep breath, square my shoulders, and look him straight in the eyes.

'I am not afraid of you, your kind, or your god.'

There's a part of me that cringes at the lightning strike that I am sure will come. But it doesn't. There isn't even dramatic thunder outside in the storm. It doesn't make me feel any less afraid, though. I am an ant on the battlefield of the gods. There's no room for pride or ego, and barely enough room for survival. But I can't help myself. Who do they think they are? We may be ants, but this field is our home, and we have every right to live in it.

His expression changes just a fraction before he shutters it in his godlike way. I'm not sure what it means, but I do know that my insane statement has some kind of an effect on him, even if it's just amusement.

'I don't doubt it, Penryn.' He says my name as though he is tasting something new, rolling it over his tongue to see how he likes it. There's an intimacy in the way he says it that makes me want to squirm.

I toss the remaining blister packets onto his lap. 'Now you know how to use them. Welcome to my world.'

I turn around, showing him my back, emphasizing my lack of fear. At least, that's what I tell myself. It's also convenient that by turning my back on him, I can let my hands shake a little as I dig through my pack for something to eat.

'Why are you guys here, anyway?' I ask as I rummage for food. 'I mean, it's obvious that you're not here for a friendly chat, but why do you want to get rid of us? What did we do to deserve extermination?'

He shrugs. 'Beats me.'

I stare at him, openmouthed.

'Hey, I don't call the shots,' he says. 'If I was good at marketing, I'd spin you an empty story that sounds profound. But the truth is that we're all just stumbling around in the dark. Sometimes we hit something terrible.'

'That's it? It can't be as random as that.' I don't know what I want to hear, but that's not it.

'It's always as random as that.'

He sounds more like a seasoned soldier than any angel I've ever heard of. One thing's for sure – I'm not going to get a lot of answers out of him.

Dinner is instant noodles and a couple of energy bars. We also have bite-sized chocolates plundered from the office for dessert. I wish we could light up the fireplace, but the smoke from the chimney would be a sure sign that the cottage is occupied. Same for the lights. I have a couple of flashlights in my bag, but remembering that it was my mother's flashlight that probably attracted the gang, we crunch our dried noodles and oversweetened energy bars in the dark.

He scarfs down his portion so fast that I can't help but stare. I don't know when he last ate, but he certainly hasn't eaten in the two days I've known him. I'm also guessing that his super-healing consumes a lot of calories too. We don't have much, but I offer him half my share. If he had been awake the last couple of days, I'd have had to feed him a lot more than this.

My hand stays out with the offered food long enough to make it awkward. 'Don't you want it?' I ask.

'That depends on why you're giving it to me.'

I shrug. 'Sometimes, as we're stumbling along in the dark, we hit something good.'

He watches me for another second before taking the offered food.

'Don't think you're getting my share of the chocolate, though.' I know I should conserve the chocolate, but I can't help eating more than I'd planned. The waxy texture and burst of sweetness in my mouth brings comfort that's too rare to pass up. I won't let us eat more than half my stash, though. I stuff the rest way down in the bottom of my pack so I won't be tempted.

My longing for the candy must show on my face because the angel asks, 'Why don't you just eat it? We can eat something else tomorrow.'

'It's for Paige.' I zip up my pack with finality, ignoring his thoughtful look.

I wonder where my mother is now. I'd always suspected that she is more clever than my father, even though he is the one with the master's degree in engineering. But all her animal cleverness won't help her when her crazy instincts are demanding her attention. Some of the worst times in my life have been because of her. But I can't help but hope that she's found a dry place out of the rain, and has managed to find something to eat for dinner.

I dig through my pack and find the last Styrofoam cup of dried noodles. I walk to the door and leave it outside.

'What are you doing?'

I think about explaining to him about my mother but decide against it. 'Nothing.'

'Why would you leave food outside in the rain?'

How did he know it was food? It's too dark for him to see the cup of noodles.

'How well can you see in the dark?'

There's a brief pause as though he's considering denying that he can see in the dark. 'Almost as well as I can see in the day.'

I squirrel away the intel. This little piece of information may have just saved my life. Who knows what I would have done once I found the other angels? I may have tried to hide in the dark as I snuck into their nest. That would have been a nasty time to find out just how well angels can see in the dark.

'So, why would you leave valuable food outside?'

'In case my mother is out there.'

'Wouldn't she just come in?'

'Maybe. Maybe not.'

He nods as if he understands, which, of course, he couldn't. Maybe to him, all humans behave as though they are crazy.

'Why don't you bring the food in, and I'll tell you if she's nearby.'

'And how would you know if she's nearby?'

'I'll hear her,' he says. 'Assuming the rain doesn't get too loud.'

'How good is your hearing?'

'What?'

'Ha ha,' I say dryly. 'Knowing this stuff could make a big difference in my chances of rescuing my sister.'

'You don't even know where she is, or if she's alive.' He says this matter-of-factly, as if he's talking about the weather.

'But I know where you are, and I know you'll be headed back to the other angels, even if it's only to get revenge.'

'Ah, is that how it is? Since you couldn't get the information out of me when I was weak and helpless, your big plan now is to follow me back to the nest of vipers to rescue your sister? You know that's about as well-thought-out as your plan to scare off those men by pretending to be an angel.'

'A girl's gotta improvise as the situation changes.'

'The situation has changed beyond your control. You'll only get yourself killed if you follow this path, so take my advice and run the other way.'

'You don't understand. This isn't about making logical, optimal decisions. It's not like I have a choice. Paige is just a helpless little girl. She's my sister. The only thing up for discussion is *how* I'll rescue her, not whether or not I'll try.'

He leans back to give me an appraising look. 'I wonder which will get you killed faster – your loyalty or your stubbornness?'

'Neither, if you'll help me.'

'And why would I do that?'

'I saved your life. Twice. You owe me. In some cultures, you'd be my slave for life.'

It's hard to see his expression in the dark, but his voice sounds both skeptical and wry. 'Granted, you did drag me out of the street while I was injured. And normally, that may qualify as saving my life, but since your intent was to kidnap me for interrogation, I don't think that counts. And if you're referring to your botched "rescue" attempt during my fight with those men, I'd have to remind you that if you hadn't slammed my back into giant nails sticking out of the wall, then chained me to a cart, I'd never have been in that position in the first place.'

He chuckles. 'I can't believe those idiots almost bought that you were an angel.'

'They didn't.'

'Only because you screwed up. I almost burst out laughing when I saw you.'

'It would have been pretty funny if our lives hadn't been at stake.'

His voice sobers. 'So you know you could have been killed?'

'So could you.'

The wind whispers outside, rustling the leaves. I open the door and retrieve the cup of noodles. I might as well believe that he'll hear my mother if she comes around. It's better if we don't risk someone else seeing the food and coming into the cabin.

I pull out a sweatshirt from my pack and put it on over the one I'm wearing. The temperature is dropping fast. Then I finally ask the question to which I dread the answer. 'What do they want with the kids?'

'There's been more than one taken?'

'I've seen the street gangs take them. I figured they wouldn't want Paige because of her legs. But now, I wonder if they're selling them to the angels.'

'I don't know what they're doing with the kids. Your sister is the first one I've heard of.' His quiet voice chills me.

The rain pounds on the windows and the wind scrapes a branch on the glass.

'Why were the other angels attacking you?'

'It's impolite to ask the victim of violence what they did to be attacked.'

'You know what I mean.'

He shrugs in the dim light. 'Angels are violent creatures.'

'So I noticed. I used to think they were all sweet and kind.'

'Why would you think that? Even in your Bible, we're harbingers of doom, willing and able to destroy entire cities. Just because we sometimes warned one or two of you before-hand doesn't make us altruistic.'

I have more questions, but I need to settle one thing first. 'You need me.'

He barks a laugh. 'How so?'

'You need to get back to your buddies to see if you can get your wings sewn back on. I saw it in your face when I mentioned it back at the office. You think it might be possible. But to get there, you have to walk. You've never traveled on the ground before, have you? You need a guide; someone who can find food and water, safe shelter.'

'You call this food?' The moonlight shows him tossing the empty Styrofoam cup into a trash can. It's too dark to see it land in the can across the room, but by the sound of things, it's a three-pointer.

'See? You would have passed that by. We have all kinds of stuff that you'd never guess was food. Besides, you need someone who'll take the suspicion off you. No one will suspect you as an angel if you're traveling with a human. Take me with you. I'll help you get home if you'll help me find my sister.'

'So you want me to lead a Trojan Horse to the aerie?'

'Hardly. I'm not out to save the world, just my sister. That's more than enough responsibility for me. Besides, what are you worried about? Little ol' me being a threat to angelkind?'

'What if she's not there?'

I have to swallow the dry lump in my throat before I can answer. 'Then I'll no longer be your problem.'

The darker shadow of his form curls up on the couch. 'Let's get some sleep while it's still dark out.'

'That's not a no, right?'

'It's not a yes either. Now let me sleep.'

'And that's another thing. It's easier to keep a watch at night when there are two of us.'

'But it's easier to sleep when there's just one.' He grabs a sofa pillow and puts it over his ear. He shifts once more, then settles in, his breathing turning heavy and regular as though already asleep.

I sigh and walk back to the bedroom. The air gets colder as I near the room, and I have second thoughts about sleeping in there.

As soon as I open the door, I see why it's so cold in the cottage. The window is broken and sheets of rain blow onto the bed. I'm so tired I could just sleep on the floor. I grab a folded blanket off the dresser. It's cold but dry. I close the bedroom door to keep the wind out and pad back into the living room. I lie down on the sofa across from the angel, wrapping myself in the blanket.

He seems to be comfortably asleep. He's still shirtless, as he has been since the first time I saw him. The bandages must provide a little warmth but not much. I wonder if he gets cold? It must be freezing when flying high up in the sky. Maybe angels are adapted to cold temperatures, just as they're light for flight.

But this is all a guess, and probably a justification to make myself feel better about taking the only blanket in the cottage. The power is out tonight, which means the heat is out. It rarely freezes in the Bay Area, but it does get pretty cold at night sometimes. This seems to be one of those times.

I fall asleep listening to the rhythm of his steady breathing and the drumming of the rain on the windows.

I dream that I am swimming in the Antarctic, surrounded by broken icebergs. The glacial towers are majestic and deadly beautiful.

I hear Paige calling for me. She's floundering in the water, coughing, barely keeping herself afloat. Having only her arms to paddle with, I know she can't tread water for long. I swim toward her, desperate to reach her, but the gut-freezing cold slows my motions, and I waste almost all my energy shivering. Paige calls to me. She's too far for me to see her face, but I can hear tears in her voice.

'I'm coming!' I try to call to her. 'It's okay, I'll be there soon.' But my voice comes out in a hoarse whisper hardly reaching my own ears. Frustration cracks through my chest. I can't even comfort her with reassurances.

Then I hear a motorboat. It cuts through the floating ice chunks as it charges toward me. My mother is on the boat, driving it. With her free hand, she throws precious survival gear overboard, splashing it into the icy water. Cans of soup and beans, life vests and blankets, even shoes and blister packs go over the side of the boat, sinking among the bobbing ice.

'You really should eat your eggs, dear,' says my mother.

The boat heads straight for me and is not slowing down. If anything, it's speeding up. If I don't get out of the way, she'll run me over.

Paige calls out for me in the distance.

'I'm coming,' I call out but only a croaked whisper comes out of my mouth. I try to swim toward her but my muscles are so cold that all I can do is flail. Flail and shiver in the path of my mother's boat.

'Hush. Shhh,' a soothing voice whispers in my ear.

I feel the sofa cushions being pulled out from against my back. Then warmth envelops me. Firm muscles embrace me from the space where the cushions used to be. I'm groggily aware of masculine arms wrapping themselves around me, their skin soft as a feather, their muscles steel velvet. Chasing away the ice in my veins and the nightmare.

'Shhh.' A husky whisper in my ear.

I relax into the cocoon of warmth and let the sound of the rain on the roof lull me back to sleep.

The warmth is gone, but I'm no longer shivering. I curl up on my own, trying to savor the heat left in the cushions by a body that is no longer there.

When I open my eyes, the morning light makes me wish I hadn't. Raffe lies on his sofa, watching me with those dark blue eyes. I swallow, suddenly feeling awkward and unkempt. Great. The world has come to an end, my mother is out there with the street gangs, crazier than ever, my sister has been kidnapped by vengeful angels, and I'm concerned that my hair is greasy and my breath smells bad.

I get up abruptly, tossing aside my blanket with more force than is necessary. I grab my toiletries and head for one of the two bathrooms.

'Good morning to you too,' he says in a lazy drawl. I have my hand on the bathroom door when he says, 'In case you're wondering, the answer is yes.'

I pause, afraid to look back. 'Yes?' Yes, it was him holding me through the night? Yes, he knows I liked it?

'Yes, you can come with me,' he says as though he already regrets it. 'I'll take you to the aerie.'

11

The water is still running in the cottage but it's not warm. I consider taking a shower anyway, not knowing how long it will be before I can take a proper one, but the thought of glacier-temperature water hitting me full force makes me hesitate.

I decide to do a thorough sponge bath with a washcloth. At least that way, I can keep various parts of me from freezing all at once.

As predicted, the water is ice-cold, and it brings back pieces of my dream from last night, which inevitably reminds me how I got warm enough to be cradled to sleep. It was probably just some kind of angel host behavior triggered by my shivering, the way penguins huddle together when it's cold. What else could it be?

But I don't want to think about that – I don't know how to think about that – so I shove it down into that dark, overstuffed place in my mind that's threatening to burst any moment now.

When I come out of the bathroom, Raffe looks freshly showered and dressed in his black pants with boots. His bandages are gone. His wet hair swings in front of his eyes as he kneels on the hardwood floor in front of the open blanket. On it, his wings are laid out.

He combs through the feathers, fluffing out the ones that are crushed and plucking out the broken ones. In a way, I suppose he's preening. His touch is gentle and reverent, although his expression is hard and unreadable as stone. The jagged ends of the wing that I chopped look ugly and abused.

I have the absurd impulse to apologize. What, exactly, am I sorry for? That his people have attacked our world and destroyed it? That they are so brutal as to cut off the wings of one of their own and leave him to be torn apart by the native savages? If we are such savages, it is only because they have made us so. So I am not sorry, I remind myself. Crushing one of the enemy's wings in a moth-eaten blanket is nothing to be sorry about.

But somehow, I still hang my head and walk softly as though I am sorry, even if I won't say it.

I walk around him so he won't see my apologetic stance, and his naked back comes into full view. It has stopped bleeding. The rest of him looks perfectly healthy now – no bruises, no swelling or cuts, except where his wings used to be.

The wounds are a couple of streaks of raw hamburger running down his back. They follow the ragged flesh where the knife sawed through the tendons and muscles. I don't like to think about it, but I suppose the other angel sawed through joints, severing bones away from the rest of him. I suppose I should have sewn the wounds shut, but I had assumed he'd die.

'Should I, like, try to sew your wounds shut?' I ask, hoping the answer will be no. I'm a pretty tough girl, but sewing chunks of flesh together pushes the limits of my comfort zone, to say the least.

'No,' he says without looking up from his work. 'It'll eventually heal on its own.'

'Why hasn't it healed already? I mean, the rest of you healed in no time.'

'Angel sword wounds take a long time to heal. If you're ever going to kill an angel, slice him up with an angel sword.'

'You're lying. Why would you tell me that?'

'Maybe I'm not afraid of you.'

'Maybe you should be.'

'My sword would never hurt me. And my sword is the only one you can wield.' He gently plucks out another broken feather and lays it on the blanket.

'How's that?'

'You need permission to use an angel sword. It'll weigh a ton if you try to lift it without permission.'

'But you never gave me permission.'

'You don't get permission from the angel. You get it from the sword. And some swords get grouchy just for asking.'

'Yeah, right.'

He runs his hand over the feathers, feeling for broken ones. Why doesn't he look like he's kidding?

'I never asked permission and I managed to lift the sword no problem.'

'That's because you wanted to throw it to me so I could defend myself. Apparently, she took that as permission asked and given.'

'What, it read my mind?'

'Your intentions, at least. She does that sometimes.'

'O-kay. Right.' I let it go. I've heard plenty of wacky things in my time and you just have to learn to roll with them without directly challenging the person spewing the weirdness. Challenging weirdness is a pointless and sometimes dangerous exercise. At least, it is with my mom. I must say, though, that Raffe is even more inventive than my mother.

'So . . . you want me to bandage your back?'

'Why?'

'To try to keep infection out,' I say, rummaging through my pack for the first aid kit.

'Infection shouldn't be a problem.'

'You can't be infected?'

'I should be resistant to your germs.'

The words 'should' and 'your' catch my attention. We know next to nothing about the angels. Any information might give us an advantage. Once we organize again, that is.

It occurs to me that I might be in the unprecedented position of being able to glean some intelligence on them. Despite what the gang leaders would have the rest of us believe, angel parts are always taken from dead or dying angels, I'm sure of it. What I would do with angel intel, I don't know. But it can't hurt to gain a little knowledge.

Tell that to Adam and Eve.

I ignore the cautionary voice in my head. 'So . . . are you immunized or something?' I try to make my voice casual as though the answer means nothing to me.

'It's probably a good idea to bandage me up anyway,' he says, sending me a clear signal that he knows that I'm fishing for information. 'I can probably pass for human so long as my wounds are covered.' He pulls out a broken feather, putting it reluctantly into a growing pile.

I use up the last of the first aid supplies to patch up his wounds. His skin is like silk-covered steel. I'm a little rougher than I need to be because it helps keep my hands steady.

'Try not to move around too much so you don't bleed again. The bandages aren't that thick and blood will soak through pretty quickly.'

'No problem,' he says. 'Shouldn't be too hard not to move around as we run for our lives.'

'I'm serious. That's the last of our bandages. You'll have to make them last.'

'Any chance we can find more?'

'Maybe.' Our best chance is from first aid kits in houses, since the stores are either cleaned out or claimed by gangs.

We fill up my water bottle. I didn't have much time to pack supplies from the office. The supplies I carried with me are a random assortment. I sigh, wishing I'd had time to pack more food. Other than the single dried noodle cup, we're out except for the handful of fun-sized chocolates I'm saving for Paige. We share the noodles, which is about two bites per person. By the time we leave the cottage, it is midmorning. The first place we hit is the main house.

I have high hopes of a stocked kitchen, but one glance at the gaping cupboards in the sea of granite and stainless steel tells me we'll have to scrounge for leftovers. Rich people may have lived here, but even the rich didn't have enough currency to buy food once things got bad. Either they ate all the food they could before packing up and hitting the road, or they took it with them. Drawer after drawer, cupboard after cupboard, there is nothing but crumbs.

'Is this edible?' Raffe stands at the kitchen entrance, framed by the Mediterranean archway. He could easily be at home in a place like this. He stands with the fluid grace of an aristocrat who's used to rich surroundings. Although the quarter-bag of cat food he's holding up does mess with the image a little.

I dip my hand into the bag and bring out a few pieces of red and yellow kibbles. I pop them in my mouth. Crunchy, with a vaguely fishy taste. I pretend they're crackers as I chew and swallow. 'Not exactly gourmet, but it probably won't kill us.'

That's the best we can do in the food department, but we do find supplies in the garage. A backpack that doubles as a duffel bag, which is great since he can't carry a backpack right now but might be able to later. A couple of boys' sleeping bags all rolled and ready to go. No tent, but there are flashlights with extra batteries. A slick camp knife that's more expensive than any I've ever managed to buy. I give mine to Raffe and keep this one for myself.

Since my clothes are dirty, I simply trade them in for clean ones from the closets. We also grab some extra clothes and jackets. I find a sweatshirt that comes close to fitting Raffe. I also make him change from his telltale black pants and laced boots to jeans and ordinary hiking boots.

Luckily, there are three bedrooms stocked with various sizes of men's clothing. There must have been a family with two teen boys here once, but the only sign of them now is what's in the closets and garage. The fit of Raffe's hiking boots are what concern me the most. His blisters are already healed from yesterday, but even with his super-healing, we can't have him tearing up his feet every day.

I tell myself I care because I can't have him holding me back by limping, and refuse to think further than that.

'You look almost human dressed like that,' I say.

Actually, he looks exactly like a gorgeous Olympian champion. It's more than a little disturbing just how much he looks like a supreme example of a human being. I mean, shouldn't an angel that's part of a legion to eradicate humanity look, well, evil and alien?

'So long as you don't bleed in the shape of wing joints, you should pass for human. Oh, and don't let anyone pick you up. They'll know you're not right as soon as they feel how light you are.'

'I'll be sure not to let anyone but you carry me in her arms.' He turns and leaves the kitchen before I can figure out what to make of his comment. A sense of humor is one more thing I don't think angels should have. The fact that his sense of humor is corny makes it even more wrong.

It's late morning by the time we leave the big house. We're in a little cul-de-sac off Page Mill Road. The road is dark and slick with last night's downpour. The sky is heavy with broken gray clouds, but if we're lucky, we should be in the hills under a warm roof by the time the rains start again.

Our packs sit on Paige's chair, and if I close my eyes, I can almost pretend it's her I'm pushing. I catch myself humming what I thought was a meaningless tune. I stop when I realize it's my mother's apology song.

I put one foot in front of the other, trying to ignore the too-light weight of the wheelchair and the wingless angel beside me.

There are a lot of cars strewn on the road until we hit the freeway entrance. After that, there are only a couple of cars pointed up the hill. Everyone tried to get on the freeway to get away in the early days. I'm not sure where they were going. I guess they weren't either since the freeway is clogged in both directions.

It's not long before we see the first body.

12

A family lying in a pool of blood.

A man, a woman, a girl about ten years old. The child is at the edge of the woods while the adults are in the middle of the road. Either the kid ran for it when the parents were attacked, or she hid during the attack and was caught when she came out.

They haven't been dead for long. I know because the blood on their tattered clothes is still bright red. I have to swallow and fight to keep the cat food in my stomach.

Their heads are intact. Thankfully, the girl's hair has been blown over her face. Their bodies, though, are in bad shape. For one thing, parts of their torsos have been chewed down to the bones with bits of flesh still stuck to them. For another, a few arms and legs are missing. I don't have the guts to take a closer look but Raffe does.

'Teeth marks,' he says as he kneels on the asphalt in front of the man's body.

'What kind of animal are we talking about?'

He sits crouched near the bodies, considering my question. 'The kind with two legs and flat teeth.'

My stomach roils. 'What are you saying? That they're human?'

'Maybe. Unusually sharp, but human-shaped.'

'Can't be.' But I know it can. Humans will do what is needed to survive. Still, it doesn't add up. 'This is too wasteful. If you're desperate enough to cannibalize, you wouldn't just take a few bites and leave.' But these bodies have more than a few bites taken out of them. Now that I make myself really look, I can see they are half-eaten. Still, why leave half behind?

Raffe peers at the place where the kid's leg should be. 'The limbs have been ripped right out of their sockets.'

'Enough,' I say as I take two steps back. I scan our surroundings. We're in an open field, and I feel as nervous as a field mouse looking at a sky full of hawks.

'Well,' he says as he gets up, scanning the trees. 'Let's hope whoever did this is still in control of this area.'

'Why?'

'Because they won't be hungry.'

That doesn't make me feel better. 'You're pretty sick, you know that?'

'Me? It isn't my people who did this.'

'How do you know? You have the same teeth we do.'

'But my people aren't desperate.' He says this as if the angels had nothing to do with us being desperate. 'Nor are they insane.'

That's when I see the broken egg.

It lies on the side of the road near the kid, the yolk brown and the egg white congealed. The stench of sulfur hits my nose. It's the familiar reek that infused my clothes, pillow, and hair for the last two years throughout Mom's rotten egg kick. Beside it, there is a small bouquet of wild sprigs.

Rosemary and sage. Either my mother thought they were pretty, or her insanity has taken on a very dark sense of humor.

It doesn't mean anything other than she was here. That's all. She couldn't take on an entire family.

But she could overtake a ten-year-old coming back from her hiding place after her parents were killed.

She was here and walked by the bodies, just as we are doing. That's all.

Really, that's all.

'Penryn?'

I realize Raffe's been talking to me.

'What?'

'Could they be kids?'

'Could what be kids?'

'The attackers,' he says slowly. Obviously, I've missed a piece of the conversation. 'As I've said, the bite marks seem too small to be adults.'

'They must be animals.'

'Animals with flat teeth?'

'Yes,' I say with more conviction than I feel. 'That makes more sense than a kid taking down an entire family.'

'But not more sense than a gang of feral children attacking them.' I try to shoot him a look that says he's crazy, but I suspect I only succeed in looking scared. My brain buzzes with images of what might have happened here.

He says something about avoiding the road and heading uphill through the forest. I nod without really hearing the details and follow him into the trees.

13

We mostly have evergreens in California, but there's enough fall foliage that covers the forest. We can't help but crunch at every step. I don't know about other parts of the world, but at least in our hills, I'm convinced that the whole story of skilled woodsmen walking silently through the woods is a myth. For one thing, there's simply no place to walk during autumn where you can avoid the fallen leaves. For another, even the squirrels and deer, birds and lizards make enough noise in these hills to make them seem like much larger animals.

The good news is that the rain drenched the leaves, which dampens the sound. The bad news is that I can't navigate the wheelchair on the wet hillside.

Dead leaves get trapped in the spokes as I struggle to force it forward. To lighten the load, I strap the sword onto my pack and carry them on my back. I throw the other pack to Raffe to carry. Still the chair skids and slips on the wet leaves, constantly heading downhill as I struggle to roll it crosswise. Our progress slows to a crawl. Raffe offers no help but neither does he offer sarcastic suggestions.

We eventually pick out a clear path that seems to go in the general direction we want to head. The ground is mostly level on the trail and there is far less foliage on it. But the rains have turned the dirt trail into a mud bath. I don't know how well the chair will work in the mud, and I'd rather keep it running in smooth condition. So I fold the chair and carry it. That works for a while, in an uncomfortable, awkward way. The most I've ever carried the chair before was a flight or two of stairs.

It becomes obvious very quickly that I won't be able to continue to hike carrying a wheelchair. Even if Raffe offered to help – which he doesn't – we wouldn't make it very far lugging an awkward metal and plastic contraption.

I finally unfold it and set it down. It sinks in, the mud greedily sucking at the wheels. It only takes a few feet for the chair to get completely clumped in mud to the point where the wheels freeze.

I grab a stick and knock off as much of it as I can. I have to do that a couple more times. Each time, the mud clumps faster on the wheels. Once churned, it's more like clay than mud. Finally, it only takes a couple of spins of the wheels before the chair is good and stuck.

I stand beside it, tears stinging my eyes. How can I rescue Paige without her chair?

I'll have to figure something out, even if I have to carry her. The important thing is that I find her. Still, I stand there for another minute, my head bowed in defeat.

'You still have her chocolate,' says Raffe, his voice not ungentle. 'The rest is just logistics.'

I don't lift my eyes to look at him because the tears haven't gone away yet. I brush my fingers along the leather seat in a good-bye as I walk away from Paige's chair.

We walk for about an hour before Raffe whispers, 'Does moping actually help humans feel better?' We've been whispering since we saw the victims on the road.

'I'm not moping,' I whisper back.

'Of course you're not. A girl like you, spending time with a warrior demigod like me. What's to mope about? Leaving a wheelchair behind couldn't possibly show up on the radar compared to that.'

I nearly stumble over a fallen branch. 'You have got to be kidding me.'

'I never kid about my warrior demigod status.'

'Oh. My. God.' I lower my voice, having forgotten to whisper. 'You are nothing but a bird with an attitude. Okay, so you have a few muscles, I'll grant you that. But you know, a bird is nothing but a barely evolved lizard. That's what you are.'

He chuckles. 'Evolution.' He leans over as if telling me a secret. 'I'll have you know that I've been this perfect since the beginning of time.' He is so close that his breath caresses my ear.

'Oh, please. Your giant head is getting too big for this forest. Pretty soon, you're going to get stuck trying to walk between two trees. And then, I'll have to rescue you.' I give him a weary look. '*Again.*'

I pick up my pace, trying to discourage the smart comeback that I'm sure will come.

But it doesn't. Could he be letting me have the last say?

When I look back, Raffe has a smug grin on his face. That's when I realize I've been manipulated into feeling better. I stubbornly try to resist but it's already too late.

I do feel a little better.

From the map, I remember that Skyline Boulevard is an artery that runs through the woods into South San Francisco or thereabouts. Skyline is uphill from where we are. Although Raffe hasn't said where the aerie is located, he's told me we need to head north. That means going through San Francisco. So if we just head uphill, then follow Skyline into the city, we can stay out of highly populated areas until we can no longer avoid it.

I have a lot of questions for Raffe now that I've realized I should collect as much knowledge of angels as possible. But cannibals take precedence, and we keep our conversation to a whispered minimum.

I thought that it could take all day for us to get to Skyline, but we reach it by midafternoon. Good thing too, because I don't think I can handle another meal of cat food. We have plenty of time to rummage through the houses on Skyline for dinner before it gets dark. These houses are nowhere near as close to each other as houses in the suburbs, but they are still regularly spaced along the road. Most of them are hidden behind redwood trees, which is great for surreptitious supply searching.

I wonder how long we should wait for my mother and how we'll ever find her again. She knew to come up to the hills, but we had no plans beyond that. Like everything else in life right now, all I can do is hope for the best.

Skyline is a beautiful road along the hilltop of the mountain range that divides Silicon Valley from the ocean. It's a two-lane highway that gives glimpses of both the valley on one side and the ocean on the other. It's the only road I've walked on since the attacks that doesn't feel *wrong* in its deserted state. Flanked by redwoods and smelling of eucalyptus, this road would feel more wrong with traffic on it.

Not long after we reach Skyline, though, we see cars piled up crosswise on the road, blocking any potential traffic. This is obviously not something that happened by accident. The cars are angled ninety degrees to the road and staggered for several car lengths, just in case someone decides to crash through them, I suppose. There is a community here, and it does not welcome strangers.

The angel who now looks human takes in the sight. He angles his head like a dog that hears something in the distance. He nods his chin slightly, ahead and to the left of the road.

'They're over there, watching us,' he whispers.

All I can see is an empty road running through redwoods. 'How can you tell?'

'I hear them.'

'How far?' I whisper. *How far are they, and how far can you hear?*

He looks at me as though knowing what I'm thinking. He can't read minds as well as have amazing hearing, can he? He shrugs, then turns to head back into the cover of the trees.

As an experiment, I call him all kinds of names in my head. When he doesn't respond, I come up with random images in my head to see if I can get him to give me a funny look. Somehow, my thoughts drift to how he held me during the night, when I dreamed I was freezing in the water. My imagination has me waking up on that couch and turning to face him. He's so close that his breath feathers my cheek . . .

I stop. I think about bananas, oranges, and strawberries, mortified that he might actually sense what I am thinking. But he continues through the forest, giving no sign that he can read my mind. That's the good news. The bad news is he doesn't know what *they* are thinking either. Unlike him, I don't hear, see, or smell anything that might indicate that anyone is out to ambush us.

'What did you hear?' I whisper.

He turns around and whispers back, 'Two people whispering.'

After that, I keep my mouth shut and just follow him.

The woods up here are all redwoods. There are no leaves on the forest floor to crunch as we walk. Instead, the forest gives us exactly what we need – a thick carpet of soft needles that muffles our footsteps.

I want to ask if the voices he heard are coming our way, but am afraid to speak unnecessarily. We can try to go around their territory, but we need to continue in the same general direction if we are to reach San Francisco.

Raffe picks up his pace downhill almost to a run. I follow blindly, assuming he hears something I don't. Then I hear it too.

Dogs.

By the sound of their barking, they're heading straight for us.

14

We break into a sprint, skidding on the needles almost as much as running over them. Could these people keep dogs? Or is this a wild pack? If they're wild, then climbing up a tree would keep us safe until they wander away. But if they're kept . . . The thought boggles my mind. They would need enough food to keep themselves and their dogs fed. Who has that kind of wealth and how did they get it?

An image of the cannibalized family comes back to me, and my brain shuts off while my instincts take over.

It's clear by the sound of the dogs that they're gaining on us. The road is far behind us now so we can't dive into a car. A tree will have to do.

I frantically scan the forest for a climbable tree. There are none that I can see. Redwoods grow tall and straight around us, with branches shooting out perpendicular to the trunk high above the ground. I'd have to be at least double my height to reach the lowest limb of any of these trees.

Raffe jumps, trying to reach one. Although he springs much higher than a normal man could, it is still not enough. He slams his fist into the trunk in frustration. He's probably never needed to jump before. Why hop when you can fly?

'Get on my shoulders,' he says.

I'm not sure what his plan is, but the dogs are getting louder. I can't tell how many of them there are, but it's not one or two, it's a pack.

He grabs my waist and lifts me up. He's strong. Strong enough to lift me all the way up until I'm standing on his shoulders. I can barely reach the lowest branch this way, but it's enough to get a grip when I push off from him. I hope the skinny limb is strong enough to hold my weight.

He puts his hands below my feet, supporting and pushing me up until I'm securely on the branch. It wobbles but holds my weight. I look around for an offshoot to break so that I can lower it to him to help him climb up.

But before I can do anything, he takes off running. I almost call out his name, but catch myself before I do. The last thing we need is me giving away our position.

I watch him disappear down the hill. Now it's my turn to pound on the tree in frustration. What's he doing? If he stayed nearby, maybe I could have managed to get him up here somehow. I could have at least helped him fight off the dogs by throwing things down on them. I have no projectile weapons but from this height, anything I throw would be a weapon.

Did he run to distract the dogs so I could be safe? Did he do it to protect me?

I slam my fist into the trunk again.

A six-pack of dogs comes snarling at the tree. A couple linger, sniffing around the base, but the rest take off after Raffe. It only takes a moment before the loitering pair run off after the pack.

My branch leans precariously toward the ground. The limbs are so sparse and thin here that all anyone would have to do is look up to see me. The lower stems only have leaves at their ends so that there is very little coverage near the trunk. I reach up for another branch and start climbing. The boughs get stronger and thicker as I head up. It's a long way up to one with enough leaves to give me any cover.

When a dog yelps in pain, I know they have caught up to him. I curl up and cling to the tree, trying to guess what's happening.

Below me, something large crashes through the underbrush. It turns out to be several large men. Five of them. They are in camouflage and carry rifles like they know how to use them.

One of them signals with his hand and the rest fan out. These men don't give the impression of weekend hunters shooting rabbits with one hand while drinking beer with the other. They are organized. Trained. Deadly. They move with an ease and confidence that makes me suspect they've worked together before. That they've hunted together before.

My chest drains of all heat thinking about what a rogue military group would do to an angel prisoner. I consider yelling at them, distracting them to give Raffe a chance to run. But dogs are still growling and yelping. He's fighting for his life and my yelling will only distract him and get us both caught.

If I die, Paige is as good as dead too. And I won't die for an angel, no matter what crazy things he does that coincidentally save my skin. If he could have climbed on my shoulders to get up here, would he have?

But deep inside, I know better. If he was just out to save himself, he would have outrun me at the first sign of danger. As the old joke goes, he doesn't need to outrun the bear, he just needs to outrun me. That, he could easily do.

The vicious growl of a dog lunging makes me cringe. The men shouldn't be able to tell that Raffe is not human unless they strip his shirt or unless the wounds on his back open and bleed. But if he's getting torn up by the dogs, he will heal completely within a day and that will be a dead giveaway if they keep him that long. Of course, if they're cannibals, none of it will matter.

I don't know what to do. I need to help Raffe. But I also need to stay alive and not do anything stupid. I just want to curl up and put my hands over my ears.

A sharp command silences the dogs. The men have found Raffe. I can't hear what they're saying, only that they're talking. Not surprisingly, the tone doesn't sound friendly. Not much is said, and I can't hear Raffe talking at all.

A few minutes later, the dogs run past my tree. The same two diligent dogs sniff at the base below me before running to catch up with the rest of the pack. Then the men come.

The one that made the hand signal earlier leads the group. Raffe walks behind him.

His hands are tied behind his back and blood runs down his face and leg. He stares straight ahead, careful not to look up at me. Two men flank him on either side, their hands on his arms as though just waiting for him to fall so they can drag him up the hill. The last two men follow, holding their rifles at forty-five degree angles and looking around for something to shoot. One of them carries Raffe's bag.

The blue blanket holding the wings is nowhere in sight. The last I saw, Raffe had it strapped to his bag. Could he have taken the time to hide the wings before the dogs reached him? If so, that could buy him a few more hours of life.

He's alive. I repeat this fact in my head to keep other, more disturbing thoughts from taking over. I can't do anything if I'm frozen by thoughts of what's happening to Raffe or Paige or my mother.

I clear my mind. Forget plans. I don't have enough information to formulate a plan. My instincts will have to do.

And my instincts tell me that Raffe is mine. I found him first. If these testosterone-poisoned baboons want a piece of him, they're going to have to wait until after he gets me into the aerie.

When I can't hear the men anymore I climb down from my branch. It's a long way and I'm careful to get my feet in the right positions before swinging down. The last thing I need is a broken ankle. The needles cushion my fall and I land without mishap.

I run downhill in the direction Raffe ran. In about five minutes, I have the wrapped wings. He must have tossed the bundle into a bush as he ran because it lies partially hidden in the underbrush. I strap it to my pack and run after the men.

15

The dogs are a problem. I'll need my brain for that one. I may be able to hide from the men as I lurk, but I won't be able to hide from the dogs. I keep running anyway. I'll have to worry about things one at a time. I'm gripped by a surprisingly strong fear that I won't be able to find them at all, so I pick up my pace from jogging to sprinting.

I'm practically doubled over breathless by the time I see them. I'm breathing so hard, I'm surprised they can't hear me.

They approach what at first looks like a dilapidated group of buildings. But a closer look shows that the buildings are actually fine. They only look dilapidated because there are branches leaning against the buildings and woven in a net above the compound. The branches are carefully placed so that they look like they fell naturally. I bet from above it looks just like the rest of the forest. I bet from above you can't see the buildings at all.

Hidden beneath redwood lean-tos around the buildings are machine guns. They are all pointed up at the sky.

This does not have the feel of an angel-friendly camp.

Raffe and the five hunters are met by more men in camouflage. There are women here too, but they're not all in uniform. Some don't look like they belong here. Some lurk around in the shadows, looking greasy and scared.

I get lucky because one of the guys ushers the dogs into a kennel. Several of the dogs are barking so if some of them bark at me, it shouldn't be noticeable.

I look around to make sure I haven't been spotted. I take my pack off and hide it in a tree hollow. I consider keeping the sword with me but decide against it. Only angels carry swords. The last thing we need is for me to nudge their thinking in that direction. I put the blanket-wrapped wings beside the pack and mentally mark the location of the tree.

I find a good spot where I can see most of the camp and flatten myself on a piece of ground covered in enough leaves to buffer me from the mud. The cold and wetness seep through my sweatshirt anyway. I throw some leaves and needles over myself for good measure. I wish I had one of their camouflage outfits. Luckily, my dark brown hair blends in with my surroundings.

They shove Raffe onto his knees in the middle of their camp.

I'm too far away to hear what they're saying, but I can tell the men are debating what to do with him. One of them bends over and talks to Raffe.

Please, please don't make him take his shirt off.

I frantically try to think of a way to rescue him and still keep myself alive, but there's nothing I can do in broad daylight with a dozen trigger-happy guys in uniform swarming the area. Unless there's an angel attack that distracts them, the best I can hope for is that he'll still be alive and somehow accessible once it gets dark.

Whatever it is Raffe tells them must at least satisfy them for now because they pull him up to his feet and take him inside the smallest building in the center. These buildings don't look like houses, they look like a compound. The two buildings on either side of the one into which they take Raffe look big enough to house at least thirty people each. The one in the center looks like it could house maybe half that. My guess is that one of them is for sleeping, another for communal use, and maybe the small one for storage.

I lie there, trying to ignore the wet cold seeping in from the ground, wishing the sun would go down faster. Maybe these people are as afraid of the dark as the street gangs in my neighborhood. Maybe they'll go to bed as soon as the sun sets.

After what seems like a long time, but is probably only about twenty minutes, a young guy in uniform walks by only a few feet away from me. He holds a rifle at a forty-five degree angle across his chest as he scans the forest. He looks like he's ready for action. I stay perfectly still as I watch the soldier walk by. I'm surprised and immensely relieved that he doesn't have a dog with him. I wonder why they don't use them to guard the compound.

After that, a soldier walks by every few minutes, too close for comfort. Their patrols are regular enough that after a while, I get the rhythm of it and know when they're coming.

About an hour after they take Raffe into the center building, I smell meat and onions, garlic and greens. The delicious smell has my stomach clenching so hard that it feels like I have cramps.

I pray that it is not Raffe I'm smelling.

People file into the building on the right. I don't hear an announcement so they must have a set dinnertime. There are far more people here than I realized. Soldiers, mostly men in uniform, trudge out of the forest in groups of two, three, or five. They come from every direction and a pair of them almost step on me on their way to dinner.

By the time night rolls around, and the people disappear into the building on the left, I am almost numb with the cold seeping in from the ground. Combined with the fact that I've had nothing but a handful of dried cat food all day, I don't feel as ready as I'd like to be for a rescue.

There are no lights in any of the buildings. This group is careful, obviously hiding themselves well at night. The compound is silent except for the sound of crickets, which is a pretty amazing feat considering how many people live there. At least there are no screams coming from Raffe's building.

I make myself wait for what I think is about an hour in the dark before making my move.

I wait until the patrol walks by. At that point, I know that the other soldier is on the other side of the compound.

I count to one hundred before I get up and run as quietly as I can toward the buildings.

My legs are as cold and stiff as gunmetal, but they limber up real fast at the thought of being caught. I have to take the long way around, skittering from moon shadow to shadow, working my way in a zigzag pattern toward the center building. The crisscross of the canopy works to my advantage, speckling the whole area with shifting camouflage.

I flatten myself against the side of the mess hall. One guard takes measured steps to my right, and in the distance, the other walks slowly on the far side of the compound. Their footsteps sound dull and slow, as if they're bored. A good sign. If they heard anything unusual, their steps would be quicker, more urgent. At least I hope so.

I try to see the back of the center building, looking for a back door. But with the moon shadow on that side, I can't tell if there's a door or even a window.

I dart from my cover to Raffe's building.

I pause there, expecting to hear a shout. But all is quiet. I stand plastered to the wall, holding my breath. I hear nothing and see no movement. There's nothing but my fear telling me to abort. So I go on.

On the backside of the building, there are four windows and a back door. I peek through a window but see nothing but darkness. I resist the temptation to tap on it to see if I get a response from Raffe. I don't know who else might be in there with him.

I have no plan, not even a harebrained one, and no real idea of how to overcome anyone who might be in there. Self-defense training usually doesn't include sneaking up on someone from behind and choking them quietly to death – a skill that could be pretty handy right now.

Still, I've consistently managed to beat sparring partners much bigger than me, and I hold on to that fact to warm me against the chill of panic.

I take a deep breath and whisper as softly as I can. 'Raffe?'

If I can just get an indication of which room he's in, it would make this a whole lot easier. But I hear nothing. No tapping on the window, no muffled calls, no chair scrapings to lead me to him. The awful thought that he might be dead comes back to me again. Without him, I have no way of finding Paige. Without him, I am alone. I give myself a mental kick to distract me from following that dangerous line of thought.

I inch over to the door and put my ear to it. I hear nothing. I try the doorknob just in case it's unlocked.

I have my handy lock picking set in my back pocket as usual. I found the kit in a teenager's room during my first week of foraging for food. It didn't take me long to realize that picking a lock is a whole lot quieter than breaking a window. Stealth is everything when you're trying to avoid street gangs. So I've been getting a lot of practice picking locks the past couple of weeks.

The doorknob turns smoothly.

These guys are cocky. I crack it open the tiniest bit and pause. There are no sounds, and I slip into the darkness. I pause, letting my eyes adjust. The only light is the mottled moonlight streaming in through the windows at the back of the house.

I'm getting used to seeing by dim moonlight now. It seems to have turned into a way of life for me. I'm in a hallway with four doors. One door stands open into a bathroom. The other three are closed. I grip my knife as if that could stop a bullet from a semi-automatic. I put my ear to the first door on the left and hear nothing. As I reach for the doorknob, I hear a very quiet voice whispering through the last door.

I freeze. Then I walk over to the last door and put my ear against it. Was that my imagination, or did that sound like, 'Run, Penryn?'

I crack open the door.

'Why don't you ever listen to me?' Raffe asks quietly.

I slip in and close the door. 'You're welcome for rescuing you.'

'You're not rescuing me, you're getting yourself caught.' Raffe sits in the middle of the room, tied to a chair. There's a lot of dried blood on his face, streaking from a wound on his forehead.

'They're asleep.' I run over to his chair and put my knife to the rope around his wrists.

'No, they're not.' The conviction in his voice trips alarms in my head. But before I can think of the word *trap*, a flash-light beam blinds me.

16

'I can't let you cut that,' says a deep voice behind the flashlight. 'We have a limited supply of rope.'

Someone grabs my knife out of my hand and shoves me roughly into a chair. The flashlight turns off and it takes several blinks for me to adjust my vision again to the night. By the time I can see again, someone is tying my hands behind my back.

There are three of them. One checks Raffe's ropes, while the remaining one leans against the doorway as though here for just a casual visit. I tense up my muscles to try to make the rope as loose as possible as the guy behind me ties me up. My captor grips my wrists so hard that I'm half-convinced that they will snap.

'You'll have to excuse the lack of light,' says the guy leaning against the doorjamb. 'We're trying to avoid unwanted visitors.' Everything about him – from his commanding voice to his casual stance – makes it clear he's the leader.

'Am I really that clumsy?' I ask.

The leader leans down toward me so that we're eye to eye. 'Actually, no. Our guards didn't see you, and they were under orders to be on the lookout for you. Not bad, overall.' There's approval in his voice.

Raffe makes a low sound in his throat that reminds me of a dog's growl.

'You knew I was here?' I ask.

The guy stands straight again. The moonlight isn't bright enough to show me details of what he looks like, but he's tall and broad-shouldered. His hair is military short, making Raffe's hair look ragged and disreputable by comparison. His profile is clean, the lines of his face sharp and defined.

He nods. 'We didn't know for sure, but the gear in his bag looked like half the supplies that a pair might carry. He has a camping stove but no matches, no pots or pans. He has two bowls, two spoons. Stuff like that. We figured someone else was carrying the matching half of the supplies. Although, frankly, I wasn't expecting a rescue attempt. And certainly not from a girl. No offense meant. I've always been a modern guy.' He shrugs. 'But times have changed. And we are a camp full of men.' He shrugs again. 'That takes guts. Or desperation.'

'You forgot lack of brains,' growls Raffe. 'I'm your target here, not her.'

'How do you figure?' asks the leader.

'You need men like me as soldiers,' says Raffe. 'Not a skinny little girl like her.'

The leader leans back with his arms crossed. 'What makes you think we're looking for soldiers?'

'You used five men and a pack of dogs to catch one guy,' says Raffe. 'At that rate, you're going to need three armies to get done whatever it is you're trying to do here.'

The leader nods. 'You obviously have prior military experience.' I raise my brows at this, wondering what happened when they captured him.

'You didn't bat an eye when we pointed the guns at you,' says the leader.

'So maybe he's not as good he thinks he is if he's been captured before,' says Raffe's guard. Raffe doesn't rise to the bait.

'Or maybe he's special ops, trained for the worst situations,' says the leader. He pauses, waiting for Raffe to confirm or deny. The moonbeams filtering through the window are bright enough to show the leader watching Raffe with the intensity of a wolf watching a rabbit. Or maybe it's like a rabbit watching a wolf. But Raffe says nothing.

The leader turns to me. 'You hungry?'

My stomach picks that time to growl loudly. It would have been funny in any other situation.

'Let's get these folks some dinner.' The three men leave.

I test the ropes around my wrists. 'Tall, dark, and friendly. What more could a girl ask for?'

Raffe snorts. 'They got a lot friendlier once you showed up. They haven't offered me food all day.'

'Are they just skittish, or are they really bad guys?'

'Anybody who ties you to a chair at gunpoint is a bad guy. Do I really need to explain this?'

I feel like a little girl who did something stupid.

'So what are you doing here?' he asks. 'I risk getting chewed to pieces by a pack of dogs so you can escape, and then you run back here? Your sense of judgment could use a dash of common sense.'

'Sorry, I'll be sure and never do that again.' I'm beginning to wish they had gagged us.

'That's the sanest thing I've ever heard you say.'

'So who are these guys?' Raffe's super hearing has no doubt gained him a lot of information on what they're up to.

'Why? You planning on enlisting?'

'I'm not much of a joiner.'

Despite his usual handsome features, he looks rather grotesque in the moonlight with all those streaks of dried blood running down his face. For a second, I envision him as the classic fallen angel out to damn your soul.

But then he asks, 'You all right?' His voice is surprisingly gentle.

'I'm fine. You know we need to get out of here by morning, right? They'll be able to tell by then.' All that blood with no wound. No human heals that fast.

The door opens and the smell of stew almost drives me mad. I haven't starved since the attacks, but I haven't exactly been gaining weight either.

The leader pulls up a chair next to mine and lifts the bowl under my nose. My stomach grumbles as soon as the scent of meat and vegetables hits me.

He lifts a heaping spoonful and stops halfway between the bowl and my mouth. I have to suppress a groan of pleasure at the anticipation for decorum's sake. A pimply faced soldier pulls up a chair next to Raffe and does the same with his stew.

'What's your name?' asks the leader. There is something intimate about the way he asks me this question as he is about to feed me.

'My friends call me Wrath,' says Raffe. 'My enemies call me Please Have Mercy. What's your name, soldier boy?' Raffe's mocking tone brings a flush to my cheeks for no reason.

But the leader isn't flustered. 'Obadiah West. You can call me Obi.' The spoon moves away from me just a fraction.

'Obadiah. How biblical,' says Raffe. 'Obadiah hid the prophets from persecution.' Raffe stares at his own suspended spoon of stew.

'A Bible expert,' says Obi. 'Too bad we already have one.' He looks at me. 'And what's your name?'

'Penryn,' I say quickly before Raffe can open his mouth to say something sarcastic. 'Penryn Young.' I'd rather not antagonize our captors, especially if they're about to feed us.

'Penryn.' He whispers it as though making it his own. I'm somehow embarrassed to have Raffe witness this moment, though I'm not sure why.

'When was the last time you had a real meal, Penryn?' asks Obi. He holds the spoon just out of reach of my mouth. I swallow the saliva before answering.

'It's been a while.' I give him an encouraging smile, wondering if he'll let me have that bite. He moves the spoon to his own mouth and I watch him eat it. My stomach grumbles in protest.

'Tell me, Obi,' says Raffe. 'Just what kind of meat is this?'

I look back and forth between the soldiers, suddenly unsure if I'm hungry.

'You'd have to catch a lot of animals to feed this many people,' says Raffe.

'I was just about to ask you what kind of animals you've been hunting,' says Obi. 'A guy your size must need a lot of protein to maintain your muscle mass.'

'What are you implying?' I ask. 'We're not the ones attacking people, if that's what you're getting at.'

Obi looks sharply at me. 'How do you know about that? I didn't say anything about attacking people.'

'Oh, don't give me that look.' I give him my best grossed-out-teenager expression. 'You couldn't possibly imagine that I'd want to eat a person, could you? That's totally disgusting.'

'We saw a family,' says Raffe. 'Half-eaten on the road.'

'Where?' asks Obi. He seems surprised.

'Not too far from here. You're sure it wasn't you or one of your men?' Raffe shifts in his chair as though to remind Obi he and his men are not exactly the friendly sort.

'None of mine would do it. They don't need to. We have sufficient supplies and firepower to support everyone here. Besides, they got two of our men last week. Trained men with rifles. Why do you think we hunted you? We don't normally go after strangers. We'd like to know who did it.'

'It wasn't us,' I say.

'No, I don't suppose it was *you*.'

'He didn't do it either, Obi,' I say. His name tastes foreign in my mouth. Different, but not bad.

'How do I know that?'

'We have to prove our innocence now?'

'It's a new world.'

'What are you, the sheriff of the New Order? Arrest first, then ask questions later?' I ask.

'What would you do if you caught them?' asks Raffe.

'We could use people who are, shall we say, a little less civilized than the rest of us. Precautions would have to be taken, of course.' Obi sighs. It's clear he doesn't like the idea but seems resigned to do what needs to be done.

'I don't get it,' I say. 'What would you do with a bunch of cannibals?'

'Sic them on the angels, of course.'

'That's crazy,' I say.

'In case you hadn't noticed, the whole world has gone crazy. It's time to adapt or die.'

'By throwing crazy at crazy?'

'By throwing whatever we have that might confuse or distract, or maybe even repulse them, if that's even possible. Anything to keep their attention from the rest of us while we organize,' says Obi.

'Organize into what?' asks Raffe.

'Into an army strong enough to launch them off our world.'

All the heat drains out of my body. 'You're gathering a resistance army?' I try desperately not to look at Raffe. I've been casually trying to collect information on the angels just in case it might come in handy. The hope of an organized resistance, though, went up in smoke along with DC and New York.

And here is Raffe, in the middle of a rebel camp that is desperately trying to keep itself a secret from the angels. If the angels knew about this, they would crush it in its infancy, and who knows how long it could take for another resistance to organize.

'We prefer to think of ourselves as simply a human army, but yes, I suppose we are considered the resistance since we are the underdog by a long shot. Right now, we're gathering forces, recruiting and organizing. But we have something big planned. Something the angels won't soon forget.'

'You're striking back?' The thought boggles my mind.

'We're striking back.'

17

'How much damage can you do?' asks Raffe. My stomach turns cold knowing that I'm the only human in the room who knows that Raffe is one of the enemy.

'Enough damage to make a point,' says the resistance leader. 'Not to the angels. We don't care what they think. But to the people. Let them know that we are here, that we exist, and together, we will not be pushed aside.'

'You're attacking the angels as a recruiting campaign?'

'They think they've won already. More importantly, our own people feel like that too. We need to let them know the war has just begun. This is our home. Our land. Nobody gets to waltz in and take over.'

My mind swirls with conflicting emotions. Who is the enemy in this room? Whose side am I on? I stare carefully at the floor, desperately trying to avoid looking at either Raffe or Obi.

If Obi senses something, then he might start to suspect Raffe. If Raffe senses something then I can't really expect him to trust me. Oh God, if I piss off Raffe, he might renege on our deal and disappear to the aerie without me.

'My head hurts,' I whimper.

There's a long pause where I'm convinced Obi is working things out. I'm almost positive that he's about to shout, 'My God, he's an angel!'

But he doesn't. Instead, he gets up and puts my bowl of stew on his chair. 'We'll talk more in the morning,' says Obi. He guides me up and over a couple of steps to a cot in the shadows I hadn't noticed before. Raffe's guard does the same across the room.

I lie down awkwardly on my side with my wrists tied behind my back. Obi sits on the cot and ties my ankles together. I'm tempted to make a quip about requiring dinner and a movie before getting so kinky, but I don't. The last thing I need is to start making sex jokes while I'm being held prisoner in a camp full of armed men in a world where there are no laws.

He puts a pillow under my head. As he's doing this, he brushes hair out of my face and sweeps it behind my ear. His touch is warm and smooth. I should be scared, but I'm not. 'You'll be all right,' he says. 'The men will have strict orders to be gentlemanly toward you.'

I guess it doesn't take a mind reader to know that I might be worried about that. 'Thank you,' I say.

Obi and his man collect the bowls of stew and leave. The lock clicks behind them.

'Thank you?' asks Raffe.

'Shut up. I'm exhausted. I really need to get some sleep.'

'What you need is to decide who's on your side and who's not.'

'Will you tell them?' I don't want to get specific in case someone's listening. I hope he understands what I mean. If

Raffe and I make it to the aerie, he'll have intel on the infant resistance movement. If he tells the other angels and they kill off the movement, I'll be the Judas of my kind.

There's a long pause.

If he doesn't tell, will he be the Judas of his kind?

'Why did you come here?' he asks, blatantly changing the subject. 'Why didn't you run away like we both know you should have?'

'Stupid, huh?'

'Very.'

'I just . . . couldn't.'

I want to ask him why he risked his life to save mine when his people kill us every day. But I can't. Not here, not now. Not while someone may be listening.

We lie in silence, listening to the crickets.

After a long time, as I drift away to a numb place, he whispers in the dark. 'They're all asleep except for the guards.'

I'm instantly alert. 'You have a plan?'

'Sure. Don't you? You're the rescuer.' The moon has moved, and the light coming through the window is dimmer now. But it's still enough for me to see the darker shadow of his form getting up from his cot. He comes over to me and starts untying me.

'How the hell did you do that?'

'When you're storming the aerie, remember that ropes won't hold angels.' He whispers the last word.

I'd forgotten how much stronger he is than a man.

'You mean you could have gotten out all that time? You don't even need me. Why didn't you do it already?'

'What, and miss the fun of rattling their tiny little brains wondering what happened?' He swiftly unties me and pulls me to my feet.

'Ah, I get it. You can escape at night, but not during the day. You can't outrun bullets, can you?'

Like most people, my first introduction to angels was through the looping footage of the Archangel Gabriel being shot. I can't help but wonder if the angels would have been less hostile if we hadn't immediately killed their leader. At least, they think he was killed. No one knows for sure because the body wasn't recovered, or so they said. The legion of winged men floating behind him dispersed with the panicked crowd, quickly disappearing into the smoky sky. I wonder if Raffe was part of that legion.

He arches his brow at me, clearly refusing to discuss the effects of bullets on angels.

I give him a smug smile. *You're not as perfect as you look.*

I walk over to the door and put my ear to it. 'Is there anyone else in the building?'

'No.'

I try to turn the knob but it's locked.

Raffe sighs. 'I was hoping not to show excessive strength and raise suspicion.' He reaches for the knob, but I stop him.

'Well then, good thing I got us covered.' I pull a slim lock-pick and tension wrench out of my back pocket. The soldier who searched me before tying me up did a fast job. He was looking for guns or bulky knives, not skinny little picks.

'What's that?'

I get to work on the lock. It feels good to surprise him with a talent that angels don't have.

Click.

'Voila.'

'Talkative, but talented. Who would have thought?'

I open my mouth to make a smartass comeback, then realize I'd only be proving his point, so I stay quiet, just to prove that I can.

We sneak out into the hallway and stop at the back door.

'Can you hear the guards?'

He listens briefly. He points to eleven o'clock and five o'clock. We wait.

'What's in here?' I ask, pointing at the closed doors.

'Who knows? Supplies maybe?'

I start for one of the doors, thinking of venison or even guns.

He grabs my arm and shakes his head. 'Don't get greedy. If we raid them on our way out, they're less likely to just forget about us. We don't want trouble if we can avoid it.'

He's right, of course. Besides, who'd be stupid enough to store guns in the same place as their prisoners? But the thought of venison makes my mouth water. Oh, I should have bargained for that stew while I had the chance.

After a minute, Raffe nods and we slip out into the night.

We make a run for it, Raffe and me. My heart flip-flops in my chest as I pump my legs as fast as they will go. The air frosts from my mouth. The smell of soil and trees beckons us toward the forest. The trees rustling in the wind mask the sound of our pounding feet.

Raffe could run much faster, but he stays close.

The moon disappears behind clouds, and the forest turns dark. I slow to a walk once we're inside the canopy, not wanting to smash into a tree.

My breathing is so heavy, I'm afraid the guards will hear it. The adrenaline rush of a run for freedom drains, and I'm back to being scared and tired. I pause, bending over to catch my breath. Raffe puts his hand on my back, urging me to keep going with gentle pressure. He's not even out of breath.

He points deeper into the forest. I shake my head and point to the other side of the camp. We need to go around to retrieve his wings. My pack is replaceable; the wings and sword are not. He pauses, then nods. I don't know if he knows what I'm after, but I know that his wings are never far from his mind, the way little Paige is never far from mine.

We skirt around the camp, going as deep into the forest as we can without losing sight of the camp. This gets tricky several times since the moonlight is so dim now, and the camp itself is mostly under canopy. I have to rely more heavily on Raffe's night vision than I like.

Even knowing he can see, I can only go so fast without walking into a branch or losing my footing. It takes a long time to navigate the forest in the dark, and even longer to find my stash.

Just when I see the tree hiding our goods, I hear the distinctive click of a gun's safety latch behind me.

My hands are up in the air before the guy can say, 'Freeze.'

18

'Just for interrupting my night, you're getting latrine duty.' Obi is clearly not an early morning guy, and he doesn't bother to hide that he'd much rather be sleeping than dealing with us.

'What do you want with us?' I ask. 'I told you we didn't kill those people.'

We're right back where we started – Raffe and I sit tied to our chairs in what I'm starting to think of as our room.

'It's now more about what we don't want. We don't want you telling others our numbers, our location, our arsenal. Now that you've seen our camp, we can't let you go until we move.'

'How long will that be?'

'A while.' Obi shrugs noncommittally. 'Won't be too long.'

'We don't have a while.'

'You'll have as long as we say you have,' says Boden, the guard who caught us. Or at least that's what the name on his uniform says. It could, of course, just be a uniform that he took from a dead soldier that already had that name on it. 'You'll do everything the resistance movement says. Because without it, we'd all be doomed to the hell those angelic motherfu—'

'Enough, Jim,' says Obi. There's enough weariness in his voice that I'm guessing that good ol' Jim and maybe several of the other soldiers have repeated these exact same lines a million times over with the zeal of the newly converted.

'It's true,' says Obi. 'The resistance founders warned us this time would come, told us where to go to survive, galvanized us while the rest of the world was falling apart. We owe the resistance everything. It's our greatest hope of surviving this massacre.'

'There's more than just this camp?' I ask.

'It's a network that's all over the world in pockets. We're just becoming aware of the others, trying to organize, trying to coordinate.'

'Great,' says Raffe. 'Does this mean we have to stay until we forget we ever heard of this resistance movement?'

'That's the one thing you should spread,' says Obi. 'Knowing about the resistance brings hope and community. We can all use as much of that as possible.'

'Aren't you worried that if word gets out, that the angels will just destroy it?' I ask.

'Those pigeons couldn't take us out if they sent their entire chirping flock,' Boden scoffs. His face is red and he looks ready for a fight. 'Just let 'em try.' The white-knuckled grip on his rifle is making me nervous.

'We've had to detain a fair number of people here since the cannibal attacks started,' says Obi. 'You're the only ones who managed to make it out. There could be a place for the two of you here. A place with meals and friends, a life with meaning and purpose. Right now, we're fractured. They have us eating each other, for God's sake. We can't make a stand if we're bashing each other over the head and killing each other for cans of dog food.'

He leans toward us in earnest. 'This camp is just the start, and we need everyone to pitch in if we're going to have a chance in hell of taking back our world from the angels. We could use people like you. People with the skills and determination to be humanity's greatest heroes.'

Boden snorts. 'They can't be that good. They stumbled in a big semicircle around the compound like a couple of dildos. How skilled can they be?'

What dildos have to do with it, I have no idea. But he does have a point in that we did get caught by an idiot.

It turns out I don't really get latrine duty. Only Raffe gets that honor. I end up with laundry duty. I'm not sure that's much better. I've never worked so hard in my life. You know the world has ended when manual labor in America is cheaper and easier than using machines. Men can seriously grime up jeans and other heavy clothes when they're out in the forest. Not to mention unmentionables.

I have more than a few 'eww' moments during the day. But I do learn a few things from the other laundry women.

After a long stretch of wary silence, the women begin to talk. A couple of them have only been at the camp for a few days. They seem surprised and still mistrustful of finding themselves unharmed and unmolested. There's a wariness about the way they keep their voices low and their eyes scanning their surroundings that keeps me from relaxing even when they begin to gossip.

While working our butts off – or more accurately, our arms and backs – I learn that Obi is an absolute favorite among the women. And that Boden and his buddies should be avoided. Obi is in charge of the camp, but not of the entire resistance movement. There's apparently talk, at least among the women, that Obi would be a great worldwide leader of the freedom fighters.

I love the idea of a leader destined to lead us out of our dark times. Love the romance of being part of something good, and right, led by a group of people fated to be heroes.

Only, it isn't my fight. My fight is getting my sister back safe and sound. My fight is keeping my mother out of trouble and shepherding her to a safe place. My fight is feeding and sheltering what remains of my family. Until those battles are permanently won, I don't have the luxury of looking beyond them to the grander picture of wars with gods and romantic heroes.

My fight at the moment is struggling to get stains out of sheets that are taller and wider than me by yards. Nothing takes the romance and grandeur out of life more than scrubbing stains out of sheets.

One of the women worries over her husband, who she says is 'playing soldier' even though he's barely moved out of his computer programmer's chair in twenty years. She also frets over her golden retriever, which is in the kennel with the rest of the dogs.

It turns out that most of the guard dogs are actually just pets of the people in the camp. They're trying to train them into the mean, vicious guard dogs that chased Raffe, but in reality, they haven't had enough time to train most of them. Besides, they've spent their whole lives being pampered and played with, and it's apparently not easy to turn them into vicious killers when they'd rather lick you to death or chase squirrels.

Dolores assures me that her dog, Checkers, is of the lick-you-to-death variety, and that most of the dogs are in doggie paradise out here in the forest. I nod in more understanding than she realizes. This is the reason the guards are dog-free. It's hard to patrol when your K9 partner keeps running off to chase after rodents and barks all night long. Thank goodness for small favors.

I casually try to turn the conversation toward what might be gnawing on the refugees on the road. All I get are wary glances and frightened expressions. One woman crosses herself. Talk about a conversation killer.

I pick up a grimy pair of pants to dunk in the dingy water, and we go back to working in silence.

Although Raffe and I are prisoners here, no one is really guarding us. That is to say, no one is specifically assigned to guard us. Everyone knows we're the newbies, and as such, everyone keeps an eye on us.

To avoid notice of Raffe's head injury healing too fast, we managed to put two adhesive bandages at his hairline first thing this morning. We were prepared to say that head injuries bleed a lot so the injury itself was smaller than it seemed last night, but no one asked. I also took a quick peek at his bandages. There was blood in the shape of wing joints. Dried but unmistakable. Nothing we could do about that.

Raffe digs a ditch by the portable toilets along with other men. He's one of the few still wearing his shirt. There's a dry band around his chest outlining his bandages but no one seems to notice. I note the filth on his shirt with a professional eye and hope that someone else ends up having to wash it for him.

The sun glints off something shiny on the privacy wall the men are building around the latrine. I'm pondering the perfect regularity of the rectangular boxes they're using to build the wall when I recognize them. Desktop computers. The men are stacking desktop computers and cementing them into a privacy wall.

'Yup,' says Dolores as she sees what I'm looking at. 'My husband always did call his electronic gadgets "bricks" when they got phased out.'

They got phased out, all right. Computers were the height of our technological prowess, and now we're using them as latrine walls, thanks to the angels.

I go back to scrubbing a pair of pants on my washboard.

Lunch takes several lifetimes to come. I'm about to get Raffe when a honey-haired woman saunters over to him on her long legs. Everything about her walk, her voice, and the tilt of her head invites a man to get a little closer. I change direction and head for the mess hall, pretending not to notice them walking to lunch together.

I grab a bowl of venison stew and a heel of bread and scarf them down as fast as I can. Some people grumble around me about having to eat the same old stuff each time, but I've had enough dried noodles and cat food to truly appreciate the taste of fresh meat and canned vegetables.

I know from my morning's gossip session that some of the food comes from foraging in the nearby houses, but most of it comes from a warehouse the resistance keeps hidden. By the looks of things, the resistance does a good job of providing for their people.

As soon as I finish eating, I look for Obi. I've been wanting to plead with him all day to let us go. These people don't seem that bad now that it's daylight, and maybe they'll sympathize with my urgent need to rescue my sister. Of course, I can't keep Raffe from telling the enemy about this camp, but there's no reason he'll want to tell anyone until we reach the aerie, and maybe by then, the camp will have moved. It's a lame justification, but it'll have to do.

I find Obi surrounded by men who are gingerly moving crates from the storage closets I almost peeked into last night. There are two men carefully loading each crate onto a truck.

When one loses his grip on a corner, everyone freezes.

For a few heartbeats, they all stare at the man who lost his grip. I can almost smell their fear.

They all exchange glances as if confirming that they're all still here. Then they continue their sideways crab-walking toward the truck.

I guess the things stored in that room had more bang than venison and guns.

I try to go talk to Obi, but a camouflaged chest blocks my way. When I look up, the guard who caught us last night, Boden, glares down at me.

'Get back to your washing, woman.'

'Are you kidding me? What century are you from?'

'This century. This is the new reality, sweet cheeks. Accept it before I cram it down your throat.' His eyes drop meaningfully to my mouth. 'Deep and hard.'

I can practically smell the lust and violence on him.

A needle of fear spikes in my chest. 'I need to talk to Obi.'

'Yeah, you and every other chick in camp. I got your Obi right here.' He grabs himself between his legs and sort of shakes it up and down like he is shaking hands with his dick. Then he leans his face down close to mine and wiggles his tongue in an obscene gesture so close to me that that I can feel his spittle.

That needle of fear punctures my lungs and all the air seems to go out of me. But the anger that swamps it is a tsunami taking over every cell in my body.

Here is the embodiment of the very thing that had me crawling from car to car, hiding and freezing at the slightest sound, scampering in the shadows like an animal, desperate with worry that someone like him will catch me, my sister, my mother. Here is the bigger, stronger attitude that had the nerve to steal my sister, a helpless, sweet little girl. Here is the thing literally blocking me from rescuing her.

'What did you just say to me?' The girl who used to be civilized and polite just had to give him a second chance.

'I said—'

I slam the heel of my hand into his nose. I don't just do it with my arm. The force comes all the way from my hips as I launch my whole body into the strike.

I feel the nose smash under my onslaught. Even better, he'd started to do that obscene gesture with his tongue again and it smashes between his teeth as his head whiplashes back, spraying blood from his bit tongue.

Sure, I'm pissed off. But my actions are not entirely without thought. I might regularly open my mouth without thinking, but I never start a fight without consulting my brain. For this one, I figured I'd win as soon as I made the first move. Intimidation tactics like his are common among bullies. The smaller, weaker opponent is supposed to cringe and back off.

My quick calculation went something like this: he's a foot taller and wider than me, a trained soldier, and I'm a girl. If I had been a man, people might let us fight it out. But people tend to believe that when a girl hits a big guy with a gun looming over her, it must be in self-defense. With all these macho men milling about, I give it about ten seconds before someone breaks up our fight.

So without much harm, I'd win the battle because: one, I'd get Obi's attention, which was what I was trying to do in the first place; two, I'd humiliate Knuckle Brain by showing everybody what kind of a girl-intimidating bully he is; and three, I'd make my point that I'm not easy pickin's.

What I don't count on is how much damage Boden can do in ten seconds.

He spends a few seconds staring at me in shock and gathering his fury.

Then he slams an SUV of a punch across my jaw.

Then he hurls his body into me.

I land on my back, trying desperately to catch my breath through the talons of pain gripping my lungs and face. By the time he sits on top of me, I figure I have about two seconds left. Maybe a really fast, chivalrous soldier out there would beat my estimate. Maybe Raffe is already leaping to get this gorilla off me.

Boden grabs the neck of my sweatshirt with one fist and cocks the other for another smash. Okay, I just need to survive this punch, then someone is bound to reach us.

I grab the pinkie of the hand on my sweatshirt and give it the hardest twist I can, flipping it all the way over.

It's a little known fact that where the pinkie goes, so goes the hand, wrist, arm, and body. Otherwise, something breaks along the way. He jerks with it, gritting his teeth and twisting his body to follow the pinkie.

That's when I catch a glimpse of the people around us.

I was beginning to think this camp had the slowest soldiers in history. But I was wrong. A surprising number of people made it to the fight in record time. The only problem is that they're acting like kids in a schoolyard – running to watch the fight rather than to break it up.

My surprise costs me. Boden jams his elbow into my right breast.

The intense pain just about kills me. I curl as best I can with two hundred pounds of muscle on top of me, but that doesn't protect me from the bitch-slap he whips across my face.

Now he's adding insult to injury because if I had been a man, he would have hit me with a closed fist. Great. If he just slaps me around and I still get beaten, then I'll only prove that I'm someone everyone can push around.

Where's Raffe when I need him? Out of the corner of my eye, I see him among a blur of faces, his expression utterly grim. He writes something down on money, then passes it to a guy who's collecting bills from everyone around him.

It dawns on me what they're doing. They're taking bets!

Worse, the few who are cheering for me aren't cheering for me to win; they're screaming for me to last just one more minute. Apparently, no one's even betting that I'll win, only on how long I'll last.

So much for chivalry.

19

While I'm taking in the scene, I block two more hits with Boden sitting on top of me. My forearms are taking a beating and my bruises are getting bruises.

With no rescue in sight, it's time to get serious about the fight. I lift my butt and legs off the ground like a gymnast and wrap my legs around Boden's thick neck, hooking my ankles at his throat. I rock my body forward, jerking my legs down.

Boden's eyes widen as he's yanked backward.

Entwined, we swing like a rocking chair. He lands on his back, legs spread around my waist. I'm suddenly sitting upright with my ankles wrapped around his throat.

The instant we land, I slam my fists into his groin.

Now it's his turn to curl.

The cheering crowd instantly mutes. The only noise I hear is Boden's groaning. Sounds like he's having trouble breathing.

Just to make sure he stays that way, I jump up and kick him in the face. I kick him so hard his body spins halfway on the dirt.

I wind up for another kick, this time to the stomach. When you're small enough to have to look up at everyone around you, there's no such thing as a dirty fight. That's a new motto for me. I think I'll keep it.

Before I can complete my kick, someone grabs me around my ribs, pinning my arms. My heart thunders from the adrenaline, and I'm practically panting in my need for blood. I kick and scream at whoever holds me.

'Easy, easy,' says Obi. 'That's enough.' His voice is like velvet brushing against my ears, his arms like steel bands across my ribs. 'Shhh . . . Relax, it's over . . . You won.'

He guides me out of the circle and through the crowd as he soothes me, his arms never relaxing their hold. I glare my most condemning glare at Raffe as I catch his eye. I could have been beaten to a pulp, and all he would have done was lose a bet. He still looks grim, his muscles taut, his face pale as though all the blood has drained from him.

'Where are my winnings?' asks Raffe. I realize he's not talking to me even though he's still looking at me. It's as if he wants to make sure I hear it along with everyone else.

'You didn't win,' says a guy near him. He sounds gleeful. He's the one who collected all the bets.

'What do you mean? My bet was the closest to what happened,' growls Raffe. His hands are fisted as he turns to the guy, and he looks ready for a fight himself.

'Hey buddy, you didn't bet she'd win. Close doesn't count . . .'

Their voices drift into the wind as Obi practically drags me to the mess hall. I don't know which is worse – that Raffe didn't jump in to defend me, or that he bet that I would lose.

The mess hall is a big open cabin with rows of fold-up tables and chairs. I'm guessing it would take less than half an hour to fold it all up for moving. From everything I've seen the whole camp is designed to be packed up and moved in less than an hour.

The place is deserted even though there are half-eaten food trays on the tables. I guess a fight is a not-to-be-missed event around here. Obi's grip on me relaxes once I stop struggling. He guides me to a table closest to the kitchen in the back.

'Sit. I'll be right back.'

I sit on a metal folding chair, trembling with the adrenaline crash. He heads back into the kitchen area. I take deep breaths, calming down and getting a hold of myself until he comes back with a first aid kit and a bag of frozen peas.

He hands me the peas. 'Put this on your jaw. It'll help with the swelling.'

I take the bag, staring at the familiar photo of green peas before gingerly pressing it to my tender jaw. The fact that they have the power to keep food frozen impresses me more than the rest of the camp combined. There's something awe-inspiring about the ability to maintain some aspects of civilization when the rest of the world is sinking into a dark age.

Obi cleans the blood and dirt off my scrapes. They're mostly that, scrapes.

'Your camp sucks,' I say. The peas are numbing my jaw and my words come out slurred.

'Sorry about that.' He rubs antibiotic ointment onto the scrapes on my hands. 'There's so much tension and jittery energy that we've had to accommodate our people's need to blow off steam. The trick is to let them do it under control-led conditions.'

'You call what happened out there a controlled condition?'

A half smile brightens his face. 'I'm sure Boden didn't think so.' He rubs more ointment on my scraped knuckles. 'One of the concessions we made is that if a fight breaks out, no one interferes until there's a clear winner or it becomes life-threatening. We just let people take bets on the outcome. It blows off steam for both the fighters and the spectators.'

So much for the power to maintain a piece of civilization.

'Also,' he says, 'it helps keep the number of fights down when the entire camp is taking bets on the outcome. People take fights seriously when there's no one to rescue you and the whole camp is watching your every move.'

'So everyone knew this rule but me? That no one is allowed to interfere?' Had Raffe known it? Not that it should have stopped him.

'People can jump in if they want, but that invites some-one else to jump in for the other side to keep it a fair fight. The bettors wouldn't like it if it suddenly turned one-sided.' So much for making excuses for Raffe. He could have jumped in; we just would have had to fight someone else too. Nothing we haven't done before.

'Sorry no one explained the rules of the playground to you.' He bandages my bleeding elbow. 'It's just that we haven't had a female get into a fight before.' He shrugs. 'We just didn't expect it.'

'I guess this means you lost your bet.'

He grins sourly. 'I only make big bets that involve lives and the future of humanity.' His shoulders slump as though the invisible weight on them is too much. 'Speaking of which, you handled yourself well out there. Better than anyone expected. We could really use someone like you. There are situations that a girl like you could handle better than a platoon of men.' His grin turns boyish. 'Assuming you don't clock an angel for pissing you off.'

'That's a big assumption.'

'We can work on that.' He gets up. 'Think about it.'

'Actually, I was trying to get to you when that gorilla got in my way. The angels have taken my sister. You need to let me go so I can find her. I swear I won't tell anybody about you, your location, anything. Just please, let me go.'

'I'm sorry about your sister, but I can't jeopardize everyone here based on your word. Join us, and we'll help you get her back.'

'It'll be too late by the time you can mobilize your men. She's seven years old and wheelchair-bound.' I can barely get the words out through the lump in my throat. I can't actually say what we both know, that it might already be too late.

He shakes his head, looking genuinely sympathetic. 'I'm sorry. Everyone here has had to bury someone they love. Join us and we'll make those bastards pay.'

'I don't intend to bury her. She's not dead.' I grind out the words. 'I'm going to find her and get her out.'

'Of course. I didn't mean to imply that she was.' He had, and we both know it. But I pretend to believe his pretty words. As I've heard other people's mothers tell their daughters, politeness is its own reward. 'We'll be moving soon, and you can go then if you still want to leave us. I hope you won't.'

'When is soon?'

'I can't disclose that information. All I can say is that we have something major in the works. You should be a part of it. For your sister, for humanity, for all of us.'

He's good. I feel like standing up and saluting him while humming the national anthem. But I don't think he'd appreciate that.

I am, of course, rooting for the humans. But I already have more responsibilities than I can handle. I just want to be an ordinary girl living an ordinary life. My biggest concern in life should be what dress to wear to the prom, not how to escape a paramilitary camp to rescue my sister from cruel angels, and certainly not whether to join a resistance army to beat back an invasion to save humanity. I know my limits and that goes way beyond them.

So I just nod. He can make of that what he will. I hadn't really expected him to let me go, but I had to try.

As soon as he walks out the door, the lunch crowd shuffles back in. It must be understood, either implicitly or explicitly, that when Obi talks to one of the fighters, everyone gives them privacy. Interesting that he took me to the mess hall during lunch, making everyone wait until we were finished. He sent a clear message to everyone in the camp that I am someone he has noticed.

I get up to leave with my chin up. I avoid looking into any faces so I won't have to talk to anyone. I walk with my bag of peas down so as to not bring attention to my injuries. As if people are likely to forget I'm the one who was fighting. If Raffe is in the lunch crowd, I don't see him. Just as well. I hope he lost his argument with the bookie. He deserves to lose that bet.

I'm barely out and walking between the buildings on my way to the laundry area when two redheaded guys step out from behind a building. If they didn't have matching boy-next-door smiles, I would have thought they were ambushing me.

They're identical twins. Both look scrappy and strung-out in their dirty civilian clothes, but that's not unusual these days. No doubt I look just as scrappy and strung-out. They're barely out of their teens, tall and skinny with mischievous eyes.

'Great job out there, champ,' says the first guy.

'Oh, man, you really put old Jimmy Boden in his place,' says the second one. He's practically beaming. 'Couldn't have happened to a better man.'

I stand there, nodding. I keep a polite grin on my face while still holding the frozen peas to my jaw.

'I'm Tweedledee,' says one.

'I'm Tweedledum,' says the other. 'Most people call us Dee-Dum for short since they can't tell us apart.'

'You're joking, right?' They shake their heads in unison with identical friendly smiles. They look more like a couple of underfed scarecrows than the chubby Tweedledee and Tweedledum I remember from childhood. 'Why would you call yourselves that?'

Dee shrugs. 'New world, new names. We were going to be Gog and Magog.'

'Those were our online names,' says Dum.

'But why go all doom and gloom?' asks Dee.

'Used to be fun being Gog and Magog when the world was Tiffany-twisted and suburban-simple,' says Dum. 'But now . . .'

'Not so much,' says Dee. 'Death and destruction are so passé.'

'So mainstream.'

'So in with the popular crowd.'

'We'd rather be Tweedledee and Tweedledum.'

I nod, because what other response is there?

'I'm Penryn. I'm named after an exit off Interstate 80.'

'Nice.' They nod as if to say they understand what it's like to have parents like that.

'Everyone's talking about you,' says Dum.

Not sure I like that. That whole fight thing didn't really go off the way I had planned. Then again, nothing in my life has gone the way I had planned.

'Great. If you don't mind, I'm going to go hide now.' I tip my bag of frozen peas at them like a hat as I try to step between them.

'Wait,' says Dee. He lowers his voice to a dramatic whisper. 'We have a business proposition for you.'

I pause and politely wait. Unless their proposition includes getting me out of here, there is nothing they can say to get me interested in any kind of business idea. But since they aren't moving out of my way, I don't have much of a choice but to listen.

'The crowd loved you,' says Dum.

'How about a repeat performance?' asks Dee. 'Say, for a thirty percent take of the winnings?'

'What are you talking about? Why would I risk my life for a measly thirty percent of the winnings? Besides, money doesn't buy you anything anymore.'

'Oh, it's not money,' says Dum. 'We just use money as a shortcut for the relative value of the bet.'

His face becomes animated like he's genuinely fascinated by the economics of post-apocalyptic gambling. 'You put your name and the bet you're making on, say, a five-dollar bill, and that just tells the bookie that you're willing to bet something of greater value than a dollar bill, but less than a ten-dollar bill. It's the bookie who decides who gets what and who gives what. You know, like maybe someone loses a quarter of his rations and gets extra chores for a week. Or if he wins, then he gets someone else's rations to add to his, and someone else scrubs the toilet for him for a week. Get it?'

'Got it. And the answer's still no. Besides, there's no guarantee I'll win.'

'No.' Dee gives me an over-the-top used car salesman's smile. 'We're looking for a guarantee that you'll lose.'

I burst out laughing. 'You want me to throw a fight?'

'Shhh!' Dee looks around dramatically. We're standing in the shadows between two buildings, and no one seems to notice us.

'It'll be great,' says Dum. His eyes shine with mischief. 'After what you did to Boden, the odds will be so far in your favor when you fight Anita—'

'You want me to fight a girl?' I cross my arms. 'You just want to see a catfight, don't you?'

'It's not just for us,' says Dee defensively. 'It'll be a gift to the whole camp.'

'Yeah,' says Dum. 'Who needs television when you've got all that water and laundry suds?'

'Dream on.' I shove through them.

'We'll help you get out,' says Dee in a singsong cadence.

I stop. My brain runs through half a dozen scenarios based on what he just said.

'We can get the keys to your cell.'

'We can distract the guards.'

'We can make sure no one checks on you until morning.'

'One fight, that's all we ask.'

I turn to look at them. 'Why would you risk treason for a mud fight?'

'You have no idea how much I'd risk for an honest-to-God mud fight between two hot women,' says Dee.

'It's not really treason anyway,' says Dum. 'Obi's gonna let you go, it's just a matter of timing. We're not here to keep human prisoners. He's overemphasizing your risk to us.'

'Why?' I ask.

'Because he wants to recruit you and that guy you came with. Obi's an only child, and he doesn't understand,' says Dee. 'He thinks keeping you around for a few days will get you to change your mind about leaving us.'

'But we know better. A few days of singing patriotic songs ain't going to convince you to abandon your sister,' says Dum.

'Got that right, brother,' says Dee.

They bump fists. 'Damn straight.'

I look at them. They really do understand. They'd never leave each other behind. Maybe I have genuine allies. 'Do I really have to do this silly fight to get your help?'

'Oh, yeah,' says Dee. 'No question.' They both grin at me like mischievous little boys.

'How do you know all this stuff? About my sister? What Obi's thinking?'

'It's our job,' says Dum. 'Some people call us Dee-Dum. Other people call us spymasters.' He wiggles his eyebrows up and down dramatically.

'Okay, Spymaster Dee-Dum, what did my friend bet on the fight?' It doesn't matter of course, but I still want to know.

'Interesting.' Dee arches his brow in a knowing fashion. 'Of all the things you could have asked when you found out we deal in information, you pick that one.'

My cheeks warm despite the frozen peas on my jaw. I try not to look like I wish I could take back my question. 'What are you, in kindergarten? Just tell me already.'

'He bet that you'd last in the ring for at least seven minutes.' Dum rubs his freckled cheek. 'We all thought he was crazy.' Seven minutes is a long, long time to get hammered by giant fists.

'Not crazy enough,' says Dee. His smile is so boyish and pre-disaster that it's almost possible to forget we live in a world gone mad. 'He should have bet that you'd win.

He woulda raked it in. Man, the odds were so far against you.'

'I bet he could take down Boden in two minutes,' says Dum. 'That guy's got *badass* written all over him.'

'Ninety seconds, flat,' says Dee.

I've seen Raffe fight. My bet would be on ten seconds, assuming Boden didn't have a rifle like he did the night he caught us. But I don't say that. Doesn't make me feel any better that he didn't jump in to play the hero.

'Get us out tonight and you've got a deal,' I say.

'Tonight's awfully short notice,' says Dee.

'Maybe if you could promise you'll rip Anita's shirt off . . .' Dum gives me his little-boy smile.

'Don't push your luck.'

Dee holds up a slim leather case and dangles it like bait. 'How about a bonus for ripping her shirt off?'

My hands fly to my pants pocket where my lock picking set should be. My pocket is flat and empty. 'Hey, that's mine!' I make a grab for it but it disappears from Dee's hand. I hadn't seen him move. 'How'd you do that?'

'Now you see it,' says Dum, waving the case. How it got from Dee to Dum I have no idea. They're standing next to each other but still, I should have seen something. Then it's gone again. 'Now you don't.'

'Give it back, now, you thieving bastards. Or the whole thing's off.'

Dum gives Dee a sad clown face. Dee arches his brow in a comic expression.

'Fine,' Dee sighs. He hands me back my lock picking set.

This time, I was watching for it, but I still didn't see it moving from Dum to Dee. 'Tonight it is.'

Dee-Dum flash identical grins at me.

I shake my head and stomp off before they can steal any more of my things.

20

My back snaps, crackles, and pops as I try to stand straight. It's dusk, and my workday is almost over. I put my hand on the small of my back, my body craning slowly to straighten like an ancient crone.

My hands, after only one day of scrubbing clothes in the washtub, are swollen and red. I've heard of dry, cracked hands but never really knew what that meant until now. After only a few minutes of being out of the water, my palm has cracks that look like someone took a razor blade and sliced the skin. It's freaky to see your hand all cut up, looking too dry to even bleed.

When the other laundry drudges offered me a pair of yellow rubber gloves this morning I turned them down, thinking only prissy old people used those. They gave me such know-it-all looks that my pride wouldn't let me ask for them at lunch.

Now, I'm beginning to consider getting up close and personal with the one humble bone in my body and asking for the gloves. Good thing I don't plan on having to do this again tomorrow.

I look around, stretching my arms, wondering when this Anita person is going to attack me. I'll be really pissed if she waits until my workday is over. What's the point of getting into a catfight if you can't even weasel out of an hour of hard labor?

I take my time stretching. I reach above my head and arch my back as far as it'll go.

My neck hurts, my back hurts, my arms and hands hurt, my legs and feet hurt, even my eyeballs hurt. My muscles are either screaming from hours of repetitive motion or stiff from hours of being held still. At this rate, I won't have to throw the fight, I'll lose it honestly.

I pretend not to watch the latrine duty men walking toward us as I stretch my legs. There are about ten of them with Raffe hanging in the back of the group.

When they are a few steps away, they start stripping off their filthy clothes. Grimy shirts, pants, and socks get tossed into the laundry pile. Some get tossed into the trash pile. Raffe dug the ditch instead of working on the truly toxic part of the latrines, but not everyone was that lucky. The only things they leave on are their boxer shorts.

I try very hard not to look at Raffe as I realize he'll be expected to take his shirt off. He might be able to explain away the bandages under his shirt, but there's no way he can explain away the bloodstains exactly where wings would have been.

I stretch my arms above my head, trying not to look scared. I hold my breath, hoping the men will move along and not notice Raffe lagging behind.

But instead of moving into the buildings for a shower, they grab the hose we've been using to fill our tubs. They line up to hose each other off. I could kick myself for not anticipating this. Of course they'll hose off first. Who would want latrine workers to walk straight into the shared showers?

I steal a glance at Raffe. He's keeping his cool, but I can tell by how slowly he's unbuttoning his shirt that he didn't see this coming either.

He must have figured he could slip away once they got into the building since the showers couldn't take everyone at the same time. But there is no good excuse to drift away from this part of the routine and no way to do it without being noticed.

Raffe finishes unbuttoning his shirt and instead of taking it off, he slowly starts unbuttoning his pants. Everyone around him has already stripped, and he's starting to look conspicuous. Just when I'm wondering if we should make a blatant run for it, the solution to our problem saunters toward us on long, shapely legs.

The woman who walked with Raffe to lunch tosses her honey hair as she smiles up at him.

Dee-Dum walk by as if on cue. 'Oh hi, Anita!' they both say with casual surprise. Their voices are slightly raised, as if to make sure I hear them.

Anita glares at them as if they'd just hawked and spat. I've seen that look a million times in the hallways given by a popular girl to a band geek when he gets too familiar in front of her clique. She turns back to Raffe, her face melting into a radiant smile. She puts her hand on his arm as he's about to take off his pants.

And that's all the excuse I need.

I grab a sudsy shirt out of the gray water and throw it at her.

It makes a plopping noise when it lands on her face, wrapping around her hair. Her perfect hair clumps into a stringy mass, and her mascara smears as the cloth slides wetly down her blouse. She emits a high-pitched squeal that turns every head within earshot.

'Oh, I'm sorry,' I say in a sugary voice. 'Did you not like that? I thought that's what you wanted. I mean, why else would you be getting all grabby with my man?'

The small crowd around us grows by the second. Oh yeah, baby. Step right up. Come see the freak show. Raffe fades into the growing crowd, discreetly buttoning up his shirt. And I thought he looked grim at my last fight.

Anita's enormous eyes look up helplessly at Raffe. She looks like a distressed kitten, bewildered and hurt. Poor thing. I have second thoughts about whether I can do this.

Then she looks at me. It's amazing how quickly her face can change, depending on who she's looking at. She looks spitting-mad. As she stalks toward me, anger turns into rage.

It's impressive how vicious a pretty woman can look when she sets her mind to it. Either she's one hell of an actress, or Dee-Dum had a double agenda when they set this up. I'll bet she doesn't even know about the fight. Why share the profits when you can get revenge instead? I'm sure this wasn't the first time Anita has snubbed Dee-Dum. Not that I believe for a second that their feelings were hurt.

'You think anything you do would get a guy like him to look at you twice?' Anita flings the wet shirt back at me.

'You'd be lucky to get a one-legged grandpa to be interested in you.'

Okay. Turns out I can do this.

I lean a little to make sure the shirt hits me.

Then, we go at it in all our feminine glory. Hair pulling, face slapping, shirt ripping, nail scratching. We squeal like cheerleaders who fell into a mud pit.

As we stumble around in our drunken dance, we bump into a wash basin. It comes crashing down, spraying the whole area with water.

She trips over it while clinging to me, and we come tumbling down. Our bodies contort around each other as we roll in the mud around the wash basins.

It's hard to look dignified when your head is being pulled down to your shoulder by your hair. It's embarrassing. I do my best to look as though I'm really fighting.

The crowd goes wild with their cheering and clapping. I catch a glimpse of Dee-Dum as we roll. They're practically hopping with glee.

Just how does somebody lose a fight like this? Should I break down crying? Land in the mud facedown and let her scratch me a few times while I curl into a ball? I'm at a complete loss as to how to tap out of this fight.

All thoughts of the fight are shattered by a gunshot.

It comes from somewhere past the crowd, but it's close enough to make everyone freeze in silence.

Two more shots go off in rapid succession.

Then a scream echoes through the woods. A very human, very terrified scream.

21

The wind rustles through the treetops. My blood pounds in my ears.

For a few heartbeats, everyone stares into the twilight with eyes wide as if waiting for a nightmare to come to life. Then, as though a command had been given, chaos bursts through the crowd.

Soldiers run to the trees in the direction of the scream, gripping their guns and rifles. Everyone starts talking, some crying. Some rush one way, others rush another. It's a crush of noise and confusion bordering on panic. Like the dogs, these people aren't as well trained as Obi would like.

Anita climbs off me, the whites of her eyes showing all around her irises. She takes off, running after the biggest crowd which is stampeding into the mess hall. I get up, torn between wanting to see what's happening and wanting to hide in the relative safety of numbers.

Raffe is suddenly beside me, whispering, 'Where are the wings?'

'What?'

'Where did you hide them?'

'In a tree.'

He sighs, obviously trying to be patient. 'Can you tell me?'

I point in the direction of the scream, where the last of the soldiers disappear.

'Can you tell me how to find it, or do you need to show me?'

'I'd have to show you.'

'Then let's go.'

'Now?'

'Can you think of a better time?'

I glance around. Everyone is still scrambling to grab gear and run into a building. No one gives us a second glance. No one would notice if we disappeared during the chaos.

Of course, there's whatever it is that's causing the panic.

My thoughts must show in my face because Raffe says, 'Either tell me or show me. It has to be now.'

Twilight is sliding fast into full dark around us. My skin prickles at the thought of wandering through the forest in the dark with whatever it was that caused an armed soldier to scream like that.

But I can't let Raffe run without me. I nod.

We slip into the darkening shadows for the closest path to the forest. We half tiptoe, half run through the woods.

Gunshots fire in rapid, overlapping succession. Several guns fire simultaneously in the woods. Maybe this isn't the best idea.

As if I'm not freaked out enough, screams echo through the oncoming night.

By the time we run across the camp and reach the hiding-tree area, the woods are quiet. Not a single rustle, no birds or squirrels disturb the silence. The light is fading fast, but there's enough to see the carnage.

About a dozen soldiers had run toward the scream. Now there are only five still standing.

The rest lie scattered on the ground like broken dolls tossed by an angry child. And like broken dolls, there are body parts missing. An arm, a leg, a head. The ripped joints are ragged and gory.

Blood splatters everything – the trees, the dirt, the soldiers. The dimming light has leached the color out of it, making it look like oil dripping off the branches.

The remaining soldiers stand in a circle with their rifles pointing outward.

I'm puzzled by the angle of their rifles. They don't point straight out or up, the way they would for an enemy on foot or in the air. Nor do they point to the ground the way they would if they weren't about to fire.

Instead, they point midway down as if aiming at something that's only as high as their waists. Mountain lion? There are mountain lions in these hills, although it's rare to see one. But mountain lions don't cause this kind of slaughter. Maybe wild dogs? But again, the slaughter doesn't look natural. It looks like a vicious, murderous attack rather than a hunt for food or a defensive fight.

The memory pops into my head of Raffe mentioning the possibility of kids attacking that family on the street. I dismiss that thought as soon as it comes. These armed soldiers would never be this scared of a gang of kids, no matter how feral.

Everything about the survivors looks freaky spooked, as though the only thing containing their panic is their paralyzing fear. Their white-knuckled grips on their rifles; the way they hold their elbows tight near their bodies as if to keep their arms from shaking; the way they move shoulder to shoulder, like a school of fish clustering near a predator.

Nothing natural could cause this kind of fear. It goes beyond a fear of physical harm and into the realm of mental and spiritual. Like the fear of losing your sanity, of losing your soul.

My skin prickles watching the soldiers. Fear is contagious. Maybe it's something that's evolved from our primeval days when your survival odds were better if you picked up on your buddy's fear without wasting time to discuss it. Or maybe I'm sensing something directly. Something horrifying that my reptile brain recognizes.

My stomach churns and tries to reject its contents. I swallow it back, ignoring the acid burn on the back of my throat.

We huddle out of sight behind a large tree. I glance at Raffe crouched beside me. He is looking at everything but the soldiers, as if they are the one thing in the forest we don't need to worry about. I'd feel better if he didn't look so uneasy.

What spooks an angel who's stronger, faster, and has keener senses than man?

The soldiers shift. The shape of their circle changes to a teardrop.

The men ooze nervousness as they back slowly toward the camp. Whatever had attacked them seems to be gone. Or at least, the soldiers seem to think so.

My instincts aren't convinced. I guess not all the soldiers are convinced either, because they look so freaked out that the slightest sound might be enough for them to open fire, spraying bullets every which way into the dark.

The temperature is plummeting, and my wet T-shirt clings to me like a sheet of ice. But sweat trickles down my temples anyway and pools greasily in my armpits. Watching the soldiers leave is like watching the basement door close, shutting out the only light in the house and leaving me alone in the monster-filled darkness. Every muscle in my body screams to run after the soldiers. Every instinct is frantic not to be the lone guppy separated from its school.

I look at Raffe, hoping for some kind of reassurance. He's on full alert: his body tense, his eyes searching the darkening forest, his ears perked as though listening in stereo.

'Where is it?' His whisper is so low I'm reading his lips almost as much as hearing his words.

At first, I assume he's talking about the monster that could do such damage. But before I can ask how should I know, I realize he's asking where the wings are hidden. I point beyond where the soldiers had been standing.

He silently runs to the other side of the circle of destruction, ignoring the carnage. I tiptoe-run after him, desperate not to be left behind in the woods.

I have a hard time ignoring the body parts. There aren't enough bodies and parts to account for all the missing men. Hopefully, some of them ran off and that's the reason there are fewer of them than there should be. I slip on the blood in the middle of the carnage but manage to regain my footing before I fall. The thought of falling face-first on a pile of human intestines is enough to keep me moving to reach the other side.

Raffe stands in the midst of the trees, trying to find one with a hollow. It takes a few minutes before we spot it. When he pulls out the blanket-wrapped bundle of his wings, the tension leaches out of him, and he hunches his shoulders and head protectively around the bundle.

He looks at me, and there is enough light for me to see him mouth the words *thank you*. It seems to be our fate to continually pass our debt back and forth.

I wonder how long it takes before it's too late to reattach the wings to his back. If it was a human body part, it would be past the expiration date already. But who knows about angels? And even if the angel surgeons or magicians or whatever manage to reattach them, I wonder if they'll be useable or just decorative, the way a glass eye is just so that people can look at your face without cringing.

A cold wind teases my hair, making it brush against the back of my neck like icy fingers. The forest is a mass of shifting shadows. The whipping of the leaves sounds like a thousand snakes hissing above me. I look up just to make sure there aren't really snakes up there. All I see are redwoods looming under the blackening sky.

Raffe touches my arm. I practically jump out of my skull but manage to stay quiet. He hands me my pack. He keeps the wings and the sword.

He nods in the direction of the camp and walks toward it, following the soldiers. I don't understand why he wants to head back to camp when we should be running the other way. But the forest has me so creeped out that I'm not inclined to linger alone, nor am I eager to break our silence. I slip on my pack and follow.

I stick to Raffe as close as I can manage without having to explain why I'm hugging his back. We reach the edge of the woods.

The camp is quiet under the mottled moon shadow beneath the camp's canopy. No lights glow from the windows, although if I look hard enough, I can catch a glimpse of metal glinting in the moonlight in some of the windows. I wonder how many rifles they have trained through the glass, seeking targets?

I don't envy Obi having to maintain order in those buildings. I'm sure panic in a confined space can be pretty ugly.

Raffe leans over to me and whispers so low I can barely hear him. 'I'll watch to make sure you get safely into the building. Go.'

I blink stupidly at him, trying to make sense of what he is saying. 'But what about you?'

He shakes his head. It seems reluctant, for all the good that will do me. 'You're safer in there. And you're safer without me. If you're still set on finding your sister, head for San Francisco. You'll find the aerie there.'

He's leaving me. Leaving me at Obi's camp while he goes on to the aerie.

'No.' *I need you*, I almost blurt out. 'I saved you. You owe me.'

'Listen to me. You are safer on your own than with me. This is no accident. This sort of ending . . .' He gestures toward the massacre. 'It happens too often to my companions.' He runs his hand through his hair. 'It's been so long since I had someone to watch my back . . . I'd fooled myself into believing . . . things could be different. Do you understand?'

'No.' It is more of a rejection of what he's telling me than an answer to his question.

He stares into my eyes with an intense look.

I hold my breath.

I swear he's memorizing me, as though his mental camera is firing, capturing me in this moment. He even inhales deeply as though filling up on my scent.

But the moment passes when he looks away and leaves me wondering if I imagined it.

Then he turns and melts into the darkness.

By the time I take a step, his form has completely merged with the darker shadows. I want to call out to him but I don't dare make that kind of noise.

Darkness closes around me. My heart hammers in my chest, telling me to run, run, run.

I can't believe he left me. Alone in the dark with a demon monster.

I clench my fists, digging my nails into my skin to help me focus. No time to feel sorry for myself. I've got to concentrate if I'm going to survive long enough to rescue Paige.

The safest place to spend the night is the camp. But if I run to the camp, they won't let me go until they're ready to move. That could be days, weeks. Paige doesn't have weeks. Whatever it is they're doing to her, they're doing it right now. I've already wasted too much time.

On the other hand, what are my options? Run through the forest? In the dark? Alone? With a monster that tore apart half a dozen armed men?

I frantically beat my brain for a third option. I come up with nothing.

I've hesitated long enough. Being found by the monster as I stand frozen in indecision is the stupidest way to die that I can think of. Rock or hard place?

I steel myself to ignore the creepy sensation crawling up my back. I take a deep breath and let it out slowly, hoping to calm myself. It doesn't work.

I turn away from camp and plunge into the forest.

22

I can't help but look to see if there's anything I need to worry about sneaking up behind me. Not that a monster capable of tearing apart armed soldiers would bother sneaking. I wonder why we didn't evolve with eyes in the back of our heads?

The farther I walk into the woods, the tighter the darkness closes in on me. I tell myself that this isn't really suicide. The woods are full of living creatures – squirrels, birds, deer, rabbits – and the monster can't kill them all. So my chances of being among the majority of living things in the forest that will survive tonight are pretty good. Right?

I move through the dark woods by instinct, hoping I'm heading north. Within a short time, I begin to have serious doubts about which direction I'm moving. I read somewhere that when lost and left to their own devices, people tend to walk in large circles. What if I'm walking the wrong way?

Doubts erode my reason and I can feel the panic bubbling in my chest.

I give myself a mental slap. This is not the time to freak out. I promise I'll let myself panic when I'm safe and sound, hidden in a nice house with a stocked kitchen with Paige and Mom.

Yeah, right. The thought brings a twitch to my lips as if I might grin. Maybe I really am losing it.

I see menace behind every rustle and shifting shadow, behind every bird taking flight and squirrel scrambling on a branch.

After what feels like hours of trekking through the woods in the dark, one of the shadows shifts from a tree like so many wind-blown branches. Only this one keeps moving away from the tree. It separates itself from the larger mass of shadows, then merges into another, greater darkness.

I freeze.

It could have been a deer. But the shadow legs didn't move right. It might have been something on two feet. Or more accurately, several somethings on two feet.

My hunch proves right when the shadows fan out, surrounding me. I hate being right all the time.

So, what stands on two legs, is three or four feet tall, and growls like a pack of dogs? It's hard to think of much other than those bodies scattered about the forest floor with missing parts.

A shadow rushes toward me so fast it looks like a dark blur. Something bumps into my arm. I step back, but whatever it was is already long gone.

The other shadows shift. Some dart forward and back, looking like shadows beginning to boil. Something bumps my other arm before I register that another shadow has darted out.

I stagger back.

Our neighbor Justin used to have a set of needlelike piranha teeth displayed on his mantel. He told us once that the
carnivorous and sometimes cannibalistic fish are actually
quite shy and usually bump their prey before attacking, gaining confidence as their schoolmates do the same. This feels
eerily like his description.

The chorus of growling rises. It sounds like a mix of animal
growls and disturbingly human grunting.

Another hit. This time, a sharp pain stabs up from my
thigh, like I've been sliced by razors. I shiver as a warm pool
spreads around the pain.

Then I get bumped twice more in rapid succession. Is the
blood whipping them into a frenzy?

Another hits my wrist. I cry out this time as soon as I feel
it.

This one isn't just a quick slice. It's a lingering one, if a
flashing shadow can be said to linger. The burning hits me a
second after I realize I've been – bitten? I'm sure I'd be less
scared if I could just see what they look like. There's something particularly terrifying about not being able to see the
things attacking you.

My panting is so loud now that I might as well be
screaming.

23

I catch motion out of the corner of my eye. I don't even have time to brace for another hit before Raffe stands before me. His muscles are tense holding his sword as he faces the boiling shadows. I hadn't even heard the rustle of leaves. One second he's not there, the next, he is.

'Run, Penryn.'

I don't need another invitation. I run.

But I don't run far, which is probably not my smartest move. I can't help it. I hesitate behind a tree to watch Raffe fight the demons.

Now that I know what to look for, I can tell there are about half a dozen of them. Definitely running on two feet. Definitely low to the ground. Not all of uniform size either. One is at least a foot taller than the shortest one. One seems outright chubby.

Their small forms could be human or angel, although they don't move like either. When they go into hyperdrive, their motions are fluid, as though that is their natural pace. These things are definitely not human. Maybe these are some form of nasty angel breed. Aren't cherubs always drawn as children?

Raffe catches one as it tries to whiz by him. Two others had started going for him but stop when they see Raffe slice through the little demon.

It screeches something awful as it flails on the forest ground.

The others aren't daunted, though, as they dash at Raffe to do their bump and run routine and shove him off balance. I figure it won't take long before they start biting or stinging or whatever it is they do.

'Raffe, behind you!'

I grab the nearest rock and take a heartbeat to aim. I've been known to hit the bull's-eye playing darts, but I've also been known to miss the dartboard altogether. Missing the dartboard here means hitting Raffe.

I hold my breath, take aim at the nearest shadow, and throw with as much force as I can muster.

Bull's-eye!

The rock smashes into a shadow, stopping it cold. It's almost funny how the low demon practically flips backward as it falls. Raffe never needs to know that I was aiming for the other one.

Raffe swings wildly with his sword, slicing a demon's chest. 'I told you to run!'

So much for gratitude. I bend and grab another rock. This one is jagged and so big that I can barely lift it. I might be getting greedy, but I lob it at one of the demons anyway. Sure enough, it lands a foot away from the fight.

This time, I go for a smaller, more aerodynamic stone. I'm careful to stay out of reach of the fighting circle, and the low demons let me. I guess my stone throwing doesn't even show up on their radar. I take aim at another shadow, then throw with all my might.

It hits Raffe on the back.

It must have hit him on his wound because he stumbles forward, staggers two steps, then stops just in front of two demons. His sword is down, almost low enough to trip him, and he's out of balance as he faces them. I swallow my heart, shoving it from my throat back down into my chest.

Raffe manages to lift the sword. But he doesn't have time to stop them from biting him.

He cries out. My stomach clenches in sympathetic pain.

Then, a strange thing happens. Stranger than what's been happening, that is. The low demons spit and make distinct noises of disgust. They spit as if trying to get the bad taste out of their mouths. I wish I could see what they look like. I'm sure they're making repelled expressions.

Raffe cries out again as a third one bites him on his back. He manages to bat it away after a few tries. That one makes a choking noise and spits noisily as well.

The shadows back off after that. Then, they melt into the general darkness of the forest.

Before I can wrap my mind around what just happened, Raffe does something just as strange. Instead of declaring victory and walking away safe, like any sane survivor, he chases after them into the dark woods.

'Raffe!'

All I hear are the dying screams of the low demons. The sounds are so eerily human, goose bumps prickle my spine. I suppose all dying animals sound that way.

Then, as quickly as it started, the final scream fades into the night.

I shiver alone in the dark. I take a couple of steps toward the black woods where Raffe disappeared, then stop. What am I supposed to do now?

The wind blows, chilling the sweat on my skin. After a while, even the wind falls quiet and still. I'm not sure if I should run to try to find Raffe, or run away from the whole thing. I remember that I'm supposed to be on my way to Paige, and that keeping myself alive until I rescue her is a good goal. I start to shiver more than the cold calls for. It must be the aftereffects of the battle.

My ears strain to hear something. I'd take anything, even a grunt of pain from Raffe. At least I'd know he's alive.

The wind rustles the tops of the trees and whips my hair.

I'm just about to give up and head into the dark trees to look for him when the sound of crunching leaves gets louder. It could be a deer. I take a step back away from the sound. It could be the low demons, back to finish the job.

The branches rustle as they part. A Raffe-shaped shadow steps into the clearing.

Utter relief washes over me, relaxing muscles I hadn't realized were tense.

I run to him. I put my arms out for a big hug, but he takes a step back from me. I'm sure even a man like him – that is to say, a non-man – can take comfort in a hug after a fight for his life. But apparently not from me.

I stop just in front of him and drop my arms awkwardly. My delight at seeing him, though, doesn't entirely dry up.

'So . . . did you get them?'

He nods. Black blood drips off his hair like he's been sprayed with the stuff. Blood soaks both his arms and stomach. His shirt is torn at the chest and it looks like he took some damage. I have the impulse to fuss over him, but I hold it in check.

'Are you all right?' It's a stupid question because there's not much I can do for him if he isn't all right, but it just tumbles out.

He snorts. 'Aside from being beaned with a rock, I'll live.'

'Sorry.' I feel pretty god-awful about that, but there's no point in groveling over it.

'The next time you have a quarrel with me, I'd appreciate it if you could just talk to me first before resorting to pelting me with rocks.'

'Oh, all right,' I grumble. 'You're so damned civilized.'

'Yeah, that's me. Civilized.' He shakes the blood off his hand. 'You okay?'

I nod. There's no graceful way to step back after my aborted hug attempt so we stand closer than is comfortable. I guess he thinks so too because he slips by me into the clearing. He must have been blocking the wind for me because I suddenly feel cold when he steps away. He takes a deep breath as though to clear his head and lets it out slowly.

'What the hell were those things?' I ask.

'I'm not sure.' He wipes his sword on his shirt.

'They weren't your kind, were they?'

'No.' He slides his sword back into its sheath.

'Well, they certainly weren't mine. Is there a third option?'

'There's always a third option.'

'Like freaky, evil demons? I mean, even more evil than angels?'

'Angels aren't evil.'

'Right. Gee, how could I have forgotten? Oh, wait. Maybe I got my wacky idea from that whole attack-and-destroy maneuver you guys pulled.'

He heads back out into the forest through the far side of the clearing. I hustle after him.

'Why did you chase those things?' I ask. 'We could have been miles away before they changed their minds and came back for us.'

He responds without turning around to look at me. 'They're too close to something that shouldn't exist. Let something like that get away, and they'll only come back to haunt you. Believe me, I know.'

He speeds up. I trot after him, practically clinging to him. I don't want to be left alone in the dark again. He gives me a sidelong glance.

'Don't even think about it,' I say. 'I'm sticking to you like a wet shirt, at least until daylight.' I resist reaching out and grabbing his shirt for guidance in the dark.

'How'd you get to me so fast?' I ask. It must have been seconds from the time I screamed to the time he showed up.

He continues to trek through the woods.

I open my mouth to repeat the question, but he speaks over me. 'I was tracking you.'

I stop in surprise. He keeps going so I run after him to make sure he's only two steps ahead of me. All kinds of questions float in my head but it's no use asking them all. I keep it simple. 'Why?'

'I said I would make sure you got back to camp safely.'

'I wasn't going back to camp.'

'I noticed.'

'You also said that you'd take me to the aerie. Leaving me alone in the dark was your idea of taking me there?'

'It was my idea of encouraging you to be sensible and go back to camp. Apparently, sensible is not part of your vocabulary. What are you complaining about anyway? I'm here, aren't I?'

It's hard to argue against that. He did save my life. We walk in silence for a while as I chew that over.

'So your blood must taste god-awful to ward off those things,' I say.

'Yes, that was a little weird, wasn't it?'

'A little weird? That was freakin' Bizarroville.'

He pauses and looks back at me. 'Are you speaking English?'

I open my mouth to make a smart comeback but he interrupts.

'Let's keep it quiet, shall we? There may be more out there.' That shuts me up.

Exhaustion hits me, probably some kind of post-trauma something or another. I figure having company in the dark, even if it is an angel, is as good as I can hope for tonight. Besides, for the first time since I started this nightmare trek through the woods, I don't have to worry about whether I'm going in the right direction. Raffe walks confidently in a straight line. He never hesitates, subtly adjusting our route here and there to get around some gorge or meadow.

I don't question whether he actually knows where he's going. The illusion that he does is enough to comfort me. Maybe angels have a special sense of direction the way birds do. Don't they always know which way to migrate and how to get back to their nest, even if they can't see it? Or maybe that's just my desperation making up stories to make myself feel better, like a mental version of whistling in the dark.

I quickly become hopelessly lost and exhausted to the point of delirium. After hours of trudging through the woods in the dark, I start to wonder if maybe Raffe is a fallen angel leading me into Hell. Maybe when we finally reach the aerie, I'll realize it's actually underground in a cave filled with fire and sulfur, with people skewered and roasting. It would explain a few things, anyway.

I hardly notice when he leads us into a house nestled in the woods. By that point, I feel like a walking zombie. We crunch over broken glass and some animal scurries away, disappearing into the shadows. He finds a bedroom. He pulls off my pack and gently shoves me onto the bed.

The world fades out the instant my head touches the pillow.

I dream that I'm fighting again by the laundry barrels. We're soaked in laundry suds. My hair is dripping and my clothes cling, as wet T-shirts will do. Anita is pulling my hair and screeching.

The crowd is too close, hardly giving us room to fight. Their faces are contorted, showing too much teeth and too much white around their eyes. They shout things like 'Rip off her shirt!' or 'Tear off her bra!' One guy keeps yelling frantically, 'Kiss her! Kiss her!'

We roll into a laundry barrel and it comes crashing down. Instead of dirty laundry water, foaming blood splashes everywhere. It is warm and crimson as it soaks me. We all stop and stare at the blood pouring out of the barrel. An impossible amount of it flows out like an endless river.

Laundry floats by. Shirts and pants soaked in blood, empty and crumpled, lost and soulless without their wearers.

Scorpions the size of sewer rats ride the islands of crimson clothing. They have enormous stingers with drops of blood at the tips. When they see us, they curl their tails and spread their wings with menace. I'm pretty sure scorpions are not supposed to have wings, but I don't have time to think about that because someone screams and points to the sky.

Along the horizon, the sky darkens. A dark, boiling cloud blots out the setting sun. A low buzz like the beating of a million insect wings fills the air.

The wind picks up and quickly grows to hurricane force as the churning cloud and its shadow race toward us. People run in panic, their faces suddenly lost and innocent like frightened children.

The scorpions take to the air. They congregate and pluck someone out of the crowd. Someone small with withered legs. She screams, 'Penryn!'

'Paige!' I jump up and run after them. I sprint blindly through the blood which is now ankle high and rising.

But no matter how hard I run, I can't get any closer to her as the monsters haul my little sister into the oncoming darkness.

24

When I open my eyes, dappled sunlight streams through the window. I am alone in what was once a lovely bedroom with high ceilings and arched windows. My first thought is that Raffe has left me again. Panic flutters in my stomach. But it's daylight, and I can handle myself in daylight, can't I? And I know to head for San Francisco, if Raffe is to be believed. I give it a fifty-fifty chance.

I pad out of the room, down the hall, and into the living room. With each step, I shed the remnants of my nightmare, leaving it behind in the dark where it belongs.

Raffe sits on the floor repacking my pack. The morning sun caresses his hair, highlighting strands of mahogany and honey hidden among the black. My shoulder muscles relax, the tension seeping out at the sight of him. He looks up at me, his eyes bluer than ever in the soft light.

We look at each other without saying anything. I wonder what he sees as he watches me standing in the stream of golden light filtering through the windows.

I look away first. My eyes roam the room in an effort to find something else to look at and settle on a row of photos sitting on the fireplace mantel. I wander over there to give myself something to do other than stand awkwardly under his gaze.

There's a family photo complete with mom, dad, and three kids. They are on a ski slope, all bundled up and looking happy. Another photo shows a sports field with the older boy in a football uniform doing a high-five with dad. I pick up one that shows the girl in a prom dress smiling at the camera with a cute guy in a tux.

The last photo is a close-up of the little kid hanging upside down on a tree branch. His hair spikes out below him and his mischievous smile shows two missing teeth.

The perfect family in a perfect house. I look around at what must have been a beautiful home. One of the windows is broken and rain has stained the hardwood floor in a big semicircle in front of it. We are not the first visitors here, as evidenced by scattered candy wrappers in one of the corners.

My eyes drift back to Raffe. He is still watching me with those unfathomable eyes.

I put the photo back into its place. 'What time is it?'

'Midmorning.' He goes back to rummaging through my pack.

'What are you doing?'

'Getting rid of things we don't need. Obadiah was right, we should have packed better.' He tosses a pot onto the hardwood floor. It clunks a couple of times before settling down.

'The place is cleaned out of food, every last scrap has been licked away,' he says. 'But there's still running water.' He lifts two filled water bottles. He's found a green daypack for himself, and he puts one bottle in it, the other in mine.

'Want some breakfast?' He shakes the bag of cat food that I had carried in my pack.

I grab a handful of the dried kibbles on my way to the bathroom. I'm dying for a shower but there's something too vulnerable about stripping down and soaping up right now, so I settle for an unsatisfactory wipedown, toweling around my clothes. I at least manage to wash my face and brush my teeth. I pull my hair back into a ponytail and prop a dark cap on it.

It's going to be another long day and this time, we'll be out in the sun. My feet are already sore and tired, and I wish I could have slept with my boots off. But I can see why Raffe didn't bother to take them off, and I'm grateful for it. I wouldn't have gotten far without my boots if I'd had to run into the forest.

By the time I come out of the bathroom, Raffe is ready to go. His hair is wet and dripping onto his shoulder, and his face is clean of blood. I doubt he took a shower any more than I did, but he looks fresh, much fresher than I feel.

There are no visible scars or wounds anywhere on him. He has changed from the bloodied jeans of yesterday into a pair of cargo pants that fit the curve of his body surprisingly well. He's also found a long-sleeved tee that echoes the deep blue of his eyes. It's a little tight around his broad shoulders and a little loose around his torso, but he manages to make it look good.

I snag a sweatshirt and jeans out of the closet. I have to roll up both the sleeves and legs but they fit well enough to do the job.

As we head out of the house, I wonder how my mother is doing. A part of me worries about her, a part of me is glad to be free of her, and all of me feels guilty for not taking better care of her. She's like a wounded feral cat. No one can truly take care of her without locking her in a cage. She would hate that, and so would I. I hope she's managed to stay far away from people. Both for her sake and theirs.

Raffe immediately turns right as soon as we get out of the house. I resume following him and hope he knows where we're going. Unlike me, he seems to have no stiffness or limping. I think he's adjusting to being on his feet. I don't say anything about it because I don't want to remind him why he's walking instead of flying.

My pack feels much lighter. We don't have anything for camping outside, but I do feel better knowing I can run faster. I also feel better having a new pocketknife attached to my belt. Raffe found it somewhere and gave it to me as we headed out. I also found some steak knives and stuck a couple into my boots. Whoever lived here liked their steaks. These are high-quality, all-metal German knives. After holding these, I never want to go back to serrated tin with wooden handles.

It's a beautiful day. The sky is a vivid blue above the redwoods and the air is cool but comfortable.

The sense of ease doesn't last, though. My mind soon fills with worries of what might lurk in the forest, and about whether Obi's men are hunting us. As we walk along the hillside, I catch glimpses of the gap in the forest where the road must be to our left.

Raffe stops in front of me. I follow his lead and hold my breath. Then I hear it.

Someone is crying. It's not the brokenhearted wail of someone who's just lost a family member. I've heard plenty of those in the last few weeks to know what they sound like. There is no shock or denial in this sound, just pure grief, and the pain of accepting it as a lifelong companion.

Raffe and I exchange glances. Which is safer? Go up to the road to avoid the griever? Or stay in the forest and risk an encounter with him? Probably the latter. Raffe must think so too, because he turns and continues in the forest.

It's not long before we see the little girls.

They hang from a tree. Not by their necks, but by ropes tied under their arms and around their chests.

One girl looks to be about Paige's age and the other a couple of years older. That would make them seven and nine. The older girl's hand still grips the younger girl's dress like she had tried to hold the little girl up out of harm's way.

They wear what look like matching striped dresses. It's hard to tell now that the print is stained in blood. Most of the material has been ripped and shredded. Whatever gnawed on their legs and torsos got full before it reached their chests. Or it was too low to the ground to reach them.

The worst by far are their tortured expressions. They were alive when they were eaten.

I double over and throw up kibble bits until I dry-heave.

All the while, a middle-aged man wearing thick glasses cries beneath the girls. He's a scrawny guy, with the kind of look and presence that must have had him sitting alone in the cafeteria through his high school years. His entire body trembles with his sobs. A woman with red-rimmed eyes wraps her arms around him.

'It was an accident,' says the woman, rubbing her hand over the man's back soothingly.

'This was no accident,' says the man.

'We didn't mean to.'

'That doesn't make it okay.'

'Of course it's not okay,' she says. 'But we'll get through this. All of us.'

'Who's worse? Him or us?'

'It's not his fault,' she says. 'He can't help it. He's the victim, not the monster.'

'We need to put him down,' he says. Another sob escapes him.

'You'd give up on him just like that?' Her expression turns fierce. She steps back from him.

He looks even more forlorn now that he's unable to lean on her. But anger stiffens his spine. He flings his arm toward the hanging girls. 'We fed him little girls!'

'He's just sick, that's all,' she says. 'We just need to make him better.'

'How?' He hunches to look intensely into her face. 'What are we going to do, take him to the hospital?'

She puts her hands on his face. 'When we get him back, we'll know what to do. Trust me.'

He turns from her. 'We've gone too far. He's not our boy anymore. He's a monster. We've all become monsters.'

She cocks back her hand and slaps him. The crack of her palm against his cheek is as startling as a gunshot.

They continue to argue, completely ignoring us as if any danger we might pose is so irrelevant compared to what they're dealing with that it's not worth their energy to notice us. I'm not sure what they're saying exactly, but dark suspicions edge my mind.

Raffe grabs my elbow and leads me downhill, around the mad people and the half-chewed girls hanging grotesquely from the tree.

The acid in my stomach churns and threatens to come up again. But I swallow hard and force my feet to follow him.

I keep my gaze on the ground at Raffe's feet, trying not to think about what's just uphill from us. I catch a faint odor that clenches my stomach in a familiar way. I look around, trying to pinpoint the scent. It's the sulfurous stench of rotten eggs. My nose leads me to a pair of eggs nestled in the dead leaves. They're cracked in several places where I can catch a glimpse of the brown yolk inside. The stain of faded pink still shows on the delicate eggshell where someone had dyed it long ago.

I look uphill. From here, I have a perfect view of the hanging girls between the trees.

Whether my mother placed the eggs here as a protective talisman for us, or whether she is playing out the type of fantasy the old media would have headlined, 'The Devil Made Me Do It,' I'll never know. Both are equally possible now that she is completely off her meds.

My stomach cramps and I have to double over again to dry-heave.

A warm hand touches my shoulder, and a water bottle is thrust in front of me. I take a swig, swish it around, then spit it out. The water lands on the eggs, tilting them with the force of my ejection. One egg oozes dark yolk down its side like old blood. The other wobbles unevenly down the hill until it rests safely against a tree root, its pink tint darkened by wetness, like the flush of guilt.

A warm arm circles my shoulder and helps me stand up. 'Come on,' says Raffe. 'Let's go.'

We walk away from the damaged eggs and the hanging girls.

I lean into his strength until I realize what I'm doing. I pull back abruptly. I don't have the luxury of leaning on anyone's strength, least of all an angel's.

My shoulder feels cold and vulnerable once his warmth is gone.

I bite the inside of my cheek to give myself something more demanding to feel.

25

'What do you think they were doing?' I ask.

Raffe shrugs.

'Do you think they were feeding the low demons?'

'Maybe.'

'Why would they do that?'

'I've given up trying to make sense of humans.'

'We're not all like that, you know,' I say. I don't know why I feel I have to justify our behavior to an angel.

He just gives me a knowing look and keeps walking.

'If you ever saw us before the attack, you'd know,' I say stubbornly.

'I know,' he says, not even looking at me.

'How do you know?'

'I watched TV.'

I snort a laugh. Then I realize he's not joking. 'For real?'

'Didn't everybody?'

I guess everybody did. It was on the air for free. All they had to do was catch the signal and they'd know all about us. TV wasn't exactly a manifesto of reality either, but it did reflect our greatest hopes and worst fears. I wonder how angels think of us, if they think of us at all.

I wonder what Raffe does in his spare time, other than watch TV. It's hard to imagine him sitting down on his couch after a rough day at war, watching TV shows about humans to wind down. What's his domestic life like?

'Are you married?' I instantly regret asking this question as it conjures up an image of him with a painfully beautiful angel wife with little cherubs running around some estate with Grecian pillars.

He pauses in his trek and glares at me as if I just said something totally inappropriate.

'Don't let my appearance fool you, Penryn. I am not human. The Daughters of Men are forbidden to Angels.'

'What about Daughters of Women?' I attempt a cheeky smile but it falls flat.

'This is serious business. Don't you know your religious history?'

Most of what I know about religion is through my mother. I think about all the times she raved in tongues in the middle of the night in my room. She came in so often while I slept that I'd gotten into the habit of sleeping with my back to the wall so I could see her coming in without her knowing I was awake.

She'd sit on the floor beside my bed, rock back and forth in a trancelike state, gripping her Bible and speaking in tongues for hours. The nonsensical, guttural noises had the cadence of an angry chant. Or a curse.

Really creepy stuff while you're lying in the dark, mostly asleep. That's about the extent of my religious education.

'Uh, no,' I say. 'Can't say I know much about religious history.'

He begins walking again. 'A group of angels called the Watchers were stationed on Earth to observe the humans. Over time, they got lonely and took human wives, knowing they shouldn't. Their children were called Nephilim. And they were abominations. They fed on humans, drank their blood, and terrorized the Earth. For that, the Watchers were condemned to the Pit until Judgment Day.'

He takes several steps in silence as if wondering whether to tell me more. I wait, hoping to hear as much as I can about the world of angels, even if it's ancient history.

The silence is heavy. There's more to this story than he's telling me.

'So,' I prod. 'The long and short of it is that angels aren't allowed to get together with humans? Otherwise, they're damned?'

'Very.'

'That's harsh.' I'm surprised I can feel any sympathy for angels, even ones in ancient stories.

'You think that's bad, you should have seen the punishment for their wives.'

It's almost as if he's inviting me to ask. Here's my chance to find out more. But I find that I don't really want to know the punishment for falling in love with an angel. Instead, I watch the dried needles crunch under my feet as we walk.

Skyline Boulevard abruptly ends at Highway 92, and we follow Freeway 280 north into the once highly populated area just south of San Francisco. This is a main artery into

San Francisco, so it shouldn't be a surprise to hear an actual working truck on the road below us. But it is.

It's been almost a month since I heard a moving car. There are plenty of cars that work, plenty of gas, but I hadn't realized there were any clear roads left anymore. We crouch down in the shrubs and scan the road. The wind cuts through my sweatshirt and teases hair strands loose from my ponytail.

Below us, a black Hummer weaves in and out, following a path that's been cleared between the jammed cars. It stops and idles for a while. If it turned off its engine, you'd never know that it was any different from the thousands of other cars abandoned on the streets. When it was moving, I could see the path of cleared cars that it followed. But now, I see that the path cleverly winds and even backtracks to hide the fact that it is a path.

Now that the Hummer has stopped, the path is blocked, and it would be very tough to see the trail at all unless you knew about it. The Hummer is just one in a sea of empty cars, the path just a random pattern of gaps among an infinite maze. From the ground, you could probably see the driver and passengers in the Hummer, but from the air, you'd never know. These guys are camouflaging themselves against the angels.

'Obi's men,' Raffe says, coming to the same conclusion I have. 'Clever,' he says with some respect in his voice.

It is clever. The roads are the most direct way to get anywhere. The Hummer cuts its engine, and it effectively disappears into the scene. A moment later, Raffe points up.

Tiny specs mar the otherwise clear sky. The specs move fast
and quickly turn into a squad of angels flying in a V forma-
tion. They sweep low over the freeway as if searching for
prey.

I hold my breath and crouch as low as I can in the brush,
wondering whether Raffe will call out for their attention. It
hits me again just how little I know about angels. I can't
even guess as to whether Raffe wants this new group's attention. How can he tell if they're hostile?

If I do manage to infiltrate the angels' lair, how will I find
the ones who took Paige? If I knew something about them,
like their names, or unit identification, I'd have a start.
Without realizing it, I had made the assumption that the
angels are a small community, one maybe a bit larger than
Obi's camp. I had vaguely imagined that so long as I could find
the aerie, I could observe and figure out what to do from there.

For the first time, it occurs to me that it could be much
bigger than that. Big enough for Raffe not to be able to identify whether these angels are his friends or foes. Big enough
for them to have deadly factions within their ranks. If I were
to walk into a camp the size of a Roman invading army, could
I just figure out on the spot where they kept Paige and simply
walk out with her?

Beside me, Raffe's muscles loosen and he deflates into the
ground. He's decided not to try to get the angels' attention. I
don't know if this means he's identified them as hostile, or if
he just couldn't identify them at all.

Either way, it tells me that his angel enemies are more
threatening than the risks he takes on the ground. If he

could find friendly angels, they could carry him to wherever he needs to go, and he could get medical attention that much sooner. So the threat must be severe for him to pass up that chance.

The angels turn and swing past the sea of cars again, as though to sniff the air for prey.

I can barely find the Hummer again even though I saw where they stopped. Obi's men know their camouflage all right.

I wonder what mission makes them risk getting caught on the road? It can't be us. We're not worth the risk, at least, not that they know. So they must think there's something important near or in the city. Maybe recon?

Whatever it is the angels are looking for, they don't find it. They swoop up and disappear into the horizon. The air rushing past their ears as they fly must dull their hearing. Maybe that's why it has to be so good to begin with.

I let out a deep breath. The Hummer below finally restarts its engine and resumes winding its way north toward the city.

'How did they know the angels were coming?' he asks, almost to himself.

I shrug. I could make some random guesses, but I don't see any reason to share them with him. We're smart monkeys, especially where survival is concerned. And Silicon Valley has some of the smartest, most innovative monkeys in the world. Even though I escaped Obi's camp, I feel a pang of pride at what our side might be doing.

Raffe watches me carefully, and I wonder how much of what I'm thinking is on my face.

'Why didn't you call out to them?' I ask.

It's his turn to shrug.

'You could be getting medical assistance by sunset,' I say.

He pushes himself off the ground and brushes off. 'Yes. Or I could be delivering myself back into the hands of my enemies.'

He starts walking roughly in the same direction as the road again. I follow on his heels.

'Did you recognize them?' I try to keep my tone casual. I wish I could just ask him directly how many of them there are, but that's not a question he could answer without betraying military secrets.

He shakes his head but doesn't elaborate.

'No, you didn't recognize who they were? Or no, you couldn't see them well enough to recognize them?'

He pauses to dig the remaining cat food out of his pack. 'Here. Please stuff this in your mouth. You can have my share.'

So much for my information mining. I guess I'll never be a spymaster like Tweedledee and Tweedledum.

26

'Can you drive one of those things?' he asks, pointing to the road.

'Yeah,' I say slowly.

'Let's go.' He turns downhill toward the road.

'Um, won't that be dangerous?'

'It's unlikely there will be two units flying in the same direction within an hour or two of each other. Once we're on the road, we'll be safer from the road monkeys. They'll think we're Obi's people, too well armed and too well fed to attack.'

'We're not monkeys.' Hadn't I just thought we were clever monkeys? So why does it sting that he just called me one?

He ignores me and keeps walking.

What did I expect? An apology? I let it drop and follow him down to the freeway.

As soon as we step onto the asphalt, Raffe grabs my arm and ducks behind a van. I crouch beside him, straining to hear what he hears. After a minute, I hear a car coming toward us. Another one? What's the chance of another car just happening to be on the same road only ten minutes behind the first car?

This one is a black truck with a canopy over the bed. Whatever is under there is big, lumpy, and somehow intimidating. It looks a lot like the truck they were filling with explosives yesterday. It rumbles by, slow and full of purpose, toward the city.

A caravan. It's a very spread out caravan, but I'd bet the contents of my pack that there are more cars ahead and behind. They've spread it out to be less noticeable. The Hummer probably knew about the angels flying toward them because they got word from the cars ahead of them. Even if the first car was taken out, the rest of the caravan would be all right. My respect for Obi's group goes up another notch.

When the sound of the engine fades, we get up from our crouch behind the van and start looking for our own ride. I'd prefer to drive a low-profile economy car that won't make much noise and won't run out of gas. But that's the last car Obi's men would drive, so we start looking at the large selection of beefy SUVs on the road.

Most of the cars don't have their keys in them. Even at the end of the world when a box of crackers is worth more than a Mercedes, people still took their keys with them when they abandoned their cars. Habit, I suppose.

After looking at half a dozen, we find a black SUV with tinted windows with the keys on the driver's seat. This driver must have pulled the keys out of habit, then thought better of dragging the worthless metal with him on the road. It has a quarter tank of gas. That should at least get us into San Francisco, assuming the road is clear that far. It's not enough to get us back, though.

Back? Back where?

I quiet the voice in my head and climb in. Raffe climbs in the passenger seat. It starts on the first try and we begin weaving up 280 heading north.

I never thought moving twenty miles per hour could be so exciting. My heart pounds as I grip the steering wheel like it's going to fly out of control any second now. I can't watch all the obstacles on the road and still be on the lookout for attackers. I throw a quick glance at Raffe. He's scanning the surroundings, including the side mirrors, and I relax a little.

'So where are we going, exactly?' I'm not an expert on the city's layout, but I have been there several times and have a general idea of where neighborhoods are located.

'Financial district.' He knows the area well enough to identify the city's districts. I briefly wonder how but let it go. I suspect he's been around a lot longer than I have to explore the world.

'I think the freeway goes through that, or at least near it. That's assuming that the road is clear that far, which I doubt.'

'There is order near the aerie. The roads should be clear.'

I throw him a sharp look. 'What do you mean, order?'

'There will be guards at the road near the aerie. Before we get there, we'll need to prepare.'

'Prepare? How?'

'I found something for you to change into at the last house. And I'll need to change my appearance too. Leave the details to me. Getting past the guards will be the easy part.'

'Great. Then what?'

'Then it's time to party at the aerie.'

'You're just full of information, aren't you? I won't go unless I know what I'm getting into.'

'Then don't go.' His tone is not ungentle, but the meaning is clear.

I grip the steering wheel so hard I'm surprised it doesn't crumple.

It's no secret that we're only temporary allies. Neither of us is pretending that this is a lasting partnership. I help him get home with his wings, he helps me find my sister. After that I'll be on my own. I know this. I've never for a moment forgotten about it.

But after only a couple of days of having someone watch my back, the thought of being on my own again feels . . . lonely.

I clip the open door of a truck.

'I thought you said you could drive this thing.'

I realize I've been pressing on the accelerator. We're weaving drunkenly at forty miles per hour. I pull it back down to twenty and force my fingers to relax.

'Leave the driving to me, and I'll leave the planning to you.' I still have to take a calming breath as I say this. I've been mad at my dad all this time for leaving me to make all the hard decisions. But now that Raffe is taking the lead and insisting on me following him blind, it churns my stomach.

We see some ragged people along the side of the road here and there, but not a lot. They scurry away as soon as they see our car. The way they stare, the way they hide, the way their furtive, dirty faces peer at us with burning curiosity brings to mind the hated word: monkey. This is what the angels have turned us into.

As we get closer to the city, we see more people. The path on the road is less labyrinthine.

Eventually, the road is mostly cleared of cars, although not of people. Everyone still looks at the car, but there's less interest, as though a car moving on the roads is something they see regularly. The closer we get to the city, the more people there are walking on the road. They look around warily at every sound and motion, but they're out in the open.

Once we enter the city proper, the damage is everywhere. San Francisco got pummeled along with a lot of other cities. It looks like a smoldering, post-apocalyptic, melting nightmare out of some Hollywood blockbuster.

Coming into the city, I catch glimpses of the Bay Bridge. It looks like a dashed line across the water with a few crucial chunks missing from the middle. I've seen photos of the city after the great quake of 1906. The devastation was staggering, and I'd always found it hard to imagine what that must have been like.

I don't have to imagine anymore.

Entire blocks are charred rubble. The initial meteor showers, quakes, and tsunamis only caused part of the damage. San Francisco was a city that had rows and rows of houses and buildings built so close together you couldn't fit a piece of paper between the buildings. Gas pipes burst and caused fires that raged unchecked. The sky was choked with blood-tinged smoke for days.

Now, all that's left are the skeletons of skyscrapers, an occasional brick church still standing, lots of pillars holding up nothing.

A sign proclaims that Life is G od. It's hard to tell what product the sign was selling because the sign is singed all around those words as well as on the missing letter. I assume the sign used to say Life is Good. The gutted building behind it looks melted, as if still suffering the effects of a fire that just won't stop, even now under an alien blue sky.

'How is this possible?' I don't even realize I say it aloud until I hear my voice choked with tears. 'How could you do this?'

My question sounds personal and maybe it is. For all I know, he could have been personally responsible for the ruin around me.

Raffe stays quiet for the rest of the drive.

In the middle of this charnel, a few blocks of the financial district stand tall and shiny in the sun. It looks almost completely undamaged. To my utter amazement, there is a makeshift camp in the area of the city that used to be South of Market, just outside the undamaged portion of the financial district.

I weave around another car, assuming it is dead, until it suddenly lurches in front of me. I slam on the brakes. The other driver gives me a dirty look as he drives past me. He looks about ten years old, barely tall enough to see over the dashboard.

The camp is more of a shantytown, the kind we used to see on the news where refugees flocked by the thousands after a disaster. The people – although they aren't eating each other as far as I can tell – look hungry and desperate. They touch the car windows like we have hidden riches in here that we could share with them.

'Pull over there.' Raffe points to an area where a pile of cars are stacked and spilling onto what used to be a parking lot. I drive the car there and park. 'Turn off the engine. Lock the doors and stay vigilant until they forget about us.'

'They're going to forget about us?' I ask, watching a couple of street guys climb onto our hood. They make themselves at home on the warmth of our car.

'Lots of people sleep in their cars. They probably won't make a move until they think we're asleep.'

'We're sleeping in here?' The last thing I feel like doing with all this adrenaline rushing through my veins is sleep under glass surrounded by desperate people.

'No. We're changing in here.'

He reaches to the backseat and grabs his pack. He pulls out a scarlet party dress. It's so small that at first, I think it's a scarf. It's the kind of shapely and tiny dress that I once borrowed from my friend Lisa when she talked me into going clubbing with her. She had fake IDs for both of us, and it would have been a fun night except that she got drunk and went home with some college guy, leaving me to find my way home on my own.

'What's this for?' Somehow, I don't think he has clubbing in mind.

'Put it on. Look as good as you can. It's our ticket in.' Maybe he did have clubbing in mind.

'You're not going to go home with some drunken college girl, are you?'

'What?'

'Never mind.' I take the skimpy bit of fabric, along with the skimpy matching shoes and to my surprise, a pair of silky pantyhose. Whatever Raffe doesn't know about humans, women's clothing isn't one of them. I shoot him a piercing look, wondering where he learned his expertise on the topic. He returns my glance with a cool look of his own, telling me nothing.

There's no private place to change away from the prying eyes of the homeless guys on our hood. Funny – I still think of men like that as homeless even though none of us have homes anymore. They were probably South of Market hipsters back in the day. 'The day' being only a couple of months ago.

Luckily, every girl knows how to change in public. I pull the dress over my head and under my sweatshirt. I pull my arms out from the sweatshirt's sleeves and wiggle into the dress using my sweatshirt as a personal curtain. Then I pull it down to my thighs, and then take off my boots and jeans.

The hem doesn't go as far down as I'd like, and I keep tugging it to make myself more modest. Too much of my thigh is showing, and the last place I want this kind of attention is where I'm surrounded by lawless men under desperate conditions.

When I look at Raffe with anxiety in my eyes, he says, 'It's the only way.' I can tell he doesn't like it either.

I don't want to take off my sweatshirt because I can feel the skimpiness of the dress. At a party in a civilized world, I might be comfortable in it. Might even be excited at how cute it is, although I have no idea if it's cute or not since I can't see myself. I can tell, however, that it might be a size too small for me because it's tight. I'm not sure if it's meant to be this tight, but it only adds to the sensation of being naked in front of savages.

Raffe has no qualms about stripping in front of strangers. He pulls off his T-shirt and slides out of his cargo pants to button on a white dress shirt and black dress slacks. More than anything, it's the feeling of being watched myself that keeps me from blatantly watching him. I have no brothers, and I've never seen a guy strip before. It's only natural to have the impulse to watch, isn't it?

Instead of looking at him, I look forlornly at the strappy slippers. They're the same shade of scarlet as the dress, as though the previous owner had one custom-made to match the other. The high, thin heels are made for accentuating legs while sitting cross-legged. 'I can't run in these.'

'You won't have to if things go according to plan.'

'Great. Because things always go according to plan.'

'If things go awry, running won't help you anyway.'

'Yeah, well, I can't fight in these either.'

'I brought you here. I'll protect you.'

I'm tempted to remind him that I'm the one who dragged him off the street like roadkill. 'Is this really the only way?'

'Yes.'

I sigh. I slip into the strappy, useless sandals and hope I don't break an ankle trying to walk in them. I take off the sweatshirt and flip down the car's visor to access the mirror. The dress is as tight as I'd guessed, but it looks better on me than I'd thought.

My hair and face, however, look like they'd be more at home in a ratty bathrobe. I rake my hand through my hair. It's greasy and matted. My lips are chapped and flaking, and my cheeks are sunburned. My jaw is a splash of mango colors from the bruise Boden gave me during our fight. At least the frozen peas kept the swelling down.

'Here,' he says, opening his pack. 'I didn't know what you'd need so I just grabbed some things from the bathroom cabinet.' He takes out a men's tuxedo jacket from his pack before handing the pack over to me.

I watch him staring down at the jacket, wondering what he's thinking that makes him look so somber. Then I turn to dig into the pack.

I find a comb to run through my hair. My hair is so greasy that it's actually easier to style, although I'm not fond of the look. There is also some lotion that I rub onto my face, lips, hands, and legs. I want to peel the flakes of skin off my lips, but I know from experience that doing that will make them bleed, so I leave them alone.

I smooth on lipstick and mascara. The lipstick is a neon pink, and the mascara is blue. Not my usual colors, but combined with the tight dress, it sure makes me look slutty, which I figure is exactly the look we're going for. There's no eye shadow so I just smear a tiny bit of the mascara around my eyes for that extra sultry emphasis. I take some foundation and smear it over my jaw. It's tender and the parts that need the makeup the most are the parts that are the most sensitive. This better be worth it.

When I finish, I notice that the guys on the hood are watching me put on my makeup. I look over at Raffe. He is busy rigging some sort of contraption involving his pack, wings, and some straps.

'What are you doing?'

'Making a—' He looks up and sees me.

I don't know if he noticed when I took my sweatshirt off, but I'm guessing he was busy at that time because he looks at me with surprise now. His pupils dilate when he sees me. His lips part as he momentarily forgets to marshal his expression, and I could swear he stops breathing for several heartbeats.

'I'm making it look like I have wings on my back,' he says quietly. His words come out husky and velvety as if he's saying something personal. As if he's giving me a caressing compliment.

I bite my lip to focus on the fact that he's actually just giving me a plain answer to my question. He can't help it if his voice is mesmerizingly sexy.

'I can't go where I need to go if they think I'm human.' He drops his gaze and cinches a strap around the base of one of his wings.

He puts the empty pack with the wings strapped to it onto his back. 'Help me get the jacket on.'

He has sliced the back of the jacket with parallel slashes to let the wings peek through.

Right. The jacket. The wings. 'Should the wings be outside?' I ask.

'No, just make sure the straps and pack are covered.'

The wings look securely strapped to the pack. I gently arrange the contraption so that the outside feathers cover the straps. The feathers still feel vibrant and alive, although they seem a bit wilted compared to the way they were when I first touched them a couple of days ago. I resist the urge to stroke the feathers even though he won't be able to feel it.

The wings lie molded to the empty backpack the way they would mold to his back. For such an enormous wingspan, it's amazing how tightly they compress to his body when they're folded. I once saw a seven-foot down sleeping bag get compacted into a small cube and it wasn't as impressive a change in volume as this.

I drape the jacket material between and on either side of the wings. The snowy wings peek out in two strips through the slits in the dark material with no sign of the pack and straps. The jacket is big enough that he only looks a little bulky. Not enough to bring attention to it unless someone is very familiar with Raffe's form.

He leans forward so he doesn't crush his wings with the back of the seat.

'How does it look?' His beautifully wide shoulders and clean line of his back are now accented by the wings. Around his neck is a silver bowtie shot playfully with curls of red that match my dress. It also matches his cummerbund around his waist. Aside from a little smudge of dirt on his jaw, he looks like he just walked out of a Hollywood magazine.

The shape of his back looks about right for a jacket that's not perfectly tailored for wings. I have a flash of the

magnificence of his snowy wings spreading out behind him
as he stood to face his enemies that first time I saw him. I feel
a little of what his loss must mean to him.

I nod. 'It looks good. You look right.'

His eyes look up into mine. In them, I catch a hint of
gratitude, a hint of loss, a hint of worry.

'Not that . . . you didn't look right before. I mean, you
always look . . . magnificent.' Magnificent? I almost roll my
eyes. What a dope. I don't know why I said that. I clear my
throat. 'Can we go already?'

He nods. He hides the teasing smile but I can see it in his
eyes.

'Drive past that crowd and up to the checkpoint.' He
points to our left, where it looks like a crowded, free-for-all
market. 'When the guards stop you, tell them you want to go
to the aerie. Tell them you heard they sometimes let in
women.'

He climbs into the backseat and crouches in the shadows.
He pulls the old blanket over himself, the one that used to
wrap his wings.

'I'm not here,' he says.

'So . . . explain to me again why you're hiding instead of
just walking through the gate with me?'

'Angels don't walk through the checkpoint. They fly
directly to the aerie.'

'Can't you just tell them you're injured?'

'You're like a little girl demanding answers to questions
during a covert operation. "Why is the sky blue, Daddy? Can
I ask that man with the machine gun where the bathroom

is?" If you don't stay quiet, I'm going to have to dump you. You need to do what I tell you, when I tell you, no questions or hesitation about it. If you don't like it, find someone else to pester into helping you.'

'Okay, okay. I got it. Geez, some people are so grouchy.'

I start the engine and inch out of our parking spot. The homeless guys grumble, and one of them bangs the hood with his fist as he slides off.

27

I drive through the crowd on Montgomery Street at a speed that's maybe half of what I could do on foot. People get out of the way, but reluctantly, and only after giving me assessing looks. I check the doors again to make sure they're locked. Not that the locks would stop anyone should they choose to break the windows.

Luckily, we are not the only ones in a car here. There's a small line of cars waiting at the checkpoint, surrounded by a mass of people on foot. Apparently, they are all waiting to cross the checkpoint. I go as far as I can and stop at the end of the line of cars.

There is an unusually large percentage of women waiting to cross the checkpoint. They are clean and dressed as though going to a party. Women stand in high heels and silk dresses among the ragged men, and everyone behaves as though that's normal.

The checkpoint is a breach in a tall chain-link fence that blocks the streets around the financial district. With what's left of the district, it wouldn't be too hard to permanently fence it off. But this is one of those temporary fences made of self-standing panels. The panels are connected together to make a fence, but it's not embedded into the asphalt.

It wouldn't take much for a crowd to push it over and just walk on top of it. Yet the crowd respects the boundary as though it's electrified.

Then I see that it is, in a way.

Humans patrol the fence from the other side and poke a metal rod through whenever they see someone getting too close. When someone is poked, there's a zap sound along with a blue spark of electricity. They're using some kind of cattle prod to keep people away. All of the prodders except one are grim-faced men who show no emotion as they patrol and occasionally prod.

The female prodder is my mother.

I bang my head against the steering wheel when I see her. It doesn't make me feel any better.

'What's wrong?' Raffe asks.

'My mother is here.'

'Is that a problem?'

'Probably.' I drive forward a few feet as the line moves.

My mother is more emotional about her job than her fellow prodders. She reaches as far as the fence will let her to shock as many people as possible. At one point, she even cackles as she zaps a man for as long as she can before he staggers out of her reach. She looks for all the world as though she's enjoying inflicting pain on people.

Despite appearances, I recognize fear in my mother when I see it. If you didn't know her, you'd think her zest comes from malice. But there's a good chance that she doesn't even recognize her victims as people.

She probably thinks she's trapped in a cage in Hell surrounded by monsters. Maybe as payment for a deal made with the devil. Maybe just because the world conspires against her. She probably thinks the people who get close to the fence are actually monsters in disguise stalking her cage. Someone has miraculously given her a weapon to keep those monsters at bay. So she's using this rare chance to fight back.

'How did she end up here?' I wonder out loud.

Dirt smears her cheeks and greasy hair, and her clothes are ripped at the elbow and knees. She looks like she's been sleeping on the ground. But she does look healthy and fed, with rosy coloring in her cheeks.

'Everyone on the road ends up here if they don't get themselves killed first.'

'How?'

'Beats me. You humans have always had some kind of herding instinct that seems to bring you together. And this is the largest herd around.'

'Town. Not herd. Towns are for people. Herds are for animals.'

He snorts rudely in response.

It probably is better to leave her there instead of trying to take her with me inside the aerie. It's hard to be stealthy with my mother around. That could cost us Paige's life. There's not much I can do to ease her torment when she's like this. The people will eventually learn to stay away from her while she patrols the fence. She's safer here. We're all safer with her here. For now.

My justifications don't ease my guilt about leaving her. But I can't think of a better solution.

I tear my gaze away from my mother and try to focus on my surroundings. I can't be distracted if we're all to stay alive.

In front of me, the crowd starts to show a pattern. Women and teen girls, all dressed and made up to the best of their resources, press up against the people in front of them, hoping to get the attention of the guards. Many of the girls are surrounded by people who look like parents or grandparents. The women often stand beside their men, sometimes with children.

The guards shake their heads at virtually everyone who requests entry. Occasionally, a woman or a group of women refuses to move out of the way after they've been turned down, choosing instead to beg or break down crying. The angels seem not to care one way or another, but the crowd cares. The mob shoves the offending rejects into itself, mindlessly pushing them back with their shifting and shoving bodies, until the losers are ejected out at the rear of the crowd.

Occasionally, the guards let one through. From what I can tell, the ones let through are always female. While we inch up to the gate, two are admitted.

Both are women dressed in tight dresses and high heels, like me. One of them enters without a backward glance, clicking confidently away down the empty road on the other side of the gate. The other goes hesitantly, turning around to throw kisses at a man and two grubby children gripping the

chain links of the fence. They scurry away from the fence
when a man with a cattle prod approaches them.

When these women are let through, a group at the edge of
the crowd exchanges goods. It takes me a minute to understand that they're taking bets on who gets in. A bookie points
to several women near the guards, then accepts items from the
people around him. The bettors are mostly men, but there are
women in the group too. Each time a woman is let through,
one of the bettors walks away with an armful of goods.

I want to ask what's going on, why humans want to go
into angel territory and why these people camp out here. But
I would only prove Raffe right about acting like a little girl,
so I tamp down the flood of questions and ask the one that's
operationally relevant.

'What if they don't let us go through?' I ask, trying not to
move my lips.

'They will,' he answers from the dark recesses of the backseat footwell.

'How do you know?'

'Because you have the look they're looking for.'

'What look is that?'

'Beautiful.' His voice is like a caress from the shadows.

No one has ever told me I'm beautiful before. I've been
too preoccupied with dealing with my mother and taking
care of Paige to pay much attention to my looks. Heat flushes
my cheeks, and I hope I don't look like a clown when I get
to the checkpoint. If Raffe is right and this is the only way
in, I need to look as good as I can if I want a chance of seeing
Paige again.

By the time I reach the front of the chaotic line, several women have just about thrown themselves at the guards. None of them were allowed in. It doesn't make me feel any better about my greasy hair as I drive up to the guards.

They give me a bored once-over. There are two of them. Their speckled wings look small and withered compared to Raffe's. One guard's face is lightly speckled with green, just like his wings. The word *dappled* comes to mind, like a horse. Looking into his face is a wrenching reminder that they are not human. That Raffe is not human.

Dappled waves at me to come out of the car. I hesitate for a second before slowly getting out. He didn't do that with the other girls in the cars in front of me.

I pull down my hem to make sure it covers my butt. The guards look at me up and down. I resist the urge to slouch and cross my arms across my breasts.

Dappled waves for me to spin around. I feel like a stripper and I want to kick them in the teeth, but I do a slow spin for them on my unsteady heels. *Paige. Think about Paige.*

The guards exchange a look. I frantically think about what I could do or say to try to get them to let me through. If Raffe says this is the way in, then I must find a way to get them to let me in.

Dappled waves me through.

I'm so stunned I just stand there.

Then, before they can change their minds, I turn away from them so that if they shake their heads, I can't see it. I slide back into the car as casually as I can.

The little hairs on the back of my neck stand stiff in anticipation of a whistle blowing, or a hand on my shoulder, or
German shepherds nosing in behind me just like in the old
war movies. We are, after all, at war, aren't we?

But none of that happens. I start the engine and they
wave me through. And I gain another piece of information.
The angels don't see humans as a threat. So what if a few
monkeys get in through the cracks in their fence or crawl in
little go-carts around the base of their nest? How hard would
it be for them to take us down and contain the intruding
animals?

'Where are we?' Raffe asks from the shadows behind me.

'In Hell,' I say. I keep the speed at a steady twenty miles
per hour. The streets are empty here so I could go sixty if I
want, but I don't want to call attention to us.

'If this is your idea of Hell, you're very innocent. Look for
a clublike scene. Lots of light, lots of women. Go and park
there, but not too close.'

I look around the weirdly deserted streets. A few women,
looking cold and forlorn in the howling San Franciscan wind,
stumble down the sidewalk toward some destination only
they know. I keep driving, looking at the empty streets. Then
I see people spilling out of a tall building along a side street.

As I get closer, I see a crowd of women around a 1920s-style
nightclub entrance. They must be freezing in their skimpy
party dresses, but they stand tall and attractive. The doorway
is arched in classic Art Deco, and the angels guarding the
front entrance are dressed in modified tuxedos with slits in
the backs to make room for their wings.

I park my car a couple of blocks past the club. I put the keys in a pocket on the visor and leave my boots in the passenger footwell where I can grab them in a rush if I need to. I wish I could stuff them in my sequined clutch, but there's only room in there for a tiny flashlight and my pocketknife.

I slide out of the car. Raffe crawls out from behind me. The wind hits me as soon as I'm out, whipping my hair into a frenzy around my face. I curl my arms around myself, wishing I had a coat.

Raffe straps his sword around his waist, looking like an old-fashioned gentleman in his tux. 'Sorry I can't offer my jacket. When we get closer, I need you to not look cold so no one wonders why I don't take off my jacket to give to you.'

I doubt anyone will wonder why an angel doesn't offer a girl his jacket, but I let it go.

'How come it's okay for you to be seen now?'

He gives me a tired look as though I'm exhausting him.

'Okay, okay.' I put my hands up in surrender. 'You call the shots, I follow. Just help me find my sister.' I mimic turning a key in a lock on my lips and throw away the pretend key.

He straightens his already straight jacket. Is that a nervous motion? He offers me his arm. I put my hand on the crook of his arm and we walk down the sidewalk.

At first, his muscles are stiff, and his eyes constantly scan the area. What's he looking for? Could he really have that many enemies among his own people? After a few steps, though, he relaxes. I'm not sure if it's natural or forced.

Either way, we now look to the world like a regular couple out for the evening.

As we near the crowd, I can see more details. Several of the angels going into the club are in old-fashioned gangster zoot suits complete with felt hats and jaunty feathers. Long watch chains drape to their knees.

'What is this, a costume party?' I ask.

'It's just the current fashion for the aerie.' His voice sounds a bit clipped, as though he doesn't approve.

'What happened to the rule of not fraternizing with the Daughters of Men?'

'An excellent question.' His jaw clenches into a hard line. I don't think I want to be around when he demands an answer to that question.

'So producing children with humans gets you damned because Nephilim are a big no-no,' I say. 'But anything up to that . . .?'

He shrugs. 'Apparently, they've decided that's a gray zone. It could get them all burned.' Then he adds in a whisper, almost to himself, 'But the fire can be tempting.'

The thought of superhuman beings with human temptations and flaws sends a chill through me.

We walk past the protection of a building to cross a street, and I'm back to being whipped mercilessly by the wind. Wind tunnels have nothing on the streets of San Francisco.

'Try not to look so cold.'

I stand up straight even though I'm dying to curl into myself. At least my skirt isn't long enough to whip up.

The opportunity to ask more questions dries up as we approach the crowd. The whole scene has a surreal feel to it.

It's as though I'm walking out of a refugee camp into an exclusive supper club, complete with tuxedos, women in formal wear, expensive cigars, and jewelry.

The cold doesn't seem to bother any of the angels who lazily breathe cigar smoke into the wind. Not in a million years would I have imagined angels smoking. These guys look more like gangsters than pious angels. Each one has at least two women lavishing attention on them. Some have four or more crowded around them. From the snippets of conversations I catch as we walk by, all of these women are trying their darndest to get an angel's attention.

Raffe walks right past the milling crowd toward the door. There are two angels standing on guard but Raffe ignores them and keeps walking. His hand is on the crook of my elbow and I just go where he goes. One of the guards eyes us as though his Spidey sense is sending alarm signals about us.

There's a moment when I'm sure he'll stop us.

Instead, he stops two women trying to get in. We walk past the women, leaving them to convince the guards that their angel had merely forgotten them outside and that he's expecting to meet them inside. The guard firmly shakes his head.

Apparently, you need an angel as your ticket into the aerie. I let out a breath as we glide right through the doors.

28

Inside, the two-story vaulted ceiling and Art Deco touches give the impression that the foyer was meant to welcome people of good breeding. A curved, gilded staircase dominates the area, creating a picture-perfect setting for couples with long dresses and tuxes, tasteful accents and pedigrees. Ironically, chubby cherubs look down at us from the frescoed ceiling.

To the side stands a long marbled counter that should have had several attendants behind it asking us how long we intend to stay. Now it's just an empty reminder that this building used to be a posh hotel only a couple of months ago. Well, not entirely empty. There is a single attendant looking very small and human among all that marble and angelic grace.

The lobby is spotted with small groups chatting and laughing, all dressed in evening clothes. Most of the women are human with only an occasional female angel circulating the foyer. The men are a mix of human and angel. The human men are servants carrying drinks, picking up empty glasses, and checking in coats for the few lucky women who have them.

Raffe hesitates only briefly to survey the scene. We drift
along the wall down a wide corridor with marbled floors and
velvet wallpaper. The lighting in the foyer and hallway is
more atmospheric than practical. This leaves much of the
walls in soft shadows, a fact that I'm sure doesn't escape
Raffe's notice. I can't say that we're sneaking through the
building, exactly, but we're certainly not calling attention to
ourselves.

A steady stream of people flow in and out of a pair of oversized leather doors accented in brass. We're headed in that
direction when three angels push through it. They're all
wide and solid, every graceful move, every casual bulge of
muscle, declaring them to be athletes. No, athletes isn't
quite right. *Warriors* is the word that rattles around in my
brain.

Two of them stand head and shoulders taller than the
crowd. The third is more compact, more lithe, more like a
cheetah to their bears. They all carry swords dangling along
their thighs as they walk. I realize that other than Raffe and
the guards, these are the first angels I've seen with swords.

Raffe ducks his head toward me, flashing a smile as though
I just said something funny. He bends his head close enough
to mine that I think he's going to kiss me. Instead, he simply
touches his forehead to mine.

To the men walking by, Raffe would look like a man being
affectionate. But they can't see his eyes. Despite the smile,
Raffe's expression is one of pain, the kind you can't stop with
aspirin. As the angels walk by us, Raffe subtly turns his body
so that his back is to them at all times. They laugh at

something the cheetah says, and Raffe closes his eyes, steeping in some bittersweet feeling I can't begin to understand.

His face is so close to mine our breaths mingle. Yet he's far away from me in a place where he's buffeted by emotions deep and unkind. Whatever he's feeling, it's very human. I have this strong compulsion to try to pull him out of this mood, to try to distract him.

I place my hand on his cheek. It's warm and pleasant. Maybe too pleasant. When his eyes don't open, I tentatively touch my lips to his.

At first, I get no response and I consider backing off.

Then, his kiss turns hungry.

It is not the gentle kiss of a couple on a first date, nor is it the kiss of a man driven by simple lust. He kisses me with the desperation of a dying man who believes the magic of eternal life is in this kiss. The ferocity of his grip around my waist and shoulders, the grinding pressure of his lips, has me off balance so that my thoughts whirl out of control.

The pressure eases, and the kiss turns sensual.

A tingling warmth shoots from the silken touch of his lips and tongue straight to my core. My body melts into his and I'm hyperaware of the hard muscles of his chest against my breasts, the warm grip of his hands around my waist and shoulders, the wet sliding of his mouth on mine.

Then it's over.

He pulls back from me, taking a gulp of air as if surfacing from choppy waters. His eyes are deep pools of swirling emotion.

He shuts his eyes off from mine. And eases his breath in a controlled exhale.

When he opens his eyes again, they are more black than blue and completely unreadable. Whatever is happening behind those shuttered eyes is now impenetrable.

What I saw there a moment ago is now buried so far I have to wonder if I imagined it in the first place. The only thing that hints that he feels anything at all is that his breathing is still faster than normal.

'You should know,' he says. His whisper is low enough that even angels probably can't hear it beyond the background noise of conversations in the corridor. 'I don't even like you.'

I stiffen in his arms. I don't know what I expected him to say, but that wasn't it.

Unlike him, I'm pretty sure my emotions come through loud and clear on my face. I can feel one of those emotions heating my cheeks in humiliation.

He steps away from me casually, turns, and pushes through the double doors.

I stand in the corridor watching the doors swing back and forth until they settle.

A couple pushes through from the other side. The angel has his arm around the woman. She wears a full-length silver sequined dress that hugs her body and winks at her every move. He sports a purple suit with a neon pink shirt that drapes its wide collar over his shoulders. They both stare at me as they walk by.

When a man in purple and screaming pink stares at you, you know it's time to change your appearance. Although my crimson dress is tight and short, it's not out of place here. It must be my stunned and humiliated expression that they're looking at.

I school my face back to what I hope is neutral and force my shoulders to relax, or to at least look relaxed.

I'd kissed guys before. Sometimes it got awkward afterward, but never like this. I'd always found kissing nice and pleasant, like smelling roses or laughter on a summer day. What I just experienced with Raffe was another animal. This was a knee-melting, gut-twisting, vein-tingling, nuclear meltdown compared to other kisses I'd had.

I take a deep, deep breath. Hold it. Let it out slowly.

He doesn't even like me.

I let the thought roll around in my head. Anything I feel during that time gets shoved into the vault with the ten-foot-thick door slamming as soon as it goes in, just in case something in there has any intention of crawling out.

Even if he did want me, so what? The result would be the same. A dead end. Our partnership is about to dissolve. As soon as I find Paige, I need to get out of here as fast as I can. And he needs to get his wings sewn back on, then deal with whatever enemies are causing him trouble. Then it's back to him destroying my world with his buddies, and me scrambling for survival with my family. And that's just the way it is. No room for high school fantasies.

I take another deep breath and let it out slowly, making sure all residual feelings are under control. All that matters is finding Paige. To do that, I need to work with Raffe just a little longer.

I walk to the double doors and push my way in to find him.

29

As soon as I step inside, the world fills with the roar of jazz, laughter, and chatter along with a blast of heat, the scent of pungent cigar smoke, perfume, and scrumptious food all rolled into an incomprehensible wave of sensation.

I can't shake the surreal feeling of being thrown back in time. Outside, people are starving and homeless in a world shattered by a worldwide attack. In here, though, the good times never ended. Sure, the men have wings, but other than that, it's like being in a 1920s club. Art Deco furniture, men in tuxes, women in long dresses.

Okay, the clothes don't all look 1920s. There is the occasional '70s or science fiction futuristic outfit, like a costume party where a few of the guests didn't understand what a 1920s outfit should look like. But the room and furniture are Art Deco, and most of the angels are in old-fashioned long-tailed coats.

The room glitters with gold watches, shiny silks, and sparkling jewels. The angels are dining and drinking, smoking and laughing. Through it all, an army of white-gloved human servers carry trays of champagne glasses and hors d'oeuvres under the winking chandeliers. The band members, the servants, and most of the women look human.

I feel an unreasonable blast of disgust for the humans in the room. All traitors like me. No, to be fair, what they're doing is nowhere near as bad as what I did by not disclosing Raffe at Obi's camp.

I want to dismiss them all as gold diggers, but I remember the woman with the husband and hungry kids hanging onto the fence as she walked toward the aerie. She is probably that family's best hope of getting fed. I hope she made it in. I scan the crowd, hoping to see her face.

Instead, I see Raffe.

He leans casually against the wall in a shadowy corner, watching the crowd. A brunette in a black dress with skin so white she looks like a vampire leans into him suggestively. Everything about her oozes sex.

I'm inclined to go anywhere but to Raffe right now, but I have a mission and he's a crucial part of it. I'm certainly not going to give up the chance to find Paige just because I feel socially awkward.

I steel myself and walk over to him.

The brunette puts her hand on his chest, whispering something intimately. He's watching something across the room and doesn't seem to hear her. He holds a tumbler of amber liquid that he tosses back in one swig. He places the empty glass beside a couple of others on a nearby table.

He doesn't look at me as I lean against the wall beside him, but I know he sees me, just like he sees the girl who is now giving me a death glare. As if her message isn't already clear, she drapes herself onto Raffe.

He takes a martini from a passing waiter who holds a tray of them. Raffe gulps that down and grabs another before the waiter leaves. He's downed four drinks in the short time it took for me to get myself together and find him. Either he's shaken by something or he's falling off the wagon hard and fast. Great. Just my luck to be partnered with an alcoholic angel.

Raffe finally turns to the brunette, who gives him a dazzling smile. Her eyes sparkle with an invitation that makes me embarrassed to watch.

'Go find someone else,' says Raffe. His voice is distracted, indifferent. Ouch. Even though she gave me that murderous glare, I still feel a pang of sympathy for her.

But then again, he only told her to go away. At least he didn't tell her he doesn't even like her.

She pulls back from him slowly, as if giving him a chance to say he was just kidding. When he goes back to people watching, she shoots me one last scathing look and leaves.

I scan the room to see what Raffe is watching. The club is cozy and not as big as I'd initially thought. It has the energy of a larger place because of the boisterous crowd, but it's more of a lounge than a modern club. My eyes are immediately drawn to a group sitting in a booth as though it is a king's dais and they are the chosen ones.

There are certain kinds of groups who can do that: popular kids on lunch benches, football heroes at a party, movie stars at a club. There are half a dozen angels lounging in or around the booth. They're joking and laughing, each with a drink in one hand and a glamour girl in the other. The area is thick with women. They're either rubbing their bodies on the men to get their attention, or strutting by slowly as though they're on a catwalk, watching the men with hungry eyes.

These angels are bigger than the others in the club – taller, beefier, with an aura of casual danger that the others don't have. The kind of danger tigers in the wild project. They remind me of the ones we saw coming out of the club, the ones Raffe wanted to avoid.

They all wear swords with casual elegance. I imagine Viking warriors might look like that, if Vikings were clean-shaven and modernized. Their presence and attitude remind me of Raffe. He would fit in. It's easy to visualize him sitting in the booth with that group, drinking and laughing with the gang. Well, the laughing part takes a little imagination, but I'm sure he's capable of it.

'See that guy in the white suit?' He nods his head almost imperceptibly toward the group. He's hard to miss. The guy is not only wearing a white suit, but his shoes, hair, skin, and wings are downy white. The only color on him is his eyes. From this distance, I can't tell what color they are, but I'm willing to bet they would be shocking up close, just in contrast with the rest of him.

I've never seen an albino before. I'm pretty sure that even among albinos, his total lack of color is rare. Human skin just doesn't come in that shade. Good thing he's not human.

He stands leaning on the edge of the round booth. He's the guy who doesn't quite belong. His laugh starts with a half-second lag as if he's waiting for the cue from the rest of the guys. All the women skirt around him, careful not to get too close. He is the only one without a girl draped over him. He watches them prowling by but doesn't reach out to any of them. There's something about the other women avoiding him that makes me want to avoid him too.

'I need you to go over there and get his attention,' whispers Raffe. Great. I should have known. 'Get him to follow you to the men's room.'

'Are you kidding? How am I supposed to do that?'

'You're resourceful.' His eyes roam over my tight dress. 'You'll think of something.'

'What happens in the bathroom if I get him there?' I keep my voice as low as I can. I figure if I'm loud enough for the others to hear over the roar of the club, Raffe will surely let me know.

'We convince him to help us.' He sounds grim. He doesn't sound like he believes our chances of convincing him are great.

'What happens if he says no?'

'Game over. Mission abort.'

I probably look the way the brunette did when he told her to go away. I look at him long enough to give him a chance to say he's joking. But there is no humor in his eyes. Why did I know that would be the case?

I nod. 'I'll get him to the bathroom. You do whatever it takes to get him to say yes.'

I push away from the wall and step out of the shadows, target in my sights.

30

I'm not an actress and I suck at lying. I am also far from being a seductress. It's hard to practice the art of seduction when you're always pushing your kid sister around in her wheelchair. Not to mention that daily jeans and baggy sweatshirt do not a seductress make.

My mind spins, grasping for ways to get the albino's attention. Nothing comes to mind.

I take the long way around the lounge, hoping to think of something.

Across the club, a small entourage of women and guards makes its way toward the warriors. They follow in the wake of an angel who has almost the beauty of the warriors with just enough normalcy to his looks to make him nonthreatening. He's good-looking without being intimidating. Toffee hair, warm eyes, with a nose that's a touch big for his otherwise perfect face. This one is all smiles and friendliness, a born politician.

He wears a light gray suit, circa 1920s, with polished shoes and a golden watch chain looping from his waist to his vest pocket. He pauses here and there to exchange a word or two of greeting. His voice is as warm as his eyes, as friendly as his smile. Everyone smiles back at him.

Everyone but the two women who flank him. They stand a step behind on either side of him. Dressed identically in silver dresses that pool on the floor at their feet, they are matching platinum trophies. They're human, but their eyes are dead. The only time any life comes into them is when the Politician glances toward them.

Fear flares in their eyes before it is squelched, as if showing it would invite something truly frightening. I can almost see the trembling of their muscles as they tense to keep from cringing from the Politician.

These women aren't just afraid of him. They are scream-ing-on-the-inside terrified.

I take another look at the smiling angel but see nothing but friendliness and sincerity. If I hadn't noticed the women's reactions to him, I would have thought he was best friend material. In a world where instincts matter more than ever, there's something very wrong about not being able to directly detect the person that these women know him to be.

Because of the circular flow of the club, the Politician and I walk toward each other as we near the warriors' booth.

He looks up and catches me watching him.

Interest lights up his face and he shoots me a smile. There's so much open friendliness in that smile that my lips automati-cally curve up a split second before alarms go off in my head.

The Politician has noticed me.

An image of me dressed as one of his trophy girls flashes through my mind. My face waxy and empty, desperately trying to hide the terror.

What are these women so afraid of?

My step falters as if my feet refuse to get closer to him.

A waiter in a tux and white gloves steps in front of me, breaking the eye contact between me and the Politician. He offers flutes of bubbly champagne on his tray.

To stall, I take one. I focus on the rising bubbles in the golden liquid to center myself. The waiter turns and I catch a glimpse of the Politician.

He leans into the warriors' table and talks in a low tone.

I let out a sigh of relief. Our moment has passed.

'Thank you,' I murmur to the waiter with great relief.

'You're welcome, miss.'

Something familiar about his voice makes me glance up at the waiter to see his face for the first time. Until now, I'd been so distracted by the Politician that I hadn't really looked at my savior.

My eyes widen in shock at the red haired, freckled-nosed face. It's one of the twins, Dee or Dum.

The look he gives me is one of blank professionalism. Absolutely no sign of recognition or surprise.

Wow, he's good. I never would have guessed it based on my interactions with him before. But they had mentioned that they were Obi's spymasters, hadn't they? I assumed they were joking or exaggerating, but maybe not.

He gives a little bow and drifts away. I keep expecting him to turn around and flash me a mischievous grin but he walks stiff-backed and offers drinks to people. Who would have thought?

I casually step behind a crowd to hide myself from the Politician. Did Dee-Dum know that he was rescuing me or was that a happy coincidence?

What's he doing here? An image of Obi's caravan winding its way up to the city comes back to me. The truck full of explosives. Obi's plan to recruit resistance fighters by making a showy stand against the angels.

Great. Just great. If the twins are here, they must be scoping out the place for their counterattack.

How much time do I have to get Paige out of here before they blow the place to kingdom come?

31

After a brief conversation, the Politician leaves the warriors' booth. To my relief, he cuts across the club instead of coming toward me. He seems to have forgotten all about me as he makes his way through the club, stopping here and there to say hello.

Everyone watches him go. No one in the crowd near me speaks for a while. Then, the conversation begins tentatively, as if unsure whether it's okay to talk. The warriors at the table drink grimly and silently. Whatever was said by the Politician, they didn't like it.

I wait until the conversation rises to full volume again before I go back to approaching the albino. Now that I know the resistance is here, I feel an extra surge of urgency to get things rolling.

Still, I hesitate on the outskirts of the river of women. There's a female-free zone around the albino. Once I step into it, it will be hard not to be noticed.

The angels seem more interested in socializing with one another than with the women. Despite their best efforts, the women are being treated like fashion accessories to the angels' costumes.

When the albino turns my way, I catch a glimpse of what keeps the women at bay. It's not his utter lack of pigment, although I'm sure that would bother some people. These women, after all, aren't put off by men with feathers growing out of their backs, and who knows where else. What's a little lack of pigment to them? But his eyes. One glimpse of those peepers and I understand why the humans stay away.

They are bloodred. I've never seen anything like it. His irises are so large they take up most of his eyes. They are balls of crimson shot through with white, like miniature lightning bolts sizzling over blood. Long ivory lashes frame the eyes, as if they aren't noticeable enough already.

I can't help but stare. I look away, embarrassed, and notice other humans snatching nervous glimpses of him as well. The other angels, despite all their terrible aggression, look like they were made in Heaven. This one, on the other hand, looks like he walked right out of my mother's nightmares.

I've had more than my fair share of hanging around people whose physical appearances are unnerving. Paige was a very popular kid in the disabled community. Her friend Judith was born with stumpy arms and tiny, malformed hands; Alex wobbled when he walked and had to contort his face painfully to form coherent words, which often let out an embarrassing amount of drool; Will was a quadriplegic who needed a pump to keep him breathing.

People stared and skirted around these kids the way humans behave around this albino. Whenever a particularly bad incident happened to any member of her flock, Paige gathered them together for a theme party. A pirate party, a zombie party, a come-as-you-are party where one kid showed up in pajamas with a toothbrush in his mouth.

They'd joke and giggle and know in their bones that they were strong together. Paige was their cheerleader, counselor, and best friend all rolled into one.

It's clear that the albino needs someone like Paige in his life. He shows the familiar subtle signs of someone who is supremely conscious of being stared at and judged by his appearance. His arms and shoulders stay close to his body, his head is angled slightly down, his eyes rarely look up. He stands to the side of the group in a spot where the light is dimmer, where it's more likely the curious stares might mistake his eyes for dark brown rather than bloodred.

I'm guessing that if there's one thing that might pique an angel's prejudice, it's someone who looks like he should be surrounded by hellfire.

Despite his posture and subtle vulnerability, he is unmistakably a warrior. Everything about him is imposing, from his broad shoulders to his exceptional height to his bulging muscles and enormous wings. Just like the angels in the booth. Just like Raffe.

Every member of this group looks like he was made for fighting and conquering. They enhance this impression with every confident motion, every commanding sentence, every inch of space they take. I never would have noticed the albino being just a tad uncomfortable if I wasn't already in tune with that kind of discomfort.

As soon as I step into the human-free zone around the albino, he looks my way. I look at him straight in the eyes like I would anyone else. Once I get past the shock of look-ing into a pair of alien eyes, I see assessment and subdued curiosity. I weave a little as I smile brightly up at him.

'What lovely lashes you have,' I say, slurring my words a little. I try not to overdo it.

He blinks his surprise with those ivory lashes. I walk over, tripping just enough to slop some of my drink on his pristine white suit.

'Ohmygod! I am so, so sorry! I can't believe I just did that!' I grab a napkin off the table and smear the stain around a little. 'Here, let me help you clean.'

I'm glad to see my hands are not trembling. I'm not oblivi-ous to the dangerous vibe. These angels have killed more humans than any war in history. And here I am, splashing one of them with a drink. Not the most original ploy, but it's the best I can do on the spur of the moment.

'I'm sure it'll come right out.' I'm babbling like the tipsy girl I'm supposed to be. The area around the booth has gone quiet and everyone watches us.

I hadn't planned on that. If he was uncomfortable being watched surreptitiously, he probably hates being the center of attention in a stupid scenario like this.

He grabs my wrist and pulls it away from his suit. His grip is firm but not enough to cause pain. There's no doubt that he could snap my wrist at the slightest whim.

'I'll just go and deal with this.' Irritation edges his voice. Irritation is okay. That, I can handle. I decide he must be an okay guy, if you can ignore that he's part of the team that brought fire and brimstone to Earth.

He walks smoothly toward the bathroom, ignoring the stares from angel and human alike. I follow him quietly. I consider keeping up the drunken chick act but think better of it unless someone distracts him from going to the bathroom.

No one stops him, not even to say hello. I do a quick check for Raffe but don't see him anywhere. I hope he isn't counting on me to keep the albino in there until he feels like making an appearance.

As soon as the albino pushes his way into the bathroom, Raffe appears out of the shadows with a red cone and a fold-out maintenance sign that says Temporarily Out of Order. He drops the cone and sign in front of the bathroom door and slips in after the albino.

I'm not sure what I'm supposed to do. Should I stay out here and be a lookout? If I completely trusted Raffe, that's exactly what I'd do.

I push my way into the men's bathroom. I pass three guys who are rushing out. One of them is hastily zipping his pants. They're human and probably won't be questioning why an angel is kicking them out of the bathroom.

Raffe stands by the door, staring at the albino who stares back through the mirror above the sink. The albino looks cautious and wary.

'Hello, Josiah,' says Raffe.

Josiah's bloody eyes narrow, staring hard at Raffe.

Then, the eyes widen in shock and recognition.

He spins to face Raffe. Disbelief wars with confusion, joy, and alarm. I had no idea a person could feel all those things simultaneously, much less show them on his face.

He marshals his expression back to cool and in control. It looks like it takes some effort.

'Do I know you?' asks Josiah.

'It's me, Josiah,' says Raffe, taking a step closer to him.

Josiah backs away along the marble counter. 'No.' He shakes his head, his red eyes large and full of recognition. 'I don't think I know you.'

Raffe looks puzzled. 'What's going on, Josiah? I know it's been a long time—'

'A long time?' Josiah breathes an uncomfortable laugh, still inching back as though Raffe had the plague. 'Yeah, you could say that.' He stretches his lips in a strained smile, white on white. 'A long time, that's funny. Yeah.'

Raffe stares at him, his head cocked to one side.

'Look,' says Josiah. 'I gotta go. Don't . . . don't follow me out, okay? Please. Please. I can't afford to be seen with . . . strangers.' He inhales a shaky breath and takes a determined step toward the door.

Raffe stops him with a palm on his chest. 'We haven't been strangers since I pulled you out of the slave quarters to train you as a soldier.'

The albino cringes from Raffe's touch like he's been burned. 'That was another life, another world.' He takes a shaky breath. He lowers his voice to a barely audible whisper. 'You shouldn't be here. It's too dangerous for you now.'

'Really?' Raffe sounds bored.

Josiah turns and paces back to the counter. 'A lot of things have changed. Things have gotten complicated.' Although his voice is losing its edge, I can't help but notice that Josiah paces as far away from Raffe as he can get.

'So complicated that my own men have forgotten me?'

Josiah goes into a stall and flushes the toilet. 'Oh, no one's forgotten you.' I can barely catch his words over the roaring water so I'm pretty sure no one outside the bathroom can hear anything. 'Just the opposite. You've become the talk of the aerie.' He walks into another stall and flushes. 'There's practically an anti-Raphael campaign.'

Raphael? Does he mean Raffe?

'Why? Who would bother?'

The albino shrugs. 'I'm just a soldier. The machinations of archangels are beyond me. But if I was forced to guess . . . now that Gabriel has been shot down . . .'

'There's a power vacuum. Who's the Messenger now?'

Josiah flushes another toilet. 'Nobody. There's a standoff. We'd all agree on Michael, but he doesn't want it. He likes being the general and won't give up the military. Uriel, on the other hand, wants it so badly he's practically combing our feathers with his own hands to get the supermajority support he needs.'

'That explains the nonstop party and the women. That's a dangerous road he's walking.'

'In the meantime, none of us know what in God's name is going on or why the hell we're here. As usual, Gabriel told us nothing. You know how he liked being dramatic. Everything was need-to-know only, and even then you were lucky if you got anything out of him that wasn't all cryptic.'

Raffe nods. 'So what's keeping Uri from getting the support he needs?'

The albino flushes another toilet. And even with the thunderous sound of the water, he only points to Raffe and mouths the word *you*.

Raffe arches an eyebrow.

'Sure,' says Josiah. 'There are those who don't like the idea of Uriel becoming Messenger because he has too close of a tie to Hell. He keeps telling us that visiting the Pit is part of his job, but who knows what goes on down there? You know what I mean?'

Josiah paces back to the first stall to fill the bathroom with another thunderous flush. 'But the bigger problem for Uriel is your men. Blockheaded, stubborn lot, every one of them. They're so pissed off at your abandonment of them, they'd tear you to pieces themselves, but they're not going to let an outsider do it. They're saying all the surviving archangels should be in the running for Messenger, including you. Uriel hasn't managed to win them over. Yet.'

'Them?'

Josiah closes his bloodred eyes. 'You know I'm not in a position to take a stand, Raphael. I never have been. I never will be. I'll be lucky if I'm not washing dishes by the end. I'm barely hanging on as part of the group as it is.' He spits this out with bubbling frustration.

'What are they saying about me?'

Josiah's voice turns gentle as if reluctant to be the bearer of such bad news. 'That no angel could withstand being alone for this long. That if you haven't come back to us by now, it can only mean you're dead. Or that you've joined the other side.'

'That I've fallen?' Raffe asks. A muscle in his jaw pulses as he grinds his teeth.

'There are rumors that you committed the same sin as the Watchers. That you haven't come back because you're not allowed back. That you cleverly escaped humiliation and eternal torture by concocting a story about sparing your Watchers the pain of hunting their own children. That all the Nephilim running around Earth is proof that you never even tried.'

'What Nephilim?'

'Are you serious?' Josiah looks at Raffe as though he's looking at a madman. 'They're everywhere. The humans are terrified to be out at night. Every one of the servants has stories of seeing half-eaten bodies or of their group being attacked by the Nephilim.'

Raffe blinks, taking a moment to absorb what Josiah is saying. 'Those aren't Nephilim. They don't look anything like Nephilim.'

'They sound like Nephilim. They eat like Nephilim. They terrorize like Nephilim. You and the Watchers are the only ones alive who know what they're supposed to look like. And you're not exactly credible witnesses.'

'I've seen these things and they aren't Nephilim.'

'Whatever they are, I swear it'll be easier for you to hunt down every last one of them than to convince the masses that they aren't. Because what else could they be?'

Raffe steals a glance at me. He looks at the polished floor as he answers. 'I have no idea. We've been calling them "low demons."'

'We?' Josiah glances at me as I try to become invisible by the door. 'You and your Daughter of Man?' His tone is part accusation, part disappointment.

'It's not like that. Jesus, Josiah. Come on. You know I'd be the last one to go there, not after what happened to my Watchers, not to mention their wives.' Raffe paces the marbled floor in frustration. 'Besides, this is the last place to throw that accusation.'

'No one's crossed the line here as far as I know,' says Josiah. 'Some of the guys claim to have, but those are the same guys who say they slew dragons back in the day, with their wings and hands tied up just to make it fair.'

The albino flushes again in the next stall. 'You, on the other hand, you're going to have a tougher time convincing people of – you know.' He glances my way again. 'You need to counter the propaganda against you with your own campaign before trying any kind of a comeback. Otherwise, you could face a lynch mob. So I suggest you leave by the nearest exit.'

'I can't. I need a surgeon.'

Josiah raises his white brows in surprise. 'For what?'

Raffe stares at Josiah's bloodred eyes. He doesn't want to say it. Come on, Raffe. We don't have time for delicate psychological moments. I know it's cold of me, but someone could walk through that door any minute now, and we haven't even gotten to asking about Paige yet. I'm on the verge of opening my mouth to say something when Raffe talks.

'My wings have been cut.'

Now, it's Josiah's turn to stare at Raffe. 'Cut how?'

'Cut off.'

The albino's face transforms in shock and horror. It's strange to see such an evil-looking pair of eyes fill with pity. You couldn't get a more sympathetic response if Raffe had just told him they'd castrated him. Josiah opens his mouth to say something, then closes it as though deciding it's a stupid thing to say. He glances at Raffe's jacket with his wings peeking out, then back at his face.

'I need someone who can sew them back on. Someone good enough to make them functional again.'

Josiah turns away from Raffe and leans against a sink. 'I can't help you.' There's doubt in his voice.

'All you have to do is ask around, make the introduction.'

'Raphael, only the head physician can set up surgery here.'

'Great. That makes your task a simple one.'

'The head physician is Laylah.'

Raffe looks at Josiah as if hoping he didn't hear correctly. 'She's the only one who can do it?' There is dread in his voice.

'Yeah.'

Raffe runs his hand through his hair, looking like he wants to tear it out. 'Are you still . . .?'

'Yeah,' Josiah says grudgingly, almost embarrassed.

'Can you talk her into it?'

'You know I can't afford to stick my neck out.' The albino paces, obviously agitated.

'I wouldn't ask if I had another choice.'

'You do have another choice. *They* have physicians.'

'That's not a choice, Josiah. Will you do it?'

Josiah sighs heavily, obviously regretting what he's about to say. 'I'll see what I can do. Hide out in a room. I'll find you in a couple of hours.'

Raffe nods. Josiah turns to go. I open my mouth to say something, worried that Raffe's forgotten my sister.

'Josiah,' says Raffe before I can get my question out. 'What do you know about human children being taken?'

Josiah stops on his way past us to the door. His profile is very still. Too still. 'What children?'

'I think you know what children. You don't need to tell me what's going on. I just want to know where they're being kept.'

'I don't know anything about that.' He still hasn't looked at us. He stands frozen in profile, talking to the door.

The jazz outside the door drifts in. The buzz of the party breaks into bits of conversation as a couple of men approach the bathroom, then recede into background noise as they leave the area. The maintenance sign must be working to keep people out.

'Okay,' says Raffe. 'I'll see you in a couple of hours.'

Josiah pushes out the door as if he can't get out fast enough.

32

My mind swirls with what I just heard. Not even the angels know why they are here. Does that mean there's room to convince them that they should leave? Could Raffe be the key to igniting an angel civil war? My mind stretches to make sense of angel politics and the opportunities it might present.

But I rein in my thoughts. Because none of it will help me find Paige.

'You spend all that time talking to him, and ask only one question about my sister?' I glare at him. 'He knows something.'

'Only enough to be cautious.'

'How would you know? You didn't even pump him for information.'

'I know him. Something has him spooked. This is as far as he'll go for now. And if I push, he won't even go that far.'

'You don't think he's involved?'

'In kidnapping children? Not his style. Don't worry. It's damned near impossible to keep a secret among angels. We'll find someone who's willing to tell.'

He heads for the door.

'Are you really an archangel?' I whisper.

He gives me a cocky grin. 'Impressed?'

'No,' I lie. 'But I have some complaints I'd like to file about your personnel.'

'Talk to middle management.'

I follow him out the door, giving him my death-by-glare expression.

As soon as we push through the club's double doors, we're out of the stifling heat and noise. We head into the cool marble foyer toward a row of elevators. We take the long way through the room, staying near the walls where the shadows are thickest.

Raffe makes a quick stop at the check-in counter. A blond servant stands behind it in a suit like a robot, as though his mind is elsewhere until we come near him. As soon as we're in smiling range, his face animates into a courteous and professional mask.

'What can I do for you, sir?' Up close, his smile looks a little stiff. His eyes, although deferential when looking at Raffe, turn cold when he looks at me. Good for him. He doesn't like working for the angels, and he likes humans cozying up to them even less.

'Give me a room.' Raffe's arrogance dial is cranked all the way up. He stands at his full height and doesn't bother to do more than glance at the man as he talks. Either he wants the clerk intimidated enough to not ask any questions, or all the angels behave like that toward humans and he doesn't want to be remembered as being different. I'm guessing both.

'The top floors are already all taken, sir. Will something a little lower be all right?'

Raffe sighs as though that's an imposition. 'Fine.'

The clerk glances my way, then scribbles something in his old-fashioned ledger. He hands Raffe a key and says we're in room 1712. I want to ask for an extra one for me, but think better of opening my mouth. Based on the women trying to find escorts into the building, I have a suspicion that the only humans allowed to move around on their own are the servants. So much for asking for my own room.

The clerk turns to me and says, 'Feel free to take the elevator, miss. The power is reliable here. The only reason we use keys instead of electronic cards is because the masters prefer it.'

Did he actually call the angels 'the masters'? My fingers turn cold at the thought. Despite my determination to grab Paige and get the hell out of here, I can't help but wonder if there's anything I can do to help bring down these bastards.

It's true that their control of what was once our world boggles my mind. They can power lights and elevators and ensure a steady supply of gourmet food. I suppose it could be magic. That seems to be as good an explanation as any these days. But I'm not quite ready to throw away centuries of scientific progress to start thinking like a medieval peasant.

I wonder if, a generation from now, people will assume everything in this building is run by magic. I clench my teeth at the thought. This is what the angels have reduced us to.

I take a good look at Raffe's perfectly formed profile. No human could look that good. Just one more reminder that he's not one of us.

I catch a glimpse of the clerk's face as I look away. His eyes warm just enough to let me know that he approves of the grim look on my face when I look at Raffe. Smoothing his face back to polite professionalism, he tells Raffe to call on him should he need anything.

The short elevator hall leads to a vast open area. I take a quick peek after pushing the button for the elevator. Above me are rows and rows of balconies that go all the way up to the glass domed ceiling.

Angels circle above, flying in short hops from floor to floor. An outer ring of angels spirals up, while an inner ring of angels spirals down.

I suppose they do this in order to avoid collisions, just the way our traffic patterns look organized from above. But despite its practical origins, the total effect is a stunning array of celestial bodies in a seemingly choreographed air ballet. If Michelangelo had seen this in daylight with the sun streaming down from the glass dome, he'd have fallen to his knees and painted 'til he was blind.

The elevator doors slide open with a ding, and I tear my eyes away from the splendor above me.

Raffe stands beside me watching his peers flying. Before he shutters his eyes, I catch something that might have been despair.

Or longing.

I refuse to feel bad for him. Refuse to feel anything for him other than anger and hatred for the things his people have done to mine.

But the hatred doesn't come.

Instead, sympathy trickles into me. As different as we are, we are in many ways kindred spirits. We're just two people striving to get our lives back together again.

But then I remember that he is, in fact, not a person at all.

I step into the elevator. It has the mirror, wood paneling, and red carpet you'd expect from an elevator in an expensive hotel. The doors start to slide shut with Raffe still standing outside. I put my hand out to keep the doors open.

'What's wrong?'

He glances around self-consciously. 'Angels don't go into elevators.'

Of course; they fly to their floors. I playfully grab his wrists and spin him in a drunken circle, giggling for the benefit of any who might be watching. Then, I waltz us both into the elevator.

I press the button for the seventeenth floor. My stomach lurches with the elevator at the thought of having to escape from such a high place. Raffe doesn't look so comfortable either. I suppose an elevator might seem like a steel coffin to someone who's used to flying the open sky.

When the door opens, he quickly steps out. Apparently, the need to get out of a coffinlike machine takes precedence over the issue of being seen coming out of an elevator.

The hotel room turns out to be a full suite with a bedroom, a living room, and a bar. It's all marble and soft leather, plush carpet and picture windows. Two months ago, the view would have been breathtaking. San Francisco at its finest.

Now it makes me want to weep at the panoramic view of charred destruction.

I walk over to the window like a sleepwalker. I lean into it with my forehead and palms on the cool glass the way I might with my father's gravestone.

The charred hills are strewn with leaning buildings like broken teeth in a burned jawbone. Haight-Ashbury, the Mission, North Beach, South of Market, Golden Gate Park, all gone. Something breaks deep within me like glass being crunched underfoot.

Here and there, plumes of dark smoke reach into the sky like the fingers of a drowning man reaching up for the last time.

Still, there are areas that don't look completely burned, areas that could house small neighborhood communities. San Francisco is known for its neighborhoods. Could some of them have survived the onslaught of asteroids, fires, raiders, and disease?

Raffe pulls the curtains closed around me. 'I don't know why they left the curtains open.'

I know why. The maids are human. They want to mar this illusion of civilization. They want to make sure no one ever forgets what the angels did. I would have left the curtains open too.

By the time I pull myself away from the window, Raffe is hanging up the phone. His shoulders sag as exhaustion seems to finally catch up with him. 'Why don't you hit the shower? I just ordered some food.'

'Room service? Is this place for real? It's hell on Earth now and you guys order meals through room service?'

'Do you want it or not?'

I shrug. 'Well, yeah.' I'm not even embarrassed by my double standard. Who knows when I'll get another meal? 'What about my sister?'

'In due time.'

'I don't have time, and neither does she.' *And neither do you.* How much time do we have before the freedom fighters hit the aerie?

As much as I want the resistance to hit the angels as hard as possible, the thought of Raffe being caught in the attack churns my stomach. I'm tempted to tell him about seeing resistance fighters here, but I squelch that idea as soon as it comes. I doubt he could stand by and not set off the alarm for his people any more than I could if I knew the angels were attacking the resistance camp.

'Okay, Miss Short-on-Time, where would you like to look first? Should we start on the eighth floor or the twenty-first? How about the roof, or the garage? Maybe you could just ask the clerk at the desk where they might be holding her. There are other intact buildings in this district. Maybe we should start with one of them. What do you think?'

I'm horrified to find that my determination is melting into tears. I keep my eyes wide open to stop them from falling. I will not cry in front of Raffe.

His voice loses its edge and turns gentle. 'It will take time to find her, Penryn. Being clean will keep us from being noticed, and being fed will give us strength to search. If you don't like it, the door is right there. I'll take my shower and eat while you search.' He heads for the bathroom.

I sigh. 'Fine.' I stab my heels along the carpet past him to the bathroom. 'I'll shower first.' I have the good grace not to slam the bathroom door.

The bathroom is a quiet statement of luxury in fossil stone and brass. I swear it's bigger than our condo. I stand under the hot spray and let the grime wash away. I never thought a hot shower and hair wash could be so luxurious.

During long minutes under the shower spray, I can almost forget how much the world has changed and pretend I've won the lottery and am staying the night in a penthouse in the city. The thought doesn't bring me as much comfort as remembering life in our little suburban house back before we moved into the condo. Dad was still taking care of us then and Paige hadn't lost her legs yet.

I wrap myself in a plush towel that qualifies more as a blanket. For lack of anything better, I slip back into the slinky dress, but decide the hose and heels can sit in the corner until I need them.

When I come out into the bedroom, a tray of food sits on the table. I run over and lift the domed cover. Boneless short ribs smothered in sauce, creamed spinach, mashed potatoes, and a hefty slice of German chocolate cake. The smell almost makes me faint with pleasure.

I dig in first and sit down as I chew. The fat content of this meal must be out of this world. In the old days, I would have tried to stay away from all of these dishes, except maybe the chocolate cake, but in the land of cat food and dried noodles, this meal is to die for. It's the best meal I can ever remember having.

'Please, don't wait for me,' says Raffe as he watches me stuff my face. He grabs a bite of the cake on his way to the bathroom.

'Don't worry,' I mumble through a mouthful, at his back.

By the time he comes back out, I've scarfed down my entire meal and am having a hard time trying not to steal some of his. I tear my eyes away from the feast to look at him.

Once I see him, I forget all about the food.

He stands in the bathroom doorway, steam drifting languidly around him, wearing nothing but a towel draped loosely around his hips. Beads of water cling to him like diamonds in a dream. The combined effect of the soft light behind him from the bathroom and the steam curling around his muscles gives the impression of a mythological water god visiting our world.

'You can have it all, you know,' he says.

I blink a few times, trying to grasp what he's saying.

'I figured we might as well double up on our meals while we can.' There's a knock at the door. 'There's my order now.' He heads out to the living room.

He's talking about both servings in front of me being mine. Right. Of course he'd want his dinner hot. No reason to leave it cooling while he showered, so he must have ordered mine, then his, just before I got out of the shower. Of course.

I return my attention to the food, trying to remember how badly I lusted after it only a moment ago. The food. Right, the food. I shovel in a giant mouthful of the rib meat. The creamy sauce is a sensual reminder of rare luxuries once taken for granted.

I walk out into the living room and talk with my mouth full. 'You're a genius for ordering this much—'

The albino, Josiah, walks into the living room with the most beautiful woman I have ever seen. I finally get to see a female angel up close. Her features are so fine and delicate that it's impossible not to stare. She looks like she was the mold for Venus, Goddess of Love. Her waist-length hair shimmers in the light as she moves, matching the golden plumage of her wings.

Her cornflower blue eyes would be the perfect reflection of innocence and all that is wholesome, except that there's something sliding behind them. Something that hints that she should be the poster child for the master race.

Those eyes assess me from the top of my wet and stringy hair to the tips of my bare toes.

I become acutely aware that I was overenthusiastic when I shoveled the rib meat into my mouth. My cheeks bulge and I can barely keep my lips closed as I chew as fast as I can. Rib meat is not something I can swallow in one lump. I hadn't bothered to brush my hair, or even dry it before diving into the feast after my shower, so it hangs limp and dripping onto my red dress. Her Aryan eyes see it all and judge me.

Raffe gives me a look and rubs his finger on his cheek. I swipe my hand across my face. It comes away smeared with meat sauce. Great.

The woman turns her eyes to Raffe. I have been dismissed. She gives him a long appraising look as well, drinking in his near-nakedness, his muscular shoulders, his wet hair. Her eyes slide over to me in a quick accusation.

She steps close to Raffe and runs her fingers down his glistening chest.

'So, it really is you.' Her voice is as smooth as an ice cream shake. A shake with ground glass hidden in it. 'Where have you been all this time, Raffe? And what have you done to deserve getting your wings cut off?'

'Can you sew them back on, Laylah?' asks Raffe stiffly.

'Straight to business,' says Laylah, strolling over to the picture window. 'I make room for you in my busy schedule at the last minute, and you can't even ask me how I am?'

'I don't have time for games. Can you do it or not?'

'In theory, it can be done. Assuming all the stars align, of course. And there are a lot of stars that need to align for it to work. But the real question is, why should I?' She throws back the curtains, shocking my eyes again with the panoramic view of the destroyed city. 'After all this time, is there any chance you haven't been lured to the other side? Why should I help the fallen?'

Raffe walks to the counter where his sword lies. He slides the blade out from the scabbard, managing to make the gesture nonthreatening, which is quite a feat considering the sharpness of the double edge. He flips it in the air and catches it by the handle. He slaps the blade back into its sheath while watching Laylah expectantly.

Josiah nods. 'Okay. His sword hasn't rejected him.'

'Doesn't mean she won't,' says Laylah. 'Sometimes they cling to loyalty longer than they should. Doesn't mean—'

'It means everything it's supposed to mean,' says Raffe.

'We're not made to be alone,' says Laylah. 'No more than wolves are made to be solo. No angel can endure such solitude for long, even you.'

'My sword hasn't rejected me. End of discussion.'

Josiah clears his throat. 'About those wings?'

Laylah glares at Raffe. 'I don't have kind memories of you, Raffe, in case you'd forgotten. After all this time, you show up in my life again with no warning. Making demands. Insulting me by flaunting your human toy in my presence. Why should I do this for you instead of sounding the alarm and letting everybody know you had the nerve to come back?'

'Laylah,' says Josiah nervously. 'They'd know it was me who helped him.'

'I'd keep you out of it, Josiah,' says Laylah. 'Well, Raffe? No arguments? No pleas? No flattery?'

'What do you want?' asks Raffe. 'Name your price.'

I'm so used to him taking charge of a situation, so used to his pride and control that it's hard for me to see him like this. Tense, and under the power of someone who's behaving like a scorned lover. Who says celestial beings can't be petty?

Her eyes slide to me as if she wants to say her price is to have me killed. Then she looks back at Raffe, weighing her options.

Someone knocks on the door.

Laylah stiffens in alarm. Josiah looks like he's just been condemned to Hell.

'It's just my dinner,' says Raffe. He opens the door before anyone can scramble away.

In the doorway stands Dee-Dum, looking professional and detached even though he can't miss seeing all of us in one glance. He's still in his butler's outfit with the coattails and white gloves. Beside him is a cart bearing a silver-domed tray and silverware laid out on a folded napkin. The room fills once more with the scents of warm meat and fresh vegetables.

'Where would you like this, sir?' asks Dee-Dum. He shows no sign of recognition, no judgment about Raffe's near nakedness.

'I'll take it.' Raffe picks up the tray. He also shows no sign of recognition. Maybe Raffe never noticed the twins at the camp. There's no doubt that the twins noticed Raffe.

As the door closes, Dee-Dum bows but his eyes never stop tracking the scene in the room. I'm sure he has every detail, every face, memorized.

Raffe never turns his back to him to show his scars, so Dee-Dum might still think him human. Although I wonder if he saw Raffe at the club with his wings displayed through his jacket slits. Either way, Obi's people can't be happy that two escaped 'guests' of their camp ended up in the company of angels at the aerie. I wonder if Raffe were to jerk the door open right now, would we find Dee-Dum with his ear to the door?

Laylah relaxes a little and seats herself on a leather chair, like a queen taking her throne. 'You appear uninvited, eat our food, make yourself at home in our place like a rat, and you have the nerve to ask for help?'

I meant to keep quiet. Getting back his wings is as important to Raffe as rescuing Paige is to me. But watching her lounge in front of a panoramic view of the charred city is too much for me.

'It's not your food, and it's not your place.' I practically spit out the words.

'Penryn,' says Raffe in a warning voice as he puts the tray down on the bar.

'And don't insult our rats.' My hands clench tight enough to score nail marks on my palms. 'They have a right to be here. Unlike you.'

The tension is so thick I wonder if it'll smother me. I may have just blown Raffe's chance to get his wings back. The Aryan looks like she's ready to break me in half.

'Okay,' says Josiah in a soothing voice. 'Let's just take a timeout here and focus on what's important.' Of all of them, he looks the most evil with his bloodred eyes and unnaturally white everything else. But looks aren't everything. 'Raffe needs his wings back. Now all we need to do is figure out what Beautiful Laylah can get out of this, and we'll all be happy. That's all that matters, right?'

He looks at each of us. I want to say I won't be happy, but I've said enough.

'Great, so Laylah,' says Josiah. 'What can we do to make you happy?'

Laylah's lashes sweep down coyly over her eyes. 'I'll think of something.' I have no doubt that she already knows her price. Why be coy about it? 'Come to my lab in an hour. It'll take me that long to prepare. I'll need the wings now.'

Raffe hesitates like a man about to sign a deal with the devil. Then he walks back into the bedroom, leaving me to be stared at by Laylah and Josiah.

The hell with it. I follow after Raffe. I find him in the bathroom, wrapping his wings in towels.

'I don't trust her,' I say.

'They can hear you.'

'I don't care.' I lean against the doorjamb.

'Got a better idea?'

'What if she just takes your wings?'

'Then I'll worry about it then.' He puts one wing aside and begins wrapping the other in a matching towel that's practically the size of a sheet.

'You'll have no leverage then.'

'I have no leverage now.'

'You have your wings.'

'What should I do with them, Penryn? Mount them up on the wall? They're useless to me unless I can get them sewn back on.' Raffe rubs his hand over the two folds of wings. He closes his eyes.

I feel like a jerk. No doubt this is difficult enough without me reinforcing his doubts.

He glides around me through the doorway. I stay in the bathroom until I hear the front door close behind the pair of angels.

33

I stare at the dark windows overlooking the charred city. 'Tell me about the Messenger.' This is the first chance I've had to try to make sense of the earlier conversation with Josiah.

'God commands Gabriel. He's the Messenger. Then Gabriel tells the rest of us what God wants.' Raffe takes in a heaping spoonful of his reheated mashed potatoes. 'That's the theory, anyway.'

'And God doesn't talk to any of the other angels?'

'Certainly not to me.' Raffe slices into his rare steak. 'But then again, I haven't been real popular lately.'

'He's never talked to you, not once?'

'No. And I doubt he ever will.'

'But from what Josiah said, it sounded like you could be the next Messenger.'

'Yeah, wouldn't that be the biggest joke? Not impossible, though. I am technically in the succession pool.'

'Why would that be such a joke?'

'Because, Miss Nosy, I am agnostic.'

I've had a lot of surprises in the past couple of months. But this one nearly floors me.

'You're . . . agnostic?' I look at him for signs of humor. 'As in you're not sure of the existence of God?' He's dead serious. 'How can that be? You're an angel, for chrissake.'

'So?'

'So, you're God's creature. He created you.'

'He supposedly created you too. Aren't some of you unsure of God's existence?'

'Well, yeah, but he doesn't talk to us. I mean, he doesn't talk to me.' My mother comes to mind. 'Okay, I admit there are people who claim that they talk to God or the other way around. But how am I supposed to know if that's true?'

My mom doesn't even talk to God in English. It's some made-up language that only she understands. Her religious belief is fanatical. More accurately, her belief in the devil is fanatical.

Me? Even now, with angels and all, I still can't believe in her God. Although I admit that late at night, I sort of fear her Devil. Overall, I guess that still makes me agnostic. For all anyone knows, these angels could just be an alien species from another world trying to trick us into giving up without much of a fight. I don't know, and I expect I'll never know about God, angels, or most of life's questions. And I've accepted that.

But now, I've found an agnostic angel.

'You're making my head hurt.' I sit down at the table.

'The Messenger's word is accepted as the word of God. We act on it. Always have. Whether each of us believes it or not – whether even the Messenger believes it or not – is another story.'

'So if the next Messenger says to kill off all the remaining humans just because he feels like it, then the angels would do it?'

'Without question.' He bites into the last slice of rare steak.

I let that sink in while Raffe gets up to prepare to leave for his surgery.

He puts on his pack. It is wrapped with white towels to give the impression that wings are folded beneath the jacket.

I get up to help him adjust his jacket. 'Won't this look suspicious?'

'There won't be many eyes where I'm going.'

He walks to the front door and pauses. 'If I'm not back by dawn, find Josiah. He'll help you get out of the aerie.'

Something tight and hard clenches inside my chest.

I don't even know where he's going. Probably to some back-alley butcher working with filthy surgical tools under dim lights.

'Wait.' I point to the sword lying on the counter. 'What about your sword?'

'She won't like all those scalpels and needles near me. She can't help me on the operating table.'

My insides flutter with unease at the thought of him lying helpless on a table surrounded by hostile angels. Not to mention the possibility of a resistance attack during the surgery.

Should I warn him?

And run the risk that he'll tell his people? His old friends and loyal soldiers?

What would he do if he knew anyway? Cancel the operation and give up his only hope for getting his wings back? Not a chance.

Raffe steps out the door without a word of warning from me.

34

I'm not sure what to do except pace.

I'm too worked up to think straight. My mind tumbles with what might be happening with Paige, my mother, Raffe, and the freedom fighters.

How long can I eat and sleep and lounge around in luxury while Paige is somewhere nearby? At this rate, it could be weeks before we get a lead on her. I just wish there was something I could do instead of waiting here helpless until Raffe gets out of surgery.

From what I've seen, humans aren't allowed anywhere in the aerie without an angel escort.

Unless they're servants . . .

I discard half a dozen crazy ideas that involve things like jumping a servant my size and stealing her clothes. That may work in the movies, but I would probably be condemning someone to starvation if she gets kicked out of the aerie. I may not approve of humans working for angels, but who am I to judge anyone's way of surviving this crisis and feeding their family?

I pick up the phone and order a bottle of champagne off their room service menu. I consider asking for Dee-Dum but decide to leave it to chance for now.

In the World Before, I wouldn't even legally be able to drink, much less order a bottle of champagne to be delivered to a thousand-dollar-a-night suite. I pace, thinking through all the possible scenarios. Just when I'm convinced I'm going to wear a circular track in the plush carpet, someone knocks on the door.

Please, please let it be Dee-Dum.

I open the door to a mousy looking woman. Her dark eyes gaze out from beneath a mop of frizzy brown hair. I'm so disappointed I can taste the metallic tang of it in my mouth. I'm so frustrated it's not Dee-Dum that I seriously consider jumping her for her black-and-white uniform. She wears a long black skirt with a crisp white blouse under a black waist jacket that resembles a female version of a tuxedo. She's a little bigger than me but not by much.

I open the door and indicate that she should come in. She walks to the coffee table to put down her tray.

'Do you have family?' I ask.

She turns and looks at me like a startled rabbit. She nods, causing her frizzy hair to flop over her eyes.

'Does this job keep them fed?'

She nods again, her eyes turning wary. She may have been an innocent a couple of months before, but that might as well have been a lifetime ago. The innocence in her eyes flees much too fast. This girl had to fight to get her job, and by the look of her grim expression, she's had to fight to keep it too.

'How many of you make deliveries for room service?'

'Why?'

'Just curious.' I consider telling her that I'm looking for Dee-Dum, but I don't want to jeopardize him. There's too much I don't understand about angel society and servant politics for me to start throwing around names.

'There are about half a dozen of us.' She shrugs with one shoulder, keeping her wary eyes on me as she heads back for the door.

'Do you take turns delivering things?'

She nods. Her eyes dart to the bedroom door, probably wondering where my angel is.

'Am I creeping you out?' I say it with a deliberately creepy tone. Her eyes dart back to me. I saunter toward her like a vampire with a hungry expression on my face. I'm making things up as I go, but I can tell that I'm freaking her out. I guess that's better than being laughed at for acting strange.

Her eyes widen as I approach her. She claws at the doorknob and practically runs out.

Hopefully, that takes her out of the running for making deliveries to this room. At most, I just need to order five more things.

It turns out I only have to order two more things before Dee-Dum comes to my door with a large slice of cheesecake. I close the door quickly behind him and lean against it as though this will force him to help me.

The first thing I want to ask is when the attack will happen. But he has seen me in the company of angels, and I'm afraid he'll think of me as a threat if I start asking questions about their attack plans. So I stick to the basics.

'Do you know where they're keeping the children?' I don't think my voice is very loud, but he whips his hand down in a shushing motion anyway. His eyes dart to the bedroom.

'They're gone,' I whisper. 'Please help me. I need to find my little sister.'

He stares at me long enough to make me fidget. Then he pulls out a pen and a pad of paper, the kind a waiter might use to take your order. He scribbles something on it and hands it to me. The note reads, *Leave now while you can*.

I put my hand out for his pen and write on the same piece of paper. A few months ago, it would have been natural to use a new piece of paper for a new note, but now, the paper we have may be the last we ever have. *Can't. Must rescue sister*.

He writes, *Then you'll die*.

I can tell you stuff about them you probably don't know.

He raises his eyebrow in question.

What can I say that he would be interested in? *They're in political turmoil. They don't know why they're here*.

He writes, *How many?*

Don't know.

Weapons?

Don't know.

Plan of attack?

I bite my lip. I don't know anything that's immediately relevant to military strategy, which is obviously what he's looking for.

'Please help me,' I whisper.

He gives me a long look. His eyes are calculating, devoid of emotion, which is an odd combination with his pink, freckled face. I don't need this coldhearted spymaster. What I need is the boy-next-door Dee-Dum who jokes and entertains.

I write, *You owe me, remember?* I give him a half smile, trying to nudge him back to the playful twin I met at the camp. It works, sort of. His face warms up a bit, probably remembering the girl fight. I wonder how bad the damage was after. Did the demons leave them alone after we left?

He writes, *I'll take you to where there might be kids. But then you're on your own.*

I'm so excited I hug him.

'Is there anything else I can get for you, miss?' He nods vigorously at me, telling me to order something new.

'Uh, yeah. How about . . . a chocolate bar?' Paige's bite-sized chocolates are still at the bottom of my pack in the car. I would give a lot to be able to give her chocolate as soon as I see her.

'Of course,' he says as he pulls out a lighter and ignites the paper we'd been writing on. 'I can get that for you right away, miss.' The flames quickly consume the little note, leaving behind only curling remnants and the lingering scent of burn paper.

He runs the water in the sink at the bar, where he drops the burning note until all traces of the ashes are gone. Then he picks up the fork from the tray and scoops an enormous portion of the cheesecake into his mouth. With a wink, he leaves, showing me his open palm in a signal to stay.

I wear down the carpet some more, pacing in circles until he returns. I think about his refusal to say anything out loud and what he might be doing here.

It seems like the note-writing thing is overly cautious considering the thickness of the walls and the racket in the aerie. I think Raffe would have warned me if the conversations in the rooms could be heard. But I suppose Obi's people don't have the benefit of an angel telling them they're talking too loud. Despite all of Obi's spies and contacts, it's possible that I know more about angels than any of them.

When Dee-Dum returns, he brings a servant's uniform and a large bar of milk chocolate with hazelnuts. I change into the black-and-white outfit as fast as I can. I'm grateful to see that the shoes are practical, soft-soled flats made for waitresses who are on their feet all day. Shoes I can run in. Things are looking up.

When Dee-Dum takes out his pad of paper, I tell him the angels can't hear us. He gives me a skeptical look even after I reassure him. He's finally startled into speaking when I pick up Raffe's sword.

'What the hell is that?' His voice is low but at least he's talking. Dee-Dum stares at the sword as I strap the scabbard onto my back.

'Dangerous times, Dee-Dum. Every girl should have a blade on her.' I have to strap it upside-down and at an angle so that it fits my back without the hilt sticking out through my hair.

'That looks like an angel's sword.'

'Obviously not, otherwise I wouldn't be able to lift it, right?'

He nods. 'True.'

There's too much conviction in his voice for a man who's never tried lifting one for himself. My guess is that he's tried it several times.

I test the leather thumb strap around the guard to make sure I can unlatch it easily to draw the sword one-handed.

He's still looking at me a little suspiciously, like he knows I'm lying about something but can't put his finger on what. 'Well, I guess it's quieter than a gun. But where'd you find a thing like that?'

'In a house. The owner was probably a collector.'

I throw on the short jacket that goes with the uniform. It's a little big for me so it hangs over the upside-down sword nicely. It doesn't quite cover the sword's pommel, but it'll pass a casual inspection. My back doesn't entirely look natural but close enough. My long hair hides some of the unnatural line.

Dee-Dum clearly wants to interrogate me about the sword, but can't seem to think of the right questions. I gesture for him to lead the way.

The hardest thing to remember as I walk through the party crowd in the lobby is to behave normally. I'm hyperconscious of the sword pommel gently bouncing off my hip as I walk. I keep wanting to slink into the shadows and disappear. But in the servants' uniforms, we are invisible so long as we behave as expected.

The only ones who seem to remotely notice us are other servants. Fortunately, they have no time or energy to really take note of us. The party is really in full swing now, and the servants are practically running to keep up with their work.

The only person who looks closely at me is the night clerk who checked us in. I have a bad moment when his eyes lock onto mine and I see the light of recognition. He glances at Dee-Dum. They exchange a look. Then the clerk goes back to his paperwork as if he saw nothing unusual.

'Wait here,' says Dee-Dum and leaves me in the shadows while he walks to the desk clerk.

I wonder how many resistance members have infiltrated the aerie?

They talk briefly, then Dee-Dum heads toward the entrance, waving for me to follow. His pace has picked up, his walk more urgent than before.

I'm a little surprised when Dee-Dum takes us out of the building. The crowd waiting outside has swelled and the guards are too busy to notice us.

I'm even more surprised when he leads us around the building and into a dark alley. I'm half-running to keep up.

'What's going on?' I whisper.

'Plans have changed. We have almost no time. I'll show you where to go, then I have things I need to do.'

No time.

I trot after him in silence, trying to stay calm.

For the first time, I'm unable to control the doubts eating away at me. Can I find Paige in time? How will I ever manage to get her out of here on my own without a wheelchair? I can carry her on my back, piggyback style, but I won't be able to run or fight like that. We'll just be a big, clumsy target in a shooting gallery.

And what about Raffe?

To our right, there's a gated driveway down to the underground garage of the aerie. Dee-Dum leads me toward it.

I'm acutely aware that we are humans on the street at night. I feel even more vulnerable when I catch a glimpse of watching eyes along the alley where dark lumps of people lie huddled out of the wind. Nothing about those eyes strikes me as preternatural, but I'm no expert.

'Why didn't we just go down from the lobby?' I ask.

'Someone's always watching those stairs. You have a much better chance of getting in through this back way.'

Beside the gated driveway is a metal door that leads into the garage. Dee-Dum hauls out an impressive ring of keys. He flips through the keys and hurriedly tries a few.

'You don't know which one it is? And here I thought you were the prepared type.'

'I am,' he says with a mischievous grin. 'But these aren't my keys.'

'You really have to teach me that pickpocketing trick sometime.'

He glances up to reply, but his face morphs into a troubled expression. I turn to see what he's seeing.

Shadows slip out of the dark alley, approaching us.

Dee-Dum moves out of his corner and loosens into a fighter's stance, the way a wrestler might get ready for impact. I'm still trying to decide whether to run or fight when four men surround us.

With the moon peeking in and out of storm clouds, I get impressions of sour unwashed bodies, tattered clothes, and feral eyes. I wonder how they got into the restricted area near the aerie. Then again, I might as well wonder how rats get into places. They just do.

'Hotel skanks,' says one. His eyes take in our clean clothes, our freshly showered bodies. 'Got any food on you?'

'Yeah,' says another. This one plays with heavy chains, the kind you see hanging from mechanic's garages. 'How about some of those fancy whore's d'oeuvres?'

'Hey, we're all on the same team here,' says Dee-Dum. His voice is calm, soothing. 'We're all fighting for the same thing.'

'Hey, jerkoff,' says the first guy closing the circle tighter around us. 'When was the last time you went hungry, huh? Same team, my ass.'

The guy with the chains starts waving them around like a lasso. I'm pretty sure he's showing off, but I'm not sure that's all he plans to do with them.

My muscles brace for a fight. I wish I could have had some practice with the sword before using it in a fight, but it's my best bet to deflect the chains.

I unlatch the thumb strap and slide the sword out of its scabbard.

35

'Penryn?'

Everyone turns to see the newcomer.

One of the lumps lying in the alley uncoils and steps out of the shadows.

My mother opens her arms wide as she walks toward me. Her cattle prod dangles from her wrist like an oversized charm bracelet for the insane. My heart drops to my stomach. She has a huge smile on her face, completely unaware of the danger she faces.

A cheery yellow sweater flaps in the wind around her shoulders like a short cape. She passes through the men like she doesn't see them. Maybe she doesn't. She grabs me in a bear hug and spins me around.

'I was so worried!' She strokes my hair and looks over me for injuries. She looks delighted.

I wiggle out of her grasp, wondering how I can protect her.

I'm about to bring up my sword when I realize the men have backed off, widening the circle around us. They have suddenly gone from menacing to nervous. The chain that was being used as a threatening lasso only a moment ago is now being used as worry beads as the guy anxiously fidgets with the links.

'Sorry, sorry,' says the first guy to my mother. His hands are up in surrender. 'We didn't know.'

'Yeah,' says the guy with the chain. 'We didn't mean any harm. Really.' He eases back nervously into the shadows.

They scatter into the night, leaving me and Dee-Dum to watch in wonder.

'I see you've made friends, Mom.'

She scowls heavily at Dee-Dum. 'Go away.' She grips her cattle prod and points it at him.

'He's okay. He's a friend.'

She smacks me on the head hard enough to bruise. 'I was worried about you! Where have you been? How many times have I told you not to trust anyone?'

I hate it when she does that. There's nothing more humiliating than being smacked by your crazy mother in front of your friends.

Dee-Dum stares at us, stunned. Despite his hardcore attitude and his pickpocketing skills, he's clearly not from a world where mothers hit their children.

I put my hand out to him. 'It's okay. Don't worry about it.' I turn to my mother. 'He's helping me find Paige.'

'He's lying to you. Just look at him.' Her eyes fill with tears. She knows I won't listen to her warnings. 'He'll trick you and drag you down a filthy hole into Hell and never let you out. He'll chain you to a wall and let the rats eat you alive. Can't you see that?'

Dee-Dum looks back and forth between me and my

mother with surprise. He looks more like a little kid than ever.

'That's enough, Mom.' I walk back to the metal door beside the gated driveway. 'Either be quiet or I'll leave you here and find Paige by myself.'

She runs to me, grabbing my arm in supplication. 'Don't leave me here alone.' I see in her wild eyes the rest of the sentence – *alone with the demons*.

I don't point out that she seems to be the most frightening thing on the streets. 'Then stay quiet, okay?'

She nods. Her face is filled with anguish and fright.

I gesture for Dee-Dum to lead the way. He looks at us, probably trying to make sense of it all. After a pause, he takes out his keys, keeping a careful eye on my mom. He tries several keys in the lock before one finally works. The door swings open with a squeak that makes me cringe.

'At the far end of the garage to your right, there's a door. Try that.'

'What can I expect in there?'

'No idea. All I can tell you is that there are rumors among the servants of . . . something that might be kids in that room. But who knows? Maybe they're just midgets.'

I let out a deep breath, trying to calm myself. My heart flutters in my chest like a dying bird. I hope against all odds that Dee-Dum will offer to come in with me.

'It's a suicide mission, you know,' he says. So much for my hope for an offer.

'Was that your plan all along? Show me where to go, then convince me there's nothing I can do to save my sister?'

'Actually, my plan all along was to become a rock star, travel the world collecting fan girls, and then get really fat and spend the rest of my life playing video games while the girls keep comin', thinking I look as good as I did in my music videos.' He shrugs as if to say, *Who knew the world would turn out so different?*

'Will you help me?'

'Sorry, kid. If I'm going to commit suicide, it'll be a lot more showy than being cut down in a basement trying to rescue somebody's kid sister.' He smiles in the dim light, taking the sting out of his words. 'Besides, I have a couple of very important things that need to get done.'

I nod. 'Thanks for bringing me here.'

My mother squeezes my arm, silently reminding me that she thinks everything he says is a lie. I realize I'm saying good-bye to him as though I too believe that this is a suicide mission.

I stuff all my doubts down where I can't feel them anymore. This is a lot like leaping over a chasm. If you don't think you can do it, you can't.

I step through the door.

'You're really going to do this?' asks Dee-Dum.

'If that was your brother in there, what would you do?'

He hesitates, then looks around to make sure no one is within earshot. 'Listen to me carefully. You have to get out of the area within an hour. I mean it. Get as far away as you can.'

Before I can ask him what's going on, he fades into the shadows.

An hour?

Could the resistance be planning to attack so soon?

The fact that he warned me at all puts the pressure on me. He wouldn't risk a leak, which means there's not enough time for me to do much damage if I get caught and interrogated.

Meanwhile, I can't shake the image of Raffe lying helpless on a surgeon's table. I don't even know where he is.

I take a deep, calming breath.

I head into the dark cavern that used to be a garage.

After a couple of steps, I swallow panic as I stand in utter darkness. My mother grips my arm with enough force to bruise.

'It's a trap,' she whispers into my ear. I can feel her trembling. I give her hand a reassuring squeeze.

There's nothing I can do until my eyes adjust to the blackness, assuming there's anything to adjust to. My first impression is that it is a pitch-black, cavernous space. Standing still, I wait until my eyes acclimate to the dark. All I hear is my mother's nervous breathing.

It's only a little while, but it feels like hours. My brain screams *hurry, hurry, hurry*.

As my eyes adjust, I feel less like a blind target in a spotlight.

We're standing in the underground garage, surrounded by abandoned cars hunched in the shadows. The ceiling feels both vast and too low at the same time. At first, there seem to be giants spread out in front of me, but they turn out to be concrete pillars. The garage is a maze of cars and pillars fading off into the darkness.

I hold the angel sword in front of me like a divining rod. I hate to go into the darker bowels of the garage, away from what little light comes through the bars of the gate, but that's where I have to go if I want to find Paige. The place feels so deserted, I'm tempted to just call out for her, but that's probably a very bad idea.

I step gingerly into the almost total darkness, careful of debris on the floor. I stumble over what I think is a spilled purse. I almost lose my footing, but my mother's viselike grip on my arm stabilizes me.

My footsteps echo in the dark. Not only do they give away our location, they also interfere with my ability to hear someone else sneaking up on me. My mother, on the other hand, is as silent as a cat. Even her breathing is quiet now. She's had a lot of practice sneaking around in the dark, avoiding Things That Chase Her.

I bump into a car and I feel my way around a long curve of cars in what I assume is a standard zigzag pattern parked back and forth down rows of slots. I'm using the sword more as a blind man's stick than as a weapon.

I almost trip over a suitcase. Some traveler must have been dragging it around when he realized there was nothing in it worth carrying anymore. I should have tripped over it. I'm deep enough in the belly of the garage that it should be completely dark. But I can see, just barely, the rectangular shape of the luggage. Somewhere in here is a very dim source of light.

I hunt for it, trying to find a place where the shadows seem lighter. I'm hopelessly lost in the maze of cars now. We could spend all night wandering through these rows of abandoned cars and not find anything.

We take two more turns, each turn lightening the shadows almost imperceptibly. If I wasn't looking for it, I would never have noticed.

The light, when I see it, is so dim that I probably would have missed it if the building wasn't so dark. It's a thin crack of light outlining a door. I put my ear to it but hear nothing.

I open it a crack. It opens onto a stairwell's landing. A dim light beckons below.

I close the door behind us as quietly as I can and head downstairs. I'm grateful the stairs are cement rather than the metal kind that make hollow, echoing clangs underfoot.

At the bottom of the stairs is another closed door. This door is outlined in bright slivers of light, the only light in the stairwell. I put my ear to the door. Someone is talking.

I can't hear what's being said, but I can tell there are at least two people. We wait, crouched in the dark with our ears to the door, hoping there's another door through which these people will leave.

The voices fade away and stop. After listening to the silence for several heartbeats, I crack open the door, cringing in anticipation of noise. The door opens silently.

It is a concrete space the size of a warehouse. The first thing I notice are rows upon rows of glass columns, each large enough to hold a grown man.

Only, what's in these tubes are more like twisted scorpion angels.

36

They may look a little like angels with their gossamer drag-onfly wings folded along the contours of their backs, but they are not. At least, they're not like any angel I've ever seen. Or ever want to.

There's something twisted about them. They float in columns of clear liquid, and I feel like I'm peering into the disembodied womb of an animal that shouldn't exist.

Some of them are the size of large men, bulging with muscles despite the fact that they're curled in the fetal position. Others are smaller as though struggling to survive. A few of them look like they're sucking their thumbs. I find the humanness of that gesture particularly disturbing.

From the front, they look human, but from the back and the sides, they look utterly alien. Plump scorpion tails grow out of their tailbones to curl over their heads. They end in needlelike stingers, ready for piercing. The sight of those tails brings back echoes of my nightmare and I shiver.

Most of them have their wings folded, but a few are partially unfurled, spread along the curve of the columns and twitching like they're dreaming of flying. These are easier to look at than the ones whose scorpion tails are quivering as if they're dreaming of killing.

Their eyes are closed with what look like underdeveloped eyelids. Their heads are hairless and their skin is nearly transparent, showing the network of veins and musculature beneath. Whatever these things are, they're not fully developed.

I block as much of this view as I can from my mother. She will freak if she sees any of this. For once, maybe her reaction is the sane one.

I give her a hand signal to wait for me where she is. I make my face intense so she knows I mean it, but I don't know if it will do any good. I hope she stays. The last thing I need is her freaking out. I never thought I'd be grateful for her paranoia, but I am. There's a decent chance she'll hide in the dark like a rabbit in a hole until I come for her. If something happens, at least she has her cattle prod.

My stomach clenches with icy fear at what I'm about to do. But if Paige is in here, I can't leave her.

I force myself to step into the cavernous room.

Inside, the air feels cold and clinical. There is a formaldehyde-like smell to the air. A scent I associate with long-dead things trapped in jars on a shelf. I step gingerly between the glass columns to get to the rest of the room.

As I walk by the columns, I notice what look like piles of lumpy cloth and seaweed at the bottom of the tanks. A creepy feeling crawls up my back. I quickly look away, not wanting to peer closer.

But when I glance away, I see something that curdles my creepy feeling into terror.

One of the beasts holds a woman in a lover's embrace in its tank. Its tail arches over its head down to the woman, burying its stinger in the back of her neck.

One strap of her party dress has been shoved down her painfully thin shoulder. The scorpion angel's mouth is buried in her sagging breast. Her skin crinkles against her drying flesh as if all the fluids are being drained from it.

Someone has forced an oxygen mask over her mouth and nose. The mask's black tubes reach up to the tank's cap, looking like a twisted umbilical cord. Her dark hair is the only thing moving about her. It floats ethereally around the cords and stinger.

Despite the mask, I recognize her. She is the woman whose children and husband waved good-bye to her from the fence when she came into the aerie. The woman who turned to throw a kiss to her family. She looks like she's aged twenty years since I last saw her a few hours ago. Her face is sallow, her skin sagging over her bones. She's lost weight. A lot of weight.

Below her floating feet lays a discarded pile of brightly colored material and what I now realize is skin over bones. What I initially mistook for seaweed is actually hair waving gently at the bottom of the tank.

This monster is slowly liquefying her insides and drinking them.

My feet won't move. I stand like prey waiting for a predator to grab me. Every instinct I have screams at me to run.

Just when I think it can't get any worse, I see her eyes. They look strained and unnatural in their oversized sockets.

I imagine a spark of desperation and pain in them. I hope she at least died quickly and painlessly, but I doubt it.

As I'm about to turn away, a cluster of small bubbles escapes from her air mask and floats past her hair.

I freeze. She couldn't possibly be alive, could she?

But why would someone put an air mask on her if she was dead?

I wait and watch for any signs of life. The only motion I see is caused by the scorpion as it greedily sucks her dry. Her once-vibrant skin shrivels almost before my eyes. Her hair dances in slow sweeps every time the scorpion moves.

Then, another group of air bubbles float up from her mask.

She's breathing. Extremely, impossibly slow, but still breathing.

I tear my eyes away from her and force myself to scan the room for something I can use to get her out of this tank. Now I can see other tanks here and there that have people trapped in them too. They are all in different stages of the deadly embrace with some still looking vital and fresh, while others look drained and close to empty.

One of the scorpions has a fresh woman in a party dress in its arms and is kissing her on the mouth with her oxygen mask dangling above her. Another has a man in a hotel uniform. His scorpion beast has its mouth latched onto his eye.

It's not a systematic feeding. Some tanks have a large pile at the bottom while others have very little. It shows in the various scorpion angels too. Some are large and muscular while others are puny and malformed.

As I stand there feeling stunned and ill, a door opens on the far side of the basement and I hear something rolling on the concrete.

My instinct is to hide behind a monster's tank, but I can't force myself to get close to one. So I stand in the middle of the glass column matrix, trying to decipher what is happening on the other side. Trying to see the room through the glass columns is like trying to read a note on the other side of a shark tank. Everything looks distorted and unrecognizable.

If I can't see the angels, they shouldn't be able to see me. I sneak around one of the columns and get a different perspective on the room. I steel myself to ignore the victims. I'll be no use to anyone if I'm caught.

On the other side of the matrix, an angel is berating a human servant. 'The drawers were supposed to arrive last week.' He wears a white lab coat draped over his wings.

The human stands behind an enormous steel cabinet balanced on top of a flatbed cart. It's three drawers high with each drawer large enough to hold a person. I don't want to think about what is meant to go into them.

'You picked the worst night to deliver these.' The angel vaguely waves his hand toward the far wall. 'Stack them over there against the wall. They need to be secured so they never tip over. The bodies are over there.' He points to the adjacent wall. 'I've had to pile them on the floor, thanks to your tardiness. You can put the bodies in the drawers when you're done setting up.'

The servant looks horrified but the lab angel doesn't seem to notice. The man moves to the far wall with the cabinet, while the angel walks the other way.

'The most interesting night in centuries and this idiot has to pick tonight of all nights to deliver furniture.' The lab angel mumbles to himself as he heads for the wall to my left.

I shift to stay hidden from the angel as he moves. He shoves through a pair of swinging doors and disappears.

I inch forward, looking around to see if there's anyone else in the room. There's no one other than the man unloading his cadaver drawers. I wonder if I should expose myself to him and beg for assistance. It could save a lot of time and trouble if I could get someone on the inside to help me.

On the other hand, he might decide he could earn brownie points by turning in an intruder. Frozen in indecision, I watch him roll his empty cart out through a set of double doors across the room.

After he leaves, the empty room gurgles with the sound of air bubbles from one of the tanks. My brain screams again – *hurry, hurry, hurry.* I have to find Paige before the resistance attacks.

But I can't leave these people to be sucked dry by these monsters.

I sneak through the matrix of fetal columns to look for something to try to get the victims out of the tanks. At the far end of the matrix, I see a blue ladder. Perfect. I can open the tops of the tanks and try to pull the victims out.

I slide my sword back into its scabbard to free my hands. As I run to the ladder, a new mass of colors appears and starts growing to my right. The columns of fluids distort the image, giving the impression of a blob of flesh with a hundred hands and feet, with grossly distorted faces dotted all around the mass.

I edge forward cautiously. A trick of the light makes the dancing distortions look like a hundred eyes following me.

Then I step out of the column matrix and see it for what it really is.

My chest constricts and I stop breathing for a few beats. My feet stick to the floor and I just stand there in the open, staring.

37

At first, my brain refuses to believe what my eyes see. My brain tries to interpret the scene as a wall of discarded dolls. Mere cloth and plastic, created by a toymaker with severe anger issues. But I can't convince myself of the illusion and I'm forced to see it for what it is.

Against the white wall are stacks and stacks of children.

Some stand stiffly against the wall and on each other, half a dozen deep. Some sit propped up against the wall and against the legs of the other children. And some lie on their backs and stomachs, stacked on top of each other like cords of wood.

They range from toddler size to about ten or twelve years old. They are all naked, stripped of anything that might protect them. All have distinctive autopsy stitch marks in a Y shape starting at their little chests and going down to their groins.

Most of them have additional stitch marks along their arms, legs, and throats. A few have stitches across their faces. Some of the kids' eyes are wide open, others closed. Some of their eyes have yellow or red instead of white around the irises. Some only have gaping holes where the eyes used to be, and others have their eyes sewn shut with big, clumsy stitches.

I almost lose the ongoing battle with my stomach, and all that rich food I ate earlier comes up in my throat. I have to swallow hard to keep it in. My breath feels too hot, and the air feels too cold on my prickling skin.

I want to – need to – close my eyes, to blot out what they see. But I can't. I'm searching. Scanning every brutalized child for my little sister's pixie face. I start shaking all over and I can't seem to stop.

'Paige.' My voice comes out in a broken whisper.

I can barely breathe her name, but I say it over and over as though that will somehow make it all right. I drift toward the pile of mangled corpses like a dreamer in a nightmare, unable to stop myself and unable to look away.

Please don't let her be here. Please, please. Anything but that.

'Paige?' There is horror in my voice as well as a thread of hope that maybe she's not here.

Something stirs in the pile of stitched flesh.

I take a shaky step back, all the strength seeping out of my legs.

A little boy rolls off the top of a pile and lands facedown.

Two bodies below his original position, a small hand reaches out blindly and braces itself awkwardly on the fallen boy's shoulder. The bodies above the hand rock back and forth, gaining momentum until they tumble on top of the fallen boy.

I can finally see the child that belongs to the fumbling hand. It's a small girl with disproportionately skinny legs. A curtain of brown hair hides the girl's face as she crawls painfully toward me.

She has a cruel cut above her bottom that intersects with another one sliding up her spine. Large, uneven stitches run up her spine, holding her bruised and slashed flesh together. Stitches run up both arms and down both legs. The red and blue of her cuts and bruises contrast sharply with her corpse-white skin.

I am frozen in my horror, aching to shut my eyes and pretend this is not real. But I'm incapable of anything but watching the girl's painful progress across the pile of bodies. She pulls herself forward by her arms, her legs a pair of deadweights dragging behind her.

After an eternity, the girl finally lifts her head. The stringy hair slides back from her face.

And there is my little sister.

Her tormented eyes find mine. Huge for her pixie face. Filling with tears as she sees me.

I crash to my knees, hardly feeling the slam of the concrete.

My baby sister's face has stitches running from her ears to her lips as though someone had peeled back the upper part of her face and then put it back together again. Her whole face is swollen and bruised in angry colors.

'Paige.' My voice cracks.

I crawl to her and take her in my arms. She is as cold as the concrete floor.

She curls into my arms like she used to when she was a toddler. I try to hold all of her on my lap even though she's too big for that now. Even her breath on my cheek is as cold as an arctic breeze. I have a crazy thought that maybe they drained all the blood out of her so she can never be warm again.

My tears drip down her cheeks, mixing our anguish together.

38

'Touching,' says a clinical voice behind me.

The angel walks toward us with an expression so detached that nothing human can be detected behind it. It's the kind of look a shark might give to a pair of crying girls. 'This is the first time one of you has broken in instead of trying to break out.'

Behind him, the delivery guy pushes through the double doors with another load of metal drawers. His expression is all human. Surprise, concern, fear.

Before I can answer, the angel jerks his gaze up toward the ceiling and cocks his head. He reminds me of a dog listening to something far away that only dogs can hear.

I hug my sister's scrawny body closer as if I can protect her from all things monstrous. It's all I can do keep my voice working, if not steady. 'Why would you do this?' I force out in a whisper.

Behind the angel, the delivery guy shakes his head at me in warning. He looks like he wants to shrink behind his cadaver drawers.

'I don't need to explain anything to a monkey,' says the angel. 'Put the specimen back where it was.'

The specimen?

Rage boils through my veins and my hands tremble with the need to squeeze his throat shut.

Amazingly, I rein it in.

I glare at him, dying to do so much more.

The goal is to get my sister out of here, not to get momentary satisfaction. I lift Paige in my arms and stagger toward him.

'We're leaving.' As soon as the words are out, I know it's wishful thinking.

He puts down his clipboard and steps between us and the door. 'By whose permission?' His voice is low and threatening. Utterly confident.

He suddenly cocks his head again, listening to something I can't hear. A frown mars his smooth skin.

I take two deep breaths, trying to blow the anger and fear out of my body. I gently put Paige down under a table.

Then I launch myself on him.

I hit him with everything I've got. No calculations, no thought, no plan. Just crazed, epic fury.

It isn't much compared to an angel's strength, even one that's a runt. But I have the advantage of surprise.

My blow slams him onto an exam table, and I wonder how his hollow bones don't break.

I whip out the angel sword from its scabbard. Angels are far stronger than men, but they can be vulnerable on the ground. No angel who is any good at flying would work in the basement where there are no windows for him to fly through. There is a good chance this one can't take to the air very quickly.

Before the angel can recover from his fall, I thrust my sword at him, aiming for his neck.

Or I try to.

He's faster than I thought. He grabs my wrist and slams it into the table's edge.

The pain is excruciating. My hand contracts open, letting the sword fly. It clatters across the concrete floor, far from my reach.

He gets up at leisure while I grab a scalpel from a tray. The scalpel feels flimsy and useless. I rate my chances of winning, or even injuring him, slim to none.

That just pisses me off all the more.

I throw my scalpel at him. It nicks his throat, causing blood to bubble out and stain his white coat.

I grab a chair and swing it at him before he recovers.

He tosses it aside as if I had thrown a crumpled ball of paper at him.

Almost before I can realize that he's coming for me, he slams me down on the concrete and starts strangling the life out of me. He's not just choking off my air, he's cutting off the blood to my brain.

Five seconds. That's all I'll have before losing consciousness with no blood flowing to my head.

I shoot my arms up between his like a wedge. Then I slam them out against his forearms.

It should have worked to bust me out of his stranglehold. It always worked during training.

But there isn't even a slight easing of his grip. In my panic, I didn't take into account his super-strength.

In a desperate final attempt, I clench my hands together, fingers interlaced. I draw back and hammer my fists down on the crook of his arm as hard as I can.

His elbow jerks back.

But then it pops right back into place.

Time's up.

Like an amateur, I instinctively claw at his hands. But they might as well be steel clamped around my throat.

My heart pounds thunderously in my ears, getting ever more frantic. My head feels like it's floating away.

The angel's face is cold, indifferent. Dark spots bloom on his face. My heart sinks as I realize my vision is fading.

Blurring.

The edges getting darker.

39

Something slams into the angel. I get a brief impression of hair and teeth, animal growling.

Something warm and wet splashes onto my shirt.

The pressure on my throat is suddenly gone. So is the weight of the angel.

I suck in a huge, burning breath. I curl into a ball, trying not to cough too much as the lovely cool air surges into my lungs.

There is blood on my shirt.

I become aware of wild grunts and growls. There is also the sound of retching.

The delivery man is puking behind his cadaver drawers. Despite that, his eyes keep darting to a spot behind me. His eyes are so wide they look more white than brown. He's staring at the place where the sounds are coming from. The source of all this blood soaking my clothes.

I have a strange reluctance to look even though I know I have to.

When I do look, I have trouble comprehending what I'm seeing. I don't know which sight to be shocked by, and my poor brain thrashes from one to another.

The angel's lab coat is soaked in blood. Around him lie chunks of quivering meat, like bits of liver torn and tossed on the floor.

A chunk of flesh has been ripped out of his cheek.

He's thrashing so much he looks like he's in the throes of a very bad nightmare. Maybe he is. Maybe I am too.

Paige hunches over him. Her little hands grip his shirt to get a better hold on his trembling body. Her hair and clothes are splattered in blood. Her face drips with it.

Her mouth opens, showing rows of shiny teeth. At first, I think that someone has grafted long braces onto her teeth. But they're not braces.

They're razors.

She bites into the angel's throat. Worries it like a dog with a chew toy. Pulls back from the gushing torn flesh.

She spits out a chunk of bloody meat. It lands with a wet thunk on the floor next to the other bits of flesh.

She spits and gags. She is revolted, although it's hard to tell if the revulsion is from her actions or from the taste. An unwanted memory of the way the low demons spat after biting into Raffe barges into my head.

They weren't meant to eat angel flesh. The thought slips through the cracks in my mind and I instantly shove it back.

The delivery guy retches again, and my stomach churns, wanting to join him. Paige opens her mouth again in animal ferocity, ready to dive back into the quivering flesh.

'Paige!' My voice comes out thin and panicked, the end rising as though in question.

The girl who used to be my sister stops midway down to the dying angel and looks at me.

Her eyes are the wide baby brown of innocence. Drops of blood hang suspended from her long lashes. She looks at me, attentive and docile as she's always been. There is no pride in her expression, no viciousness, no horror at her actions. She looks up at me as though I have called her name while she is eating a bowl of cereal.

My throat is raw from the strangling, and I keep swallowing back a cough, which is handy because I need to swallow back my dinner too. The puking sounds the delivery guy makes aren't helping.

Paige unfolds away from the angel. She stands up on her own feet, without leaning against anything.

Then she takes two graceful, miraculous steps toward me.

She stops, as though remembering she was crippled.

I don't dare to breathe. I stare at her, resisting the urge to run up and catch her in case she falls.

She spreads her arms out toward me in a pick-me-up gesture, the way she used to when she was a toddler. If not for the blood dripping down her face and streaking her stitched-up body, I would think her expression as sweet and innocent as it's always been.

'Ryn-Ryn.' Her voice is on the verge of tears. It's the sound of a frightened little girl, one who's sure her big sister can make the monsters under her bed go away. Paige hasn't called me Ryn-Ryn since she was a baby.

I look at the angry stitches crisscrossing her face and body. I stare at her bruises – red and blue all over her battered skin.

It's not her fault. Whatever they did to her, she's the victim, not the monster.

Where have I heard that before?

The thought triggers an image of those chewed-up girls hanging on the tree. Had that crazy couple said something similar? Is their mad conversation starting to make sense to me?

Another thought sneaks into my head like poisoned gas. If Paige could only eat human flesh and nothing else, what would I do? Would I go so far as to use human bait to lure her, thinking I could help her?

Too horrifying to even think about.

And totally irrelevant.

Because there's no reason to think Paige has to eat anything. Paige is not a low demon. She's a little girl. A vegetarian. A born humanitarian. A budding Dalai Lama, for chrissake. She only attacked the angel to defend me. That's all.

Besides, she didn't eat him, she just . . . gnawed on him a little.

The chunks of flesh quiver on the floor. My stomach roils.

Paige watches me with her warm brown eyes fringed with doe-like lashes. I concentrate on that and purposely ignore the blood dripping from her chin and the big, cruel stitches running from her lips to her ears.

Behind her, the angel convulses in earnest. His eyes roll, leaving them pure white, and his head bangs repeatedly on the concrete floor. He is having a seizure. I wonder if he can live with chunks of flesh missing and most of his blood on the floor. His body is probably frantically repairing itself even now. Is there a chance that this monster could recover from this?

I push myself up, trying to ignore the slimy fluids under my hands. My throat burns and I feel stiff and bruised all over.

'Ryn-Ryn.' Paige still has her arms up in a forlorn gesture, but I can't quite bring myself to go hug her. Instead, I lurch over to the angel sword and grab it. I walk back a little more smoothly, getting used to my body again.

I look at the angel's blank eyes, his bleeding mouth. His head trembles, tapping against the floor.

I slam the blade into his heart.

I've never killed anyone before. What frightens me isn't that I'm killing someone. What frightens me is how easy it is.

The blade cuts through him as though he is nothing but a rotten piece of fruit. I feel no sympathetic sensation of a soul or a life essence leaving. There is no guilt or shock or grief at the life that was and the person I have become. There is only the stilling of the trembling flesh and the slow exhalation of his last breath.

'Great Lord in Heaven.'

I look up, startled, at the new voice. It's another angel in a lab coat. I get a quick impression of fresh blood soaking his white coat and gloved hands before two more angels push through the door behind him. Both of the new ones also have blood on their coats and gloves.

I almost don't recognize Laylah with her golden hair pulled back in a tight bun. What is she doing here? Isn't she supposed to be performing surgery on Raffe?

They all stare at me. I wonder why they would be staring at me rather than at my blood-splattered sister until I realize that I still have my sword stuck into the lab angel. I'm sure they have no trouble recognizing the sword for what it is. There have to be at least a dozen rules against humans having an angel sword.

My brain frantically searches for a way out of this alive. But before any of them can start making accusations, they all look up at the ceiling at the same time. Like the lab angel, they hear something I don't. The nervous looks on their faces don't reassure me.

Then I feel it too. First, a rumbling, then a trembling.

Has it been an hour already?

The angels look toward me again, then turn and bolt toward the double doors that the delivery guy used.

I didn't realize I could feel even more unnerved than I was already.

The Resistance has started their attack.

40

We need to get out before the hotel comes crashing down. But I can't just let these people get sucked dry by the scorpion angels. Dragging the ladder to each tank and slowly pulling out each paralyzed person could take hours.

I pull my sword out of the lab angel. I run over to the fetal columns in frustration, holding the sword like a bat.

I swing the blade into one of the scorpion tanks. It's mostly to let out my frustration and I don't expect it to do anything other than bounce off.

Before I can even register the impact, the thick tank shatters. Fluid and glass explode onto the concrete floor.

I could get used to this sword.

The scorpion fetus unlatches from its victim. It screeches as it falls. Then it flops and writhes on the glass shards, bleeding all over them. The emaciated woman crumples to the bottom of the broken tank. Her glassy eyes stare into the air.

I have no idea if she's alive, or if she'll be in better shape once the venom wears off. This is the best I can do for her. The best I can do for any of them. All I can hope is that somehow, some of them will recover enough to get away from here before things become too explosive, because I can't drag them up the stairs.

I run over to the other tanks that are holding victims and smash them, one after another. Shards of water and glass spray all over the basement lab. The air fills with the screeching of thrashing scorpion fetuses.

Most of the monsters in the surrounding tanks wake and twitch. A few react violently and slam against their glass prisons. They are the ones that are more fully formed, staring at me through the veined membranes of their eyelids with the understanding that I am preying upon them.

While I'm doing this, a tiny part of me considers running without Paige. She's not really my sister anymore, is she? She's certainly not helpless any longer.

'Ryn-Ryn?' Paige is crying.

She calls to me as if unsure whether I would take care of her. My heart constricts like an iron hand is squeezing it as punishment for thinking of betraying her.

'Yeah, sweetie,' I say in my most reassuring voice. 'We have to get out of here. Okay?'

The building shakes again and one of the stitched-up corpses topples. The little boy's mouth opens when his head hits the floor, revealing metal teeth.

Paige looked that dead before she started moving. Is there any chance this kid could be alive too?

A weird thought pops into my head. Didn't Raffe say that sometimes, names have power?

Did Paige wake up because I called her? I scan the bodies leaning against the wall, noting their shiny teeth and long nails, their discolored eyes. If they're alive, would I wake them if I could?

I turn away and smash my blade into another tank. I can't help but be glad I don't know the kids' names.

'Paige?' My mother walks over to us as though in a dream. She crunches over broken glass and weaves to avoid the thrashing monsters as if she sees this kind of thing regularly. Maybe she does. Maybe in her world, this is normal. She sees them and avoids them, but she's not surprised by them. Her eyes are clear, her expression cautious.

'Baby?' She runs over to Paige and hugs her with no hesitation despite the blood and gore covering her.

My mother cries in big, anguished sobs. For the first time, I realize that she's been at least as worried and upset over Paige as I have. That it was no accident that she ended up here, the same dangerous place that I trekked to find Paige. That even though her love often manifests itself in ways that a mentally healthy person couldn't understand – might even declare abusive – that doesn't diminish the fact that she does care.

I swallow the tears that threaten to drown me as I watch my mother fuss over Paige.

Mom takes a good look at Paige. The blood. The stitches. The bruises. She doesn't remark on any of them but does make shocked and cooing noises as she strokes Paige's hair and skin.

Then she looks at me. In her eyes is a hard accusation. She blames me for what's happened to Paige. I want to tell her I didn't do this to her. How could she think that?

But I don't say anything. I can't. I can only look back at my mother with guilt and remorse. I look at her the way she looked at me when Dad and I found Paige broken and crippled all those years ago. I may not have held the knife to Paige, but this terrible thing happened on my watch.

For the first time, I wonder if my mother really was responsible for Paige's broken back.

'We have to get out of here,' says Mom with her arm protectively around Paige. Her voice is clear and full of purpose.

I look up at her in surprise. Before I can stop myself, hope blooms inside me. She sounds full of authority and confidence. She sounds like a mother ready and determined to lead her daughters to safety.

She sounds sane.

Then she says, 'They're after us.'

Hope shrivels and dies inside me, leaving a hard lump where my heart should be. I don't need to ask who 'they' are. According to my mother, 'they' have been after us for as long as I can remember. Her protective statement is not a step toward taking responsibility for her girls.

I nod, taking the weight of my family responsibilities back on my shoulders.

41

Mom is guiding Paige toward the exit when a loud crash from behind the double doors stops them in their tracks. It comes from the room the angels came out of. I pause midswing, wondering whether to check it out.

I can't think of a good reason to waste time looking through those doors, but something bothers me. It snags on my brain like a needle picking a weave, trying to unravel it to see something beneath. So much has been happening I haven't had time to follow up on a thought – something that might be important, something . . .

The blood.

The angels had blood all over their gloved hands and their white smocks.

And Laylah. She was supposed to be in surgery with Raffe.

Another crash comes through the doors. Metal on metal like a cart tipping over and crashing into another.

I'm running before I know it.

As I near the double doors, a body crashes through it. I only have a second to recognize Raffe hurtling through the air.

A giant of an angel slams through the doors after him.

Something about the way he moves seems familiar. His face might have been handsome once, but now his vicious expression dominates.

He has beautiful snowy wings spread out behind him. The bases of his wings are covered in dried blood where fresh stitches hold them onto his back. Oddly, though there is blood on his back, it's his stomach that's bandaged.

There's something familiar about those wings.

One of them has a notch on it where scissors have sliced through the feathers. A notch exactly like the one I cut on Raffe's wings.

My brain tries to reject the obvious conclusion.

The giant angel stands between my family and the door we came through. My mom stands frozen in terror as she stares at him. Her cattle prod shakes in her hand as she holds it out toward the giant. It looks almost more like an offering than a defense.

A low bang rumbles through the ceiling, closely followed by another, then another. Each bang gets louder. This must be what the angels were hearing. Now there's no doubt in my mind that the attacks have started.

I frantically wave at my mother to go through the doors the delivery guy used. She finally gets it and scampers off through the doors with Paige.

I'm terrified the giant will stop them, but he doesn't pay them any attention. He reserves all his attention for Raffe.

Raffe lies on the floor, his face and muscles contorted with pain. His back arches to try to keep from touching the concrete floor. Below him, spread out like a dark cape on the floor, is a pair of giant bat wings.

It looks like a film of leather stretched out over a skeletal structure that's more like a deadly weapon than a frame for wings. The wing edges are razor-sharp with a series of ever-growing hooks, the smallest of which resemble barbed fish-hooks. The largest hooks are at the wing tips. They remind me of sharp scythes.

Raffe's back drips with fresh blood as he turns around painfully and pushes himself up off the floor. His new wings droop over him as he moves, as if they are not yet under his control. He shoves one behind him the way I might shove my hair out of my face. His arm comes back bloodied with fresh slices on his forearm and a gash where one of the hooks catches his flesh.

'Careful with that, archangel,' says the giant as he stalks toward Raffe. The word 'archangel' is steeped with venom.

I recognize his voice. It is the voice of the Night Angel who cut off Raffe's wings the night we met. He walks past me without looking, as though I am a piece of furniture.

'What games are you playing, Beliel? Why not just kill me on the operating table? Why bother to sew these things onto me?' Raffe weaves a little on his feet. They must have just finished the operation, moments before the doctor angels left.

By the look of the dried blood on the giant's back, it doesn't take a genius to tell they worked on him first. He's had more time to recover than Raffe, although I'm willing to bet he's nowhere near full strength yet.

I lift my sword, trying to be as discreet as I can.

'Killing you would have been my choice,' says Beliel. 'But all those petty angel politics. You remember what that's like.'

'Been a long time.' Raffe sways on his feet.

'And it'll be longer still, now that you have those wings.' Beliel grins, but his expression still manages to be cruel. 'Women and children will run screaming from you now. And so will angels.'

He turns toward the exit, stroking his new feathers. 'Run along now while I show off my new acquisition. No one below has feathers. I'll be the envy of Hell.'

Putting his head down like a bull, Raffe charges Beliel.

With all that blood loss, I'm surprised Raffe can walk, much less run. He weaves a little as he rushes Beliel, who catches him under one massive arm and shoves him into a cart.

Raffe goes crashing down along with the cart. Vivid red slices appear on his cheek, neck, and arms as his uncontrolled wings flop around during his fall.

I run over to Raffe and hand him his sword.

A look of uncertainty crosses Beliel face, and his motions suddenly become cautious.

As soon as I let go of the hilt in Raffe's hand, the sword's tip hits the floor like a ton of lead.

Raffe holds the sword like it takes every ounce of strength for him to keep the hilt from hitting the floor as well. It's been as light as air in my hands.

Raffe looks like someone just broke his heart.

He looks at his sword in bewilderment and betrayal. He tries to lift it again but can't. Disbelief and hurt mix in his expression. This is the most emotional I've seen him, and seeing him like this makes me want to hurt something.

Beliel is the first of us to recover from the shock of seeing Raffe struggle to lift his blade. 'Your own blade rejects you. It senses my wings. You're no longer just Raphael.'

He chuckles, a dark sound that's made all the more disturbing by the undercurrent of genuine mirth. 'How sad. A leader bereft of followers. An angel with severed wings. A warrior without a sword.' Beliel circles Raffe like a shark as he taunts him. 'You have nothing left.'

'He has me,' I say. Out of the corner of my eye, I see Raffe wince.

Beliel looks at me, really seeing me for the first time. 'You've acquired a pet, archangel. When did this happen?' There's puzzlement in his voice, as if it's normal for Beliel to know of Raffe's companions.

'I'm not anyone's pet.'

'I met her tonight at the aerie,' says Raffe. 'She's been following me around. She means nothing.'

Beliel snorts. 'Funny, I didn't ask if she meant anything to you.' He looks me up and down, taking in every detail. 'Scrawny. But serviceable.' He saunters toward me.

Raffe hands the sword hilt back to me. 'Run.'

I hesitate, wondering how much of a beating Raffe can take in his state.

'Run!' Raffe positions himself between me and Beliel.

I run. I hide behind a fetal column to watch.

'Making friends, are we?' asks Beliel. 'And with a Daughter of Man. How deliciously ironic. When will the surprises end?' He actually sounds delighted. 'Pretty soon, you'll end up being a full-fledged member of my clan. I always knew you would. You'd make an excellent archdemon.' His smile dries up. 'Too bad I don't care to have you as my boss.'

He grabs Raffe in a bear hug but quickly lets go. His arms and chest bleed from fresh cuts. Raffe is apparently not the only one who is unused to his new wings.

This time he grabs Raffe by the neck, lifting him off the floor. Raffe's face turns red, veins popping on his temples as Beliel crushes his throat.

A loud boom shakes the building above us. Concrete debris crashes through the door to the garage. Several of the remaining glass columns crack, causing the monstrous occupants to gyrate in agitation.

I run toward Beliel.

The sword feels solid and well-balanced in my hands. I swing back the sword and get yet another shock.

The sword adjusts itself.

I could swear it tweaks its angle to raise my elbows higher. It's ready for battle and thirsty for blood. I blink in surprise, almost missing my timing. But I don't, because though my feet are frozen in shock, my arm moves in a smooth arc, led by the sword.

I'm not wielding the sword. It is wielding me.

I swing the sword at the same time Raffe whips his deadly wings at Beliel. My sword slices through the meat of his back, wedging in his spine.

Raffe's wings shred the demon's cheeks and lay open his forearms. He screams, letting go of Raffe's throat.

Raffe crumples to the floor, gasping for breath.

Beliel staggers away from us. Maybe if he hadn't just been through surgery, he would have been strong enough to withstand us both. Or maybe not. The bandages around his middle must be from the sword wound Raffe gave him a few days ago during their last fight. Beliel's wounds won't be healing anytime soon if Raffe is right about angel swords.

My blade swings back again, clearly wanting me to attack him again. Beliel stares at me with bewildered eyes, no less surprised than the angels who saw me kill their coworker. An angel sword isn't supposed to be in the hands of a human girl. It just isn't done.

Raffe springs up and charges Beliel.

I watch in awe as Raffe pummels Beliel with blows so fast they're almost a blur. The force of the emotion behind those blows is immense. For the first time, he doesn't bother to hide his frustration and anger, or his longing for the wings he has lost.

As Beliel staggers from the blows, Raffe grabs his old wing and pulls. Stitches begin popping out of Beliel's back, fresh blood staining the once-snowy wings. Raffe seems determined to get his wings back even if he has to rip them out of Beliel's flesh, stitch by stitch.

I grip Raffe's sword. I guess it's my sword now. If the sword rejects him as long as he has his new wings, then I'm the only one who can use it.

I move toward Raffe and Beliel, ready to slice the wings off.

Something grabs my ankle and pulls from behind. Something slimy with an iron grip.

My feet slip on the wet floor and I slam down onto the concrete. The sword skitters out of my hand. My lungs spasm so hard at the impact that I think I'll black out.

I manage to turn my head to see what has a hold of me.

I wish I hadn't.

42

Behind me, a well-muscled scorpion fetus opens its jaws to scream at me, revealing rows of piranha teeth.

Its undeveloped skin shows its veins and the shadows of muscles. It lies on its belly as if it crawled all the way from its shattered tank to get to me.

Its deadly stinger shoots up and over its back, aiming for my face.

An image of Paige and my mother running through the night flashes through my head. Alone. Terrified. Wondering if I've abandoned them.

'No!' The scream is torn from me as I twist unnaturally to avoid the onrushing barb. The tip narrowly misses my face.

Before I can even take a breath, the tip whips up and jabs down again. This time, I don't even have time to brace myself as it darts down toward me.

'No!' Raffe roars.

My body jerks as the stinger punctures my neck.

It feels like an impossibly long needle digging its way through my flesh.

Then the real pain starts.

A burning agony spreads across the side of my neck. It feels like I'm being shredded from the inside out. My breath comes in harsh gasps and my skin breaks out in a sweat.

A tormented scream bursts from my throat and my legs pump in frantic kicks.

None of that stops the scorpion fetus from coming for me. Its mouth opens as it nears, poised to give me its deadly kiss.

Our eyes meet as it pulls me to it. I can tell that it thinks sucking me dry will give it enough energy to survive outside its artificial womb. Its desperation shows in its grip, in the way it opens and shuts its mouth like a fish trying to breathe, in the way it squeezes its veined eyelids shut as if the harsh light is too much for its underdeveloped eyes.

Its venom spreads a swath of torment across my face and down my chest. I try to shove the scorpion angel away, but all I can do is feebly nudge at it.

My muscles are beginning to freeze.

The stinger suddenly rips out of my neck. It feels barbed, like it's pulling my neck inside out.

Another scream rips through me but I can't release it. My mouth only opens a crack. The muscles in my face just twitch instead of contorting in agony. My scream sounds like a weak gurgle.

I can't move my face.

Raffe whips the tail in his hands and drags the abomination off me. He is roaring, and I realize he has been screaming all this time.

He grabs the scorpion fetus, swings it like a bat, and hurls it into the scorpion tanks.

Three columns shatter as it crashes through them, one after another. The room fills with the dying screeches of aborted monsters.

Raffe crashes to his knees beside me. He looks stunned. And oddly shaken. He stares at me as if he can't believe what he sees. As if he refuses to believe what he sees.

Do I look that bad?

Am I dying?

I try to touch my neck to see how much blood is flowing, but I can't get my arm to move all the way up there. I watch it come up a third of the way, trembling with effort, then fall limp. He looks stricken when he sees my feeble attempt to move.

I try to tell him that the stinger venom paralyses and slows down breathing, but what comes out of my mouth is a mumbling that even I can't understand. My tongue feels enormous and my lips too swollen to move. None of the other victims looked swollen, so I assume I don't either, but it feels that way. Like my tongue has suddenly become large and clumsy, too heavy to move.

'Shh,' he says gently. 'I'm here.'

He pulls me into his arms and I try to concentrate on feeling his warmth. Inside, I feel like I'm trembling with the pain but outside, I'm utterly still as the paralysis spreads down my back and legs. It takes all my willpower to keep my head from drooping on his arm.

The look on his face scares me as much as the paralysis. For the first time, his face is completely unshuttered. As if it just doesn't matter anymore what I see.

Shock and grief line his face. I try to wrap my head around the fact that he is grieving. For me.

'You don't even like me, remember?' That's what I try to say. What actually comes out of my mouth is closer to a baby's first attempt at babbling.

'Shh.' He runs his fingertips along my cheek, caressing my face. 'Hush. I'm right here.' He looks at me with deep anguish in his eyes. Like there's so much he wants to tell me but feels it's too late now.

I want to stroke his face and tell him that it will be okay. That everything will be all right.

And I wish so badly that it would be.

43

'Shh,' says Raffe, rocking me in his arms.

The light around Raffe's head falls into shadow.

Behind him, Beliel's dark form rises into my field of view.

One of his new wings is mostly torn off and dangling by a few stitches. His face is contorted in rage as he lifts what looks like a refrigerator over Raffe's head the way Cain must have hefted a boulder over Abel's head.

I try to cry out. I try to warn Raffe with my expression.

But only a whispery exhale comes out.

'Beliel!'

Beliel swings to see who yells at him. Raffe also swivels to take in the scene, still holding me protectively in his arms.

Standing in the doorway is the Politician. I recognize him even without the terrified trophy women following in his wake.

'Put that down, *now*!' The Politician's friendly face is marred by a frown as he stares down the giant angel.

Beliel breathes heavily with the refrigerator hefted above him. It's not clear whether he'll comply.

'You had your chance to kill him out on the streets,' says the Politician as he marches into the room. 'But you got distracted by a pair of pretty wings, didn't you? And now that he's been seen and rumors are running wild that he's back, now you want to kill him? What is wrong with you?'

Beliel hurls the refrigerator across the room. He looks like he'd like to throw it at the Politician. It lands with a crash out of sight.

'He attacked me!' Beliel stabs his finger at Raffe like a crazed infant on steroids.

'I don't care if he poured acid down your pants. I told you not to touch him. If he dies now, his men will turn him into a martyr. Do you have any idea how hard it is to campaign against an angelic martyr? They'd forever be making up stories of how he would have opposed this policy or that.'

'What do I care about your angel politics?'

'You care because I tell you to care.' The Politician straightens his cuffs. 'Oh, why do I bother? You'll never amount to more than just a mid-demon. You just don't have the faculty to comprehend political strategy.'

'Oh, I comprehend it, Uriel.' Beliel curls his lip like a growling dog. 'You've turned him into a pariah. Everything he ever believed in, everything he ever said will be the ravings of a demon-winged fallen angel. I get it more than you'll ever understand. I've lived through it, remember? I just don't care that it gives you an advantage.'

Uriel faces off with Beliel even though he has to look up to glare at him. 'Just do as I say. You got your wings as payment for your services. Now get out.'

The building shakes as something explodes above.

The last ounce of will drains out of me, and I just can't keep my head up any longer. I wilt in Raffe's arms. My head dangles, my eyes are open but unfocused, my breathing imperceptible.

Just like a dead body.

'NO!' Raffe grips me as if he can bind my soul to my body.

An upside-down view of the doorway shows up in my field of vision. Smoke wafts through it.

Although the pain obscures Raffe's warmth, I feel the pressure of his hug, the rocking of our bodies back and forth as he repeats the word, 'No.'

His embrace comforts me and the fear ebbs a little.

'What is that he's mourning over?' asks Uriel.

'His Daughter of Man,' says Beliel. 'One of your Franken-pets killed her.'

'No.' Uriel sounds delightfully scandalized. 'Could it be? A human? After all his warnings to stay away from them? After all his crusading against their evil hybrid spawn?'

Uriel circles Raffe like a shark. 'Look at you, Raffe. The great archangel, on his knees with a pair of demon wings puddled around him. And holding a broken Daughter of Man in his arms?' He chuckles. 'Oh, God does love me after all. What happened, Raffe? Did life on Earth get too lonely for you? Century after century, with no companions but for the Nephilim you so nobly hunted?'

Raffe ignores him and continues to stroke my hair and rock back and forth gently as if putting a child to sleep.

'How long did you resist?' asks Uriel. 'Did you push her away? Did you tell her she meant no more to you than any other animal? Oh, Raffe, did she die thinking you didn't care about her? How *tragic*. That must just tear you to pieces.'

Raffe looks up with murder in his eyes. 'Don't. Talk. About. Her.'

Uriel takes an involuntary step back.

The building rocks again. Dust falls over the dying scorpions. Raffe lets me go, putting me gently on the concrete.

'We're done here,' says Uriel to Beliel. 'You can kill him after he's known as the Fallen Angel Raphael.' His shoulders are stiff with authority, but his feet beat a hasty exit. Beliel follows him with his torn wing dragging in the dust. It's a heartbreaking sight to see Raffe's snowy feathers treated that way.

Raffe takes a moment to tuck my hair out of the way so it won't tug against my head, as if that matters.

Then he takes off running after them. He roars out his rage as he tears through the doors and up the stairs like a cyclone.

Two sets of footsteps pound up the stairs ahead of Raffe's.

A door bangs shut at the top of the stairs.

Blows echo off the door and walls. Something crashes, then clangs down the stairs. Raffe yells his fury and it sounds like he's punching through the walls. He's raging like a mad dog at the end of his tether. What's he tethered to? Why isn't he going after them?

He stomps down the stairs and stands at the doorway breathing heavily. He takes one look at me lying on the cement floor and hurls himself at a scorpion tank.

He practically howls with fury. Glass shatters. Water erupts.

Things flop on the floor and screech as the scorpion monsters are separated from their victims. I can't tell which explosions and screams are from upstairs and which are from Raffe's rampage as he demolishes the lab.

Finally, after there's nothing left to smash, he stands surrounded by rubble, chest heaving, looking around for more things to break.

He kicks broken glass and lab supplies aside and stares down at something. He bends to grab it. Instead of picking it up, he drags it over to me.

It's his sword. He maneuvers me so he can slide it into the scabbard that's still on my back. I expect the weight of the blade to pull against me, but it's barely perceptible as it slides into the scabbard.

Then he picks me up in his arms. The pain has plateaued, but I'm completely paralyzed. My head and arms dangle limply like a fresh corpse's.

He shoves his way out through the door to the stairs and we head up toward the explosions.

44

At first Raffe staggers, always on the verge of collapsing. I can't tell if his stumbling is from recovering from surgery or from the adrenaline crash after his rampage.

The cuts on his neck and ear have already stopped bleeding. He's practically healing before my eyes. He should be getting stronger with every step, but his breathing is labored and uneven.

At one point, he leans against the side of the stairs and pulls me up into an embrace. 'Why didn't you run like I told you?' he whispers against my hair. 'I knew from the start that your loyalty would get you killed. I just never thought it would be your loyalty to me that would do it.'

Another explosion rocks the stairs and we move on.

He steps over the contorted railing that lies on the stairs. It's been torn out of the wall. The walls on both sides are punched and shredded with ragged holes.

We finally reach the top. Raffe leans into the door and we push out onto the ground floor.

It's a war zone.

Everyone who isn't shooting seems to be dodging bullets.

Angels are ripping off their dress coats at one end of the foyer, getting a running start to the front door and leaping into the air as soon as they get outside. But one out of every three comes down again in a bloody heap of feathers, as bullets find their marks. It's a little like shooting angels in a barrel since there's only the one big exit on this side.

Chunks of marble and light fixtures come tumbling down as something explodes.

Dust and debris shower us as the building is riddled with gunshots.

People scatter in every direction. Many of the women run in high heels, slipping and stumbling over broken glass. I swear some of the people who ran one way a minute ago are now running the other way. They have to step over people and angels who are lying limp on the ground.

Raffe is much more noticeable now with his new wings spread out to keep them from shredding us. Even in their panic, everyone stares at us as they run by.

More than a few angels stop and stare, particularly the warrior types. I see the light of recognition and shock in some of their faces. Whatever campaign Uriel is running against Raffe, it's getting a major boost in the polls. Raffe and I are like a demonic campaign poster on legs. I worry about what will happen to him, how he'll be treated if and when we get out of this madness.

I try to look for my family but it's hard to see anything in this chaos when I still can't move my eyes.

A number of angels decide to take their chances at being trapped indoors and run away from the front doors. They're probably headed to the elevator area where they can fly up and out from a higher part of the building. It gives me some satisfaction to see the party literally disintegrating, to see these aliens stripping off their highbrow costumes and running for their lives.

What's left of the front doors blows apart in a blast of shrapnel.

Everything sounds muffled after that. The floor is covered in shattered glass, and several of the people running in robes and bare feet are having a hard time of it.

I want to run to the doors and shout that we're human. Tell them to stop shooting so we can get out of there, just like hostages on TV. But even if I could, there's not a cell in my body that thinks the resistance fighters are going to pause their attack just so we can go free. The days of bending over backward to preserve life for its own sake have been over for weeks. Human life is now the cheapest commodity around, with one exception. Angels lie side by side with humans, like rag dolls strewn about the scene.

We move into the bowels of the building. Everyone gives us a wide berth.

At the elevator lobby, there is a carpet of discarded formal jackets and ripped dress shirts. They must be able to fly better without being bound by clothes, even if those clothes were custom-made for them.

Above us, the air is filled with angels. The majestic spirals of angelic grace are gone, and it's a free-for-all of flapping wings.

Our shattered reflections flow along a wall of broken mirrors, making the scene seem even more chaotic. Raffe, with his demon wings and dead girl in his arms, dominates the lobby as he glides through the pandemonium.

I catch my reflection in the mirror. Although my throat feels torn out, I can hardly see the red mark where the stinger pierced me. I'd assumed there would be bloody strips of flesh from where the stinger erupted, but instead, it looks no worse than a bad bug bite.

Despite the chaos, I start to see a pattern. The angels are generally running in one direction, while the majority of humans head another way. We follow the stream of humans. Like a zipper, the crowd opens up before us.

We push through a swinging door into an enormous kitchen full of stainless steel and industrial appliances. Dark smoke swirls through the air. The walls near the stoves rage with flames.

Smoke stings my throat and makes my eyes water. It's a special kind of torture not to be able to cough and blink. But I take it as a sign that the pain from the stinger must be receding if there's room for me to feel other sensations like smoke irritation.

At the far end of the kitchen, a stream of people shove through a delivery door. Several people move back against the wall, letting us through.

Raffe stays silent. I can't see his expression but the humans look at him as though they are seeing the devil himself.

Another blast rips through the building and the walls shift. People scream behind us in the kitchen. Someone is shouting, 'Get out! Get out! The gas is going to blow!'

We burst through the door into the cool night air.

The screams and explosions are even louder outside as we walk into the combat zone. All my senses fill with the rat-tat-tat of gunfire. The acrid smells of overheated machinery and gun smoke fill my lungs.

Ahead of us, there is a convoy of trucks surrounded by a small crowd of civilians and soldiers. Beyond them, I catch a glimpse of the apocalypse.

Now that the angels have taken to the air, the battle has taken a turn. Soldiers still lob grenades from inside retreating trucks, but the building is already on fire and the grenades only seem to add noise to the mayhem.

They also shoot machine guns at the flying enemies, but in doing so they risk being targeted by them as well. A gang of angels lifts two of the trucks into the air and drops them on top of other trucks that are trying to speed away.

Humans scatter down every alley, both on foot and by car. Angels swoop down seemingly at random and tear apart soldiers and civilians alike.

Raffe does not change his steady pace as he walks away from the building and toward the group of people crowding around the trucks.

What is he doing? The last thing we need is some berserker citizen-soldier strafing us with his machine gun just because he sees something that makes him nervous.

The soldiers seem to have been cramming civilians into the backs of large military trucks. Resistance soldiers in camouflage uniforms kneel in the truck beds with their guns pointed up. They're shooting in the air at circling angels. One of the soldiers has stopped yelling commands and is looking at us. Another truck's headlights sweep over him, giving me a glimpse of his face. It's Obi, the resistance leader.

The shooting and yelling stop the way conversation might stop at a party when you walk in with a police officer. They all freeze and stare at us. Their faces reflect the fire's glow as the kitchen behind us pours flames out the door and windows.

'What the hell is that?' asks one of the soldiers. There is deep fear in his voice. Another soldier crosses himself, completely unaware of the irony of such a gesture from a soldier fighting angels.

A third man lifts his gun and points it at us.

The soldiers in the truck beds, apparently spooked and on hair triggers, swing their machine guns toward us.

'Hold your fire,' says Obi. Another truck's headlights sweep across him and I can see his curiosity fighting his adrenaline. For now, curiosity keeps us alive, but it will only hold the bullets back for so long.

Raffe keeps moving toward them. I want to yell at him to stop, that he's going to get us killed, but of course, I can't. He thinks I'm dead already, and as for his safety, it's as if he doesn't care anymore.

A woman screams in absolute hysterics. Something about it makes me think of my mother.

Then I see the woman who is screaming. Of course, she *is* my mother. Her face glows red in the firelight, showing me the full force of her horror. She screams and screams and looks as if she'll never stop.

I can just imagine what we must look like through her eyes. Raffe's wings are spread out around him like a demonic bat out of Hell. I'm sure the firelight emphasizes the sharp scythes at their edges. Behind him, the building burns with malevolent flames against the smoke-blackened sky, shrouding his face in flickering shadows. I have no doubt that he looms dark and menacing in classic demon form.

My mother doesn't know that he's probably holding the wings that way to avoid slicing us. To her, he must look like the Thing That Hunts Her. And her worst nightmare has come true tonight. Here is the devil, walking out of flames, carrying her dead daughter in its arms.

She must have recognized me by my clothes for her to start screaming so soon. Or maybe she's imagined this scene so many times that she just has no doubt that it must be me in this demon's arms. Her horror is so genuine and so deep that I cringe inside to hear it.

A soldier twitches with his gun aimed at us. I don't know how long they'll restrain themselves. I realize that if they shoot, I won't even be able to shut my eyes.

Raffe kneels down and places me on the asphalt. He lifts my hair to one side and lets it run through his fingers as it slowly cascades over my shoulder.

His head is haloed in firelight above me, his face in shadow. He runs his fingers across my lips in a slow, gentle touch.

Then he pulls away stiffly as if every muscle is fighting him.

I want to beg him not to leave. Tell him that I'm still here. But I lie frozen. All I can do is watch as he gets up.

And disappears from my view.

Then, there's nothing but the empty sky reflecting the firelight.

45

Somewhere in the city, a dog howls. The hollow sound should have been lost in the clamor of the battle, drowned in my fear and pain. Instead, my mind draws it out until it eclipses everything else.

As I lie paralyzed on the cold pavement, all I can think is that it's the loneliest sound I've ever heard.

My mother rushes toward me, still screaming. She throws herself on me, sobbing hysterically. She thinks I am dead, but she is still afraid. Afraid for my soul. After all, she just saw a demon deliver my dead body.

Around us, people burst into frightened conversation.

'What the hell was that?'

'Is she dead?'

'Did he kill her?'

'You should have shot it!'

'I didn't know if she was dead.'

'Did we just see the devil?'

'What the hell was he doing?'

He was delivering my body to my people.

He could have been shot. He could have been attacked by other angels. If I was actually dead, he should have left me in the basement to be buried in rubble. He should have chased after Beliel and taken his wings back. He should have thwarted Uriel and avoided being seen by the other angels.

Instead, he delivered me to my family.

'It's her. Penryn.' Dee-Dum comes into my line of sight. He's smudged with soot, looking exhausted and sad.

Obi comes into view. He looks down at me solemnly for a moment.

'Let's go,' Obi says wearily. 'Move it!' he yells to the group. 'Let's get these people out of here!'

People shuffle past me onto the trucks. They all stare down at me as they walk by.

My mother grips me tighter and continues sobbing. 'Please, help me get her on the truck,' she wails.

Obi stops and gives her a sympathetic look. 'I'm sorry about your daughter, ma'am. But I'm afraid there isn't room for . . . I'm afraid you'll have to leave her.' He turns and calls to his soldiers, 'Someone help this lady onto a truck.'

A soldier comes and pries her away from me.

'No!' She screams and wails and twists in the soldier's arms.

Just when it looks like the soldier is about to give up and let her go, I feel myself being lifted. Someone is carrying me. My head lolls back and I get a glimpse of who holds me.

It's little Paige.

From my angle, I can see the crude stitches along her jawline leading up to her ear. Mom's cheery yellow sweater lies askew along the stitches on her throat and shoulder. I've carried her like this a thousand times. I never thought we would switch places one day. She walks at a normal pace rather than staggering the way she should with my weight.

The crowd goes quiet. Everyone stares at us.

She places me onto a truck bed without anyone's help. The soldier standing in the bed grips his rifle in the ready position and backs away from us. The people who are already on the truck back up into each other like animals herding together.

I hear Paige grunting as she climbs into the truck. No one helps her. She bends over to pick me up again.

She smiles a little when she looks at me, but it turns into a wince once it gets big enough to shift her stitches. I catch a glimpse of raw meat fibers caught in her even rows of razor teeth.

I wish I could close my eyes.

My baby sister places me along a bench on the side of the truck bed. People shift out of our way. My mother comes into view and sits by my head. She props my head on her lap. She is still crying but no longer hysterical. Paige sits by my feet.

Obi must be nearby because everyone on the truck looks past the truck bed as if waiting for a verdict. Will they let me stay?

'Let's get out of here,' says Obi. 'We've already wasted too much time. Get these people on the trucks! Let's go before she blows!'

She? The aerie?

The truck fills with people, but somehow, they manage to leave some space around us so we're not crowded.

Gunshots pop among the shouting. Everybody hangs on, preparing for a rough ride. The truck lurches forward, weaving through dead cars as it speeds away from the aerie.

My head bounces on my mother's thigh as we run over something. A body? The machine-gun popping of bullets shooting into the air never stops. I can only hope that the wild spray of bullets misses Raffe, wherever he is.

Not long after we leave, a large truck crashes into the building in the false dawn of the firelight.

The first floor of the aerie explodes outward in a ball of fire.

Glass and concrete spray in every direction. Through the fire, smoke, and debris, people and angels run and fly from the aerie like scattered insects.

The majestic building teeters as though in shock.

Fire flickers out from the lower windows. My heart constricts, wondering if Raffe stayed out of the aerie. I didn't see where he went after he left me. I can only hope he is safe.

Then, the aerie slowly collapses on itself.

It comes down in a heap, with a puff of dust billowing out in slow motion. The accompanying rumbling sounds like an endless earthquake. Everyone stares in awe.

Hordes of angels circle the air, viewing the carnage.

When the dust mushrooms toward them, they back off, spreading out, looking sparse and dispersed. When the crown façade of the aerie topples onto the broken heap, there is an awed silence.

Then, in twos and threes, the angels scatter into the smoky sky.

Everyone around us cheers. Some are crying. Others are hollering. People jump up and down, clapping. Strangers who would have pointed guns at each other on the street are now hugging.

We have struck back.

We have declared war on any being that dares to think they can wipe us out without a fight. No matter how celestial, no matter how powerful they are, this is our home and we will fight to keep it.

The victory is far from perfect. I know that many of the angels have escaped with only minor injuries. Maybe a few have been killed, but the rest will heal quickly.

But to look at the people celebrating, you'd think the war has been won. I understand now what Obi meant when he said this attack was not about winning over the angels. It was about winning over the humans.

Until now, no one, certainly not me, believed there was even a chance at fighting back. We thought the war was over. Obi and his resistance fighters have now shown us that it's just beginning.

I never thought about it before, but I'm proud to be human. We're ever so flawed. We're frail, confused, violent, and we struggle with so many issues. But all in all, I'm proud to be a Daughter of Man.

46

The sky glows with a blend of bloody red and soot black. The bruised light gives a surreal radiance to the charred city. The soldiers have stopped shooting, although they continue to scan the skies as if expecting to see an army of demons bearing down on us. Somewhere in the distance, the sound of machine-gun fire echoes down the streets.

We continue to weave through dead cars. The people in our truck talk excitedly in hushed voices. They're so pumped up, they each sound ready to take on an entire legion of angels all by themselves.

They still stay as much on their side of the truck as possible. It's a good thing they're so excited and happy; otherwise, I'm afraid they might just burn us all at the stake. In between the chatter, they keep glancing our way. It's hard to say whether it's my mother in her speaking-in-tongues prayer trance, my sister with her disturbing stitches and vacant stare, or the dead body that is me that keeps them glancing our way.

The pain is fading. It's starting to feel more like I was hit with an economy car running a stop sign as opposed to an eighteen-wheeler on the freeway. My eyes are beginning to come a little under my control again. I suspect some of my other muscles are thawing too, but my eyes are the easiest to move, if you call shifting a fraction of an inch moving. But it's enough to tell me that the effects of the venom are wearing off and that I will probably be okay.

The streets have turned desolate and empty of people. We are out of the aerie district and in the demolished zone. Miles of burnt-out car husks and wrecked buildings flow by. The wind whips my hair around my face as we drive through the charred and broken skeleton of our world.

We occasionally stop, blending in with the other dead cars. At one point, Obi shushes us, and we hold our breath, hoping nothing finds us. I assume angels have been spotted above and we are camouflaging ourselves.

Just when I think it's all over, someone in the back shouts, 'Look out!'

He points above him. Everyone looks up.

Against the wounded sky, a lone angel circles above us.

No, not an angel.

Light glints off curved metal on one of the edges of his wings. They are not shaped like a bird's wings. It's a giant bat-wing shape.

My heart speeds up with my need to shout out to him. Could it be?

He circles overhead, each pass spiraling him down closer. The spirals are wide and slow, almost reluctant.

To me, it's a nonthreatening look at our truck. But to the others, especially in their adrenaline-fueled states, it's an enemy attack.

They heft up their rifles and point them up at the sky.

I want to shout for them to stop. I want to tell them they're not all out to get us. I want to slam into them and mess up their aim. But all I can do is watch as they point and shoot into the air.

The lazy circles turn into evasive maneuvers. He is close enough for me to see that he has dark hair, and now that he's doing more than gliding, the way he moves seems awkward. As though he's just learning to fly with his wings.

It's Raffe. He's alive.

And he's flying!

I want to jump up and down, waving and yelling up to him. I want to cheer him on. My heart soars with him even as it is gripped with fear that he'll fall out of the sky.

The soldiers are not expert enough with their rifles to hit a moving target from that distance. Raffe flies away without injury.

My face muscles twitch a tiny bit in response to my inner joy.

47

It takes another hour before I thaw out completely. All the while, my mother clenches her hands and prays desperately over my body in the low guttural sounds that are her speaking-in-tongues utterances. They are her unique perversions of words that are undoubtedly disturbing to hear, but she chants them in a cadence that's somehow lulling at the same time. Leave it to Mom to be simultaneously frightening and soothing, as only an insane mother can be.

I know I'm getting my body back, but I just lie there until I can sit up. I start to occasionally blink and breathe normally long before I move, but no one notices. Between my sister's stitched and automaton-like presence at my feet, and my mother's nonstop prayers over my head, I suppose my still body is the least interesting thing to look at.

The day is dawning.

I never realized what a triumph it is to simply be alive. My sister is with us. Raffe is flying. Everything else is secondary.

And for now, that is enough.

Acknowledgements

A very special thanks goes out to my fantastic beta readers Nyla Adams, Jessica Lynch Alfaro, Eric Schaible, Adrian Khactu, and Travis Heermann for their amazing and insightful feedback which brought the story up to the next level. To my original copy-editor, Robert Gryphon, whose commitment to the book inspired me; to John Skotnik for catching those last minute copy-editing issues; and to Peter Adams, photographer extraordinaire, for taking such great author photos.

Thanks also goes out to my agent, Steven Axelrod, and my publishing team, Larry Kirshbaum, Tim Ditlow, Amy Hosford, Margery Cuyler, Anahid Hamparian, Diana Blough and Deborah Bass for all their hard work, support and tremendous enthusiasm for *Angelfall* as they ushered the book to a larger readership.

Hugs and thanks go out to Lee, who always does an excellent job of keeping my head from getting too big. And of course, a heartfelt hug and thanks to Aaron, whose artistic nurturing and encouragement helped me find the way. Finally, a huge thanks to the early readers and supporters of *Angelfall* who ignited the word-of-mouth about the book. You are wonderful, amazing, and I'm eternally grateful to you.

The best books live on in your head long after they are finished. As you read, you are turning the pages faster and faster to find out what happens next, only to feel bereft when you reach the end.

If that is how you feel now, you might like to join us at www.hodder.co.uk, or follow us on Twitter @hodderbooks, and be part of our community of people who love the very best of books and reading.

Whether you want to find out more about this book, or a particular author, watch trailers and interviews, have the chance to win early limited editions, or simply browse our expert readers' selection of the very best books, we think you'll find what you're looking for.

And if you don't, that's the place to tell us what's missing.

We love what we do, and we'd love you to be part of it.

www.hodder.co.uk

@hodderbooks

HodderBooks

HodderBooks